Acclaim

a novel

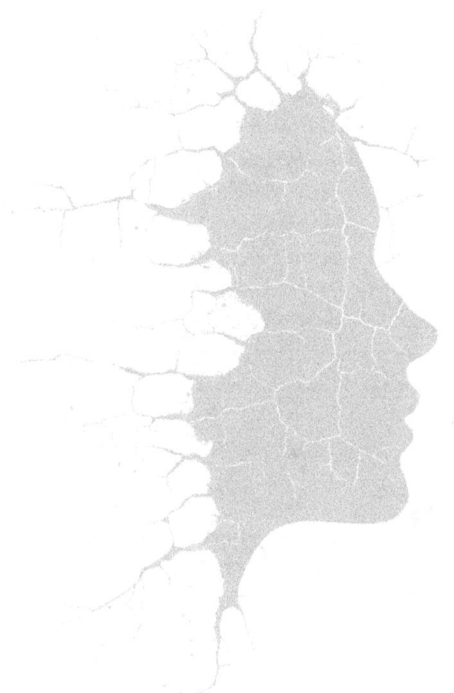

JEAN THESQUARE

Sultryverse - New York - 2026
SULTRYVERSE
https://www.sultryverse.com

Trigger Warning

This book contains explicit sexual content (including BDSM and power-exchange dynamics), psychological manipulation, public scandal, and themes of obsession and emotional coercion. Recommended for mature readers only.

LCCN TXU002513753

Interior illustrations and layout by Brady Moller

– 10 9 8 7 6 5 4 3 2 1 –

CONTENTS

For all those who helped this book get to the reader
For all the readers who will take it on the rest of its
journey

Part 1

FIRST CLAIM

CHAPTER
One

BIRTHDAY BAIT

Some people drag you to hell. Others you follow willingly, knowing they will have your back if needed.

Manon was the latter.

And now, she was calling.

I let the phone ring twice before answering.

"*Ma chérie*," she purred in that lazy, aristocratic French drawl, the one that drew people closer, as if sharing a secret. "Tell me you don't plan to stay in writing on your birthday night when the city beckons?"

"That depends." I spun my chair around, kicking my feet up on the windowsill. "Are you about to make me regret picking up?"

A throaty chuckle. "Oh, B, don't I always?"

She wasn't wrong.

Manon had been my partner-in-crime since boarding school, a fixture in my life — like fine lingerie and expensive rebellion. Born into one of the wealthiest families in France, heiress to a billion-dollar empire she had no interest in running, she treated wealth the way people treated the weather: omnipresent, unchangeable, uninteresting.

Her rebellion against the family heritage wasn't drugs or partying. It was in doing things to unsettle her parents.

Becoming a supermodel, not because she had any aspirations related to fashion, but because her father once said models were for men to enjoy, not for women to become.

Sleeping with artists, women, and men twice her age, because her mother insisted on a respectable match.

And, of course, being friends with me.

Beatrix.

We met in a European boarding school where we were *supposed* to be trained to be good stewards of our families' legacies and found a side education in the pleasure of each other's company.

I was still Beatrice, a respectable name for a respectable heir, at the time.

But one evening, as I laid on her bedroom's bed, she had crawled between my legs, her mouth curved in that feline smirk she wore when she was about to do something reckless. I had let her.

A dare. A lesson. A name given with a kiss.

She had pulled a tube of lipstick from her pocket—Dior, always Dior, that deep shade of red she swore made men weak—and dragged it across my skin; not my lips, but lower, on the inner part of my thigh, letter after letter, teasing.

"Beatrice is too prim. You, *ma chérie*, are not a Beatrice. You are..."

She paused...

"Beatrixxx," she murmured, tracing each letter like a spell, sealing the last X with a kiss from her soft lips.

"There," she said, eyes dark with mischief. "Welcome to the new you."

The triple X was a little much, so I shortened it to Beatrix.

And yet, Manon's biggest impact on me wasn't in kissing or seduction.

We were sixteen, lounging in our dormitory, the heavy French windows open to let in the thick summer air. She had been sorting through a package from her mother: boxes of silk and lace, delicate underthings wrapped in tissue paper and scented with something expensive.

I had watched, bemused, as she pulled out a slip of sheer black lace, holding it up to the light.

"That is lingerie," she had said, as if unveiling something sacred.

I rolled onto my stomach. "So? Big deal. I have lingerie, too."

"Oh B. There's the stuff *you* wear, and then there's lingerie. Mother says lingerie is what makes a woman strong."

She reached into the box again, pulling out another set: a champagne-colored bralette, scalloped lace, delicate embroidery, paired with whisper-thin panties. She tossed them at me, expectant.

I caught them, frowning. "You want me to try them on?"

"Yes," she said.

"Why?"

"Because it's better than the frump you wear."

I indulged her, as always.

Slipping it on, something shifted in me. Could it have been the soft luxurious lace sending pulses across my bare skin? Or the first real sense of being a woman?

I turned to the mirror.

Manon smiled behind me.

Her hand skimmed down my side, tracing the lace at my hip.

"Lingerie is power," she whispered. "A secret oath between you and your skin."

She stepped away, pleased with herself, leaving me in front of the mirror.

Lingerie wasn't an indulgence. It was armor, reminding me my body belonged to me first and pleasure was mine to give, to withhold, to wield as I pleased.

Now, years later, my drawers were filled with silk and lace, mesh and satin, the kind of pieces that draped against the skin like a whisper.

Power started with what touched your skin first.

That power made me more confident about my ability to write. It was around that time I started to write erotica. We'd sneak out after curfew, discovering the joys of the Paris underground. We'd slip back into bed hours later, still flushed from whatever sin we'd gotten away with that night, and I would capture the most scandalous aspects of our excursion, merging them with fantasies I could not fulfill. I had written it in a leather-bound notebook, ink pressed deep into the pages, as if the words themselves had weight.

At first, it had been indulgent—a secret between me and my own wicked thoughts.

But over time, it became something else. The notebook got filled and it became easier to type it into a private folder on my computer.

At Oxford, it was an exercise in restraint, in suggestion; in knowing that power lay not in what was written but in what was withheld.

Until...

I had been in a writing seminar, studying under a visiting professor whose praise carried weight in the literary world. One evening, I had meant to submit some crafted short story, something brooding and intelligent, something that would prove I belonged in the room.

After a late-night binge of cigarettes, caffeine, and god knows what else, I sent the wrong file as homework.

I hadn't realized my mistake until I was sitting in his office the next afternoon, the crisp pages spread across his desk, his fingers steepled beneath his chin as he looked at me.

"This," he said, tapping the paper, "is better than anything else you've given me. You should publish it."

He made all the right introductions. An agent, then an editor. Soon enough, a book contract arrived and, before I had finished my second year, I was a published author.

Erotica, but not cheap. Not tawdry. Beautiful, aching, intoxicating.

The kind of thing respectable people tucked onto their shelves in leather-bound covers, pretending they hadn't read every word.

The kind of stories that made people hungry.

The kind my parents didn't approve of.

And that made Manon and I kindred spirits, partners in parental disapproval.

The first book hit the bestseller list in the UK. Then in the US.

By the time I graduated, I was building a name and a life, independent of my family's wealth and reputation. A couple of titles to my name and enough of an income to keep going.

And the professor?

He had been useful.

For a time.

But I had never needed him.

Once I had learned everything I could, once there was nothing left for him to teach me, I let him go.

Manon's voice purred through the phone, pulling me back.

"So? Will you let me give you a proper birthday gift?"

I sighed. "What's the catch?"

"No catch. It's a private art show."

"My dear, there's got to be more to this. Sounds like you need an escort?"

"Oh B. I'd never consider you as a mere escort," she scoffed. "But it's Lucian? He's now creating sculptures and paintings that could make a nun break her vows."

I hummed. "Erotic?"

"In the most delicious way," she promised. "Not crude. Subtle. The kind of thing billionaires pay millions for so they can pretend it's about 'aesthetics.'"

My lips curled. We'd both known Lucian for a long time but I had lost touch.

"Who else will be there?"

"You'll love it," she continued. "Private penthouse. No cameras. No press. The kind of men who like to collect... rare things. Dorian Wolker will be there."

Something hot twisted low in my stomach.

I knew that name.

Everyone did.

Whispered about in elite circles, not for his business acumen, but for the way he dominated in every *other* way. Self-made, our age, and every bit in as much control as I enjoyed to be.

I was standing, crossing to my closet, my fingers trailing over silk and lace.

"Send me the details," I murmured.

CHAPTER
Two

SILK STRATEGY

I reached for the black lace set. Delicate, devastating, sheer in all the right places. The bra cupped me like a whisper, the garters snapped into place against my thighs.

Next up, a dress demanding, not begging for, attention: a charcoal silk slip, cut low in the back and high at the slit.

My hands smoothed over the fabric, clinging like a second skin, an elegant sheath over curves shaped by morning runs and nights spent stretching out in ways that left lovers breathless. My body, honed and deliberate.

Jewelry next. A fine thread of diamonds at my throat, subtle but precise.

Perfume. A hint, devastating in its placement. A whisper at my wrists, my throat, between my thighs.

With a final touch, heels.

Black, high, with straps wrapping my ankles like a promise.

I stepped back from the mirror, taking myself in.

Tonight, I'd meet him.

Ruthless. Exacting. Disciplinarian in all the right ways.

Would he notice me tonight?

Would he let me see him looking?

Would he wait until I drew to him, until I played into his hands?

I wasn't looking for a man who wanted to own me. In fact, I'd avoided the type.

I had grown up around men who saw women as accessories, bargaining chips, status symbols.

Dorian Wolker wasn't like them.

He was much more intriguing.

My phone buzzed. A message from Manon.

Car downstairs. Get your perfect ass down here.

I reached for my clutch, slipping inside the essentials: lipstick, condom, a sleek switchblade hidden, just in case, and a smaller phone.

My eyes flickered to the bookshelf.

To a row of hardcovers, pristine but well-loved.

My books.

My bestsellers.

They had made me a small fortune, independent from my family's wealth, and ensured I would never need anyone to support me.

But money didn't feel the gap I was yearning for. I wanted an adventure, a partner who would not just sweep me off my feet but discover new worlds within my own body. I knew how to control but yearned for release and tonight, the man who could grant me that may be there.

The black sedan purred beneath us, gliding through the city streets with the smooth precision of a well-oiled machine. The driver remained silent, the privacy glass firm in place, separating us from the world outside.

Manon stretched beside me, at ease, the picture of effortless decadence.

She draped herself in black silk, the kind of slip dress that looked like she had stolen it from a lover's bed and let it cling to her body out of pure indulgence. Thin straps slid over her bronzed shoulders, the fabric a whisper skimming her hips, the hem indecent when she crossed her legs.

Over it, she had thrown a cropped leather jacket, draped over her shoulders, making it clear she didn't dress for anyone but herself.

Her legs crossed at the knee, the faintest glimpse of stockings—black, sheer, ending mid-thigh, with lace peeking out when she moved.

And sharp heels. Louboutin, of course. Black patent stilettos with red soles flashing like a warning sign.

She smelled expensive, something smoky and warm with hints of vanilla and sandalwood, the kind of perfume that clung to sheets long after she had gone.

She smirked at me, catching me.

"What?" she drawled.

I shook my head, amused. "You look like you're about to ruin someone's life tonight."

She stretched, languid and unbothered, the leather of her jacket slipping off one shoulder.

"Darling," she murmured, eyes gleaming, "when don't I?"

As if that settled the matter, she turned toward me, eyes sharp with curiosity.

"What have you been up to?"

I exhaled, the blur of city lights outside the tinted glass.

A club in London. Exclusive, discreet. The kind of place where the right people gathered, where you had to prove yourself to get in. The kind of place where power and pleasure intertwined in the dark, where bodies moved against each other in sin.

A man caught my eye. He was older, dangerous in the way he studied me, his patience a sharper blade than his desire.

I let him follow me upstairs. Let him press me against the wall, his breath warm at my ear, his fingers wrapping around my wrists.

"I stayed in London," I admitted, my voice smooth. "Private club. Interesting company."

Manon made a sound of approval. "And?"

"And," I shrugged, "I got bored before anything worth mentioning happened."

She *tsk*ed, shaking her head. "You're impossible."

I smirked. "Selective isn't impossible."

Her gaze turned speculative. "Are you waiting for something?"

I tilted my head, considering.

Not something. Someone.

I deflected instead. "What about you?"

Manon stretched her arms above her head, arching her back like a lazy cat, her dress shifting high against her thigh. "Mmm. There was a sheikh in Dubai."

I raised a brow. "Another royal?"

"Technically." She waved a hand, dismissing it. "But his wives were more fun."

I laughed, shaking my head. "Of course they were."

She shot me a wicked grin. "And last week, there was a villa in Tuscany. A party. A few... distractions."

"Distractions?"

She tapped a manicured nail against her lip. "Three of them. Beautiful, eager, devoted."

I exhaled a slow breath, my lips curving. "You do live such a hard knocks life."

She sighed dramatically. "I do."

For a moment, silence settled between us, the kind of ease that came with understanding someone too well.

She glanced at me, her expression turning shrewd. "So, no birthday plans? And all it took was a name to get you onboard?"

I looked at her, unreadable.

She grinned.

"Dorian Wolker?"

The name slid through me like a slow, electric pulse.

I held her gaze, my fingers tracing the stem of my champagne flute.

Manon studied me, amusement flickering in her eyes. "You want to experience it, don't you? To be in his sights."

I didn't answer.

She smirked, swirling the liquid in her glass.

I took a slow sip, the warmth of the champagne sliding down my throat.

"Good thing I don't chase either."

Manon laughed, tipping her head back. "Oh, *ma chérie*. The two of you are going to go around in circles if one of you doesn't take the initiative."

The car slowed as we approached the building, a stunning penthouse gallery hidden in the heart of the city, the kind of place that shunned gaudy signs or public invitations. This was an event for those who didn't need an invitation, the ones who existed in a world where exclusivity remained understood, not granted.

A place for people like Manon and Dorian Wolker.

And even though I've tried to run away from it all my life, a place for me.

CHAPTER
Three

THE COLLECTOR

The valet opened my door first. Cool night air brushed against my skin as I stepped onto the marble, my heels clicking softly against stone.

Manon unfolded herself from the car with lazy elegance.

People noticed.

Subtle, not overt — the shift of attention that happens when something enters a room that was never meant to be ignored.

The doorman stepped aside wordlessly.

The penthouse glowed gold, champagne catching the light as smooth laughter moved through the air.

The art was sensual without confession. Sculptures of intertwined bodies, brushstrokes hinting at skin and sweat and pleasure without ever surrendering to it.

Billionaires would spend millions on a single piece because they liked owning things that made people wonder if they were admiring or being seduced by something they couldn't quite place.

Manon adjusted the strap of her dress, lips already curved in mischief.

"See anyone worth ruining?"

"They all look so breakable."

She smiled.

No cameras. No social media. Only discretion.

Not the kind of event where influencers flaunted borrowed jewels or the wealthy their power for the public.

A world where indulgences were taken in private, where power was understood rather than broadcast, where everything was for the pleasure of those who belonged.

Manon thrived in rooms like this one because it was home territory, the world she had both grown into and subsequently rebelled against. The attention, however, aroused her.

She had that look, where her pupils dilated a fraction, where her breathing changed so minutely, only I would notice.

"If I don't have someone's hands under my dress before midnight, I will be personally offended."

I smirked, taking a sip of champagne. "Anyone in mind?"

She hummed, eyes flicking over the crowd. "Anaïs told me she'd be here. But if I can't find her..."

She turned toward me, her sharp gaze flicking over me. "What's your next book about?"

I gave her a knowing look. "Depends. What else have you been up to?"

Manon grinned, swirling the liquid in her glass. "Oh, so you need more material, do you?"

"Always."

She took a slow sip, considering. "There was the art collector in Vienna who had a thing for watching. Interesting."

"How many of you were involved?"

She shrugged, smirking. "Only three. Intimate, you know?"

I hummed, already tucking the idea away in my mind.

"Ah oui," she continued, eyes flicking toward the crowd as if she were already searching for her next conquest. "The actress. French, married, desperate for something wasn't her husband. She had the softest skin, B. Like velvet."

I could use this.

I leaned in, lowering my voice. "And what did she taste like?"

"Like strawberries and sin."

I exhaled a slow breath, my lips curving. "You do live a blessed life."

She sighed dramatically. "I really do."

"And you? Who is your next muse?"

I didn't answer but sensed a presence.

It came slowly, a ghost of awareness and uncomfortable proximity before your turned. An apparition above it all, apart from the men circling, waiting for their chance.

Dorian stood near the far end of the gallery, partially shadowed in dim lighting, yet somehow, he was the only thing in the room that truly existed.

Tall, commanding, and effortlessly dressed in a dark suit worn as a second skin.

He was speaking to someone without really engaging, scanning the room, his eyes landing on me as if assessing me.

Not in the way men usually looked at me, all hunger, admiration, or unchecked lust.

No shift in expression or polite smile. Raw, unshaken awareness.

A lesser man would have come to me immediately. He didn't, forcing me to sit in the weight of his gaze.

Turning his head as effortlessly as he had acknowledged me, he looked away.

My pulse had already quickened.

Manon leaned in, her voice a whisper at my ear.

"Oh, *ma chérie*," she purred, amusement laced with something darker. "You're in so much trouble now."

"Beatrix Winslow-Hale."

A voice, smooth and European, interrupted my hunt.

I turned, my gaze snapping to the man addressing me.

Lucian Moreau.

The artist of the evening and an old schoolmate of ours. French, dark-eyed, and elegant in the way only men who had spent their entire lives surrounded by beauty could be. He had the look of a man who had been indulged, not in a spoiled way, but in the way of someone who understood his own worth.

"I thought that shape looked familiar."

Manon arched a brow, intrigued. "Ah, so you read."

Lucian's smirk deepened. "Only the very best lines."

His eyes returned to me, dark and interested. "Your recent work is... dripping with that *je ne sais quoi.*"

I smiled, sipping my drink. "And is yours supposed to make us drip with that *je sais quoi*?"

The corners of his lips twitched.

"Erotica and fine art," he mused, stepping a fraction closer. "Both deal in desire, in power. The right balance of restraint and indulgence."

I let the moment stretch. I murmured, "Desire is most potent when left a hair beyond reach."

Lucian's expression sharpened, his gaze flickering with something deeper. "Yes. It is the suggestion, not the revelation, that captivates."

Manon, standing beside me, studied Lucian with something close to approval.

"So tell me, Lucian," she murmured, voice dipped in honey, offering him something neither of us had quite named yet. "Are you the kind of artist who prefers to observe? Or participate?"

His lips twitched. "They say two's company and three's a crowd. There are times where crowds are fun, but after tonight, I may be more interested in just company."

Lucian's eyes gleamed, focus locked onto me.

Manon sighed, feigning mild disappointment, before running a single manicured finger along the edge of his sleeve.

"Well," she murmured, amusement dancing in her voice, "if you ever change your mind, you can always find me."

Lucian gave a slow nod of acknowledgment. Not dismissal. Not disinterested. Understanding.

She accepted it for what it was and stepped away.

"Enjoy your chat, *ma chérie*," she whispered in my ear, her breath warm, before disappearing into the crowd.

I turned my attention back to Lucian, who still held his drink loosely, eyes studying me with something measured.

But I was only half-present.

I had lost sight of Dorian.

I didn't like losing sight of men like him.

Lucian said something smooth, something flirtatious, but my mind was only half on him.

Where was he?

Where had he gone?

I forced my focus back to Lucian, giving him a soft, knowing smile, continuing our game.

He leaned in, lowering his voice, eyes glinting. "Do you always hold a man's attention so carelessly?"

I took a slow sip of champagne, letting the bubbles linger against my tongue before answering. "Carelessly?" I echoed. "Or deliberately?"

Lucian smiled. "Ah. A game, then?"

"Aren't you playing one, too?"

Before he could respond, someone interrupted.

A sleekly dressed assistant stepped up beside him, murmuring something in his ear.

The auction was about to begin.

Lucian straightened, his expression shifting from flirtation to something more self-assured, something amused.

"Everything has a price, Beatrix," he murmured. "Even things you think they don't."

The words lingered, curling around my spine like silk and something sharper.

Lucian took his leave, leaving me standing there, still holding my drink, still searching the crowd for someone else entirely.

The host took the stage, speaking smoothly into the microphone.

"All proceeds from tonight's auction will go toward the Aegis Foundation, supporting education and arts programs worldwide. A reminder that not only are you collecting exquisite pieces tonight, you're also giving back to something greater."

There were polite nods, murmurs of approval, a few raised glasses.

The early pieces passed in a blur of polite indulgence. Applause and champagne, numbers large enough to impress but small enough to remain civilized.

Then a sculpture was unveiled—curved marble, feminine, suggestive without apology.

My attention lingered.

Across the room, Dorian lifted his paddle.

$100,000.

The movement was unhurried, almost absentminded, as if the decision had been made long before the piece appeared.

He didn't look at me.

The bidding climbed. Men tested one another as the numbers rose.

$200,000.

$300,000.

$1 million.

The hammer fell.

He still hadn't acknowledged me.

Another piece followed. Smaller. Intimate. The kind of object meant for private rooms and locked doors.

Manon leaned closer. "I like this one."

"So do I," I murmured.

She raised her paddle. I followed, amused by the game.

$75,000.
$125,000.
A pause.
Then—
$1 million.
Dorian.
A quiet ripple moved through the room, laughter edged with disbelief.

The final piece appeared like a secret revealed too late.
The room shifted. Conversations died mid-sentence.
Bidding opened at $2 million.
$3 million.
Someone pushed higher.
A breathless pause followed.
Then Dorian lifted his paddle once more.
$5 million.
No flourish nor smile.
The hammer struck. Applause followed as the awareness that he had taken every piece that stirred me and never once given me the satisfaction of being seen crawled up my spine.
Manon's voice brushed my ear, soft with delight.
"Oh, *ma chérie*... you're not being ignored."
"You're being studied."
I lifted my glass to hide the heat rising beneath my composure and hated how much I enjoyed it.

CHAPTER
Four

CRATE EXPECTATIONS

The morning hung heavy with sleep, silk negligee warm against my bare skin when my phone rang.

I groaned, reaching for it, knowing who called.

Manon.

I swiped to answer.

"You sound flushed," I murmured, stretching against the pillows.

She exhaled, something unreadable in her tone. "Oh, *ma chérie*, you flatter me."

I smirked. "So? Which lucky soul warmed your bed last night?"

Manon scoffed. "Not why I'm calling."

A twist, unexpected.

I pushed up on one elbow, rubbing my temple. "Go on."

"A box arrived for me this morning."

I frowned. "From whom?"

"At first? Unclear."

"Unclear?"

Manon let out a soft hum, and I pictured the wicked glint in her eyes.

"The woman who delivered it had the hottest ass I've seen in years," she mused. "Put together like a dream. Not your run-of-the-mill courier, trust me."

I smirked. "You'd sleep with your own reflection if physics allowed it."

"I'd consider it," she shot back. "But I digress."

I rolled my eyes. "The box, Manon. The box."

"Inside," she said, "was the piece I liked at the auction."

My fingers tightened around the phone.

The one Dorian had outbid her on.

The one he had claimed.

"A card came with it."

She paused.

"Thank you for last night."

I sat up, pulse thrumming.

Last night.

My brain conjured images I tried to ignore.

Manon. Dorian.

Together.

In ways I refused to imagine—or maybe, ways I craved to see.

I swallowed, gripping the sheets.

"Manon," I said, my voice sharp. "Did you…?"

The doorman buzzed on the other line.

I ignored it.

"Did you and Dorian…?"

Manon laughed, or at least I imagined she did.

But before she could answer…

A knock at my door.

Loud. Firm.

I jerked, startled, heart spiking.

I glanced toward the door and back at my phone.

Manon had said something, lost to me.

The knock came again, harder.

I took a breath, fingers tight around the phone.

I switched the call, pressing it to my ear.

"Miss Beatrix," the doorman said, his voice measured.

I exhaled, irritated. "I was going to call you back."

"A large delivery awaits you downstairs."

I frowned. "Large?"

"Five boxes."

My stomach tightened.

"And," the doorman continued, "the building needs the freight elevator to bring them up."

Five boxes.

Freight elevator.

Dorian.

I swallowed, pressing my thumbnail to my lip.

"What's in them?"

Pause on the line.

"The sender's representatives made themselves clear," the doorman said. "They must go to your apartment. Now."

I exhaled, pulse racing.

"Fine," I said, voice even. "Send them up."

I ended the call, staring at my ceiling.

Behind me, my phone flickered, Manon still on the line.

"Well?" she purred, voice rich with amusement.

"We both received gifts this morning," I murmured, pressing cool water glass against my lips, "but mine might overshadow yours."

Manon laughed. "I never mind second place when the show promises to be this good."

My lips twitched, but my mind circled what Dorian had done.

The knock at my door came five minutes later.

I expected men.

Movers. A logistics team.

But five composed Amazons stood at my door, dressed in identical tailored uniforms: black pencil skirts, white silk blouses, fitted black blazers.

Stockings. Ballet flats wrapped tight around their ankles.

They looked like executives entering a boardroom, not couriers delivering crates in a hurried but unstrained fashion.

Their short-cropped hair. Their flawless makeup. A trace of elegant and intentional perfume.

Not movers. A message.

The woman in front met my gaze with a neutral expression.

"Miss Winslow-Hale?"

"Yes?"

"We have your delivery."

My gaze flicked to the five massive crates behind them before returning to her.

I stepped aside.

The first woman nodded once, motioning to the others.

They entered in silent precision, steps fluid, posture controlled.

The weight they carried? Nothing to them.

Within moments, the boxes rested in the center of my apartment, positioned with eerie grace.

I crossed my arms, watching them move.

Without hesitation, they began opening them.

One by one, crates peeled open.

One by one, latches clicked.

As they did, the air shifted.

Not a single piece.

Every piece that caught my eye, now laid bare before me.

Hundreds of millions in art.

Each piece was removed and placed as if it belonged.

As if I belonged to them.

As if I belonged to *him*.

A shiver curled down my spine.

I scanned the room.

One piece was missing.

I scanned the collection again.

The one Manon and I both liked.

My stomach tightened.

I took a breath, pressing my fingers against my lips.

As I stepped closer to the final crate, I saw the envelope.

Thick, heavy stationery, pristine white, sealed with wax.

My name, written in precise, elegant script.

I exhaled, picking it up, my fingers sliding beneath the seal, breaking it.

Inside, a single card.

Dinner. Tonight.

8pm.

D.

I pressed my lips together, heat unfurling low in my stomach.

I stared at the card, my thumb tracing the smooth edge of the stationery.

Dinner. Tonight.

8pm.

D.

I exhaled, dropping the card onto my coffee table, where it sat among hundreds of millions of dollars in art.

I grabbed my phone, dialing Manon.

She answered at once, her voice dripping with the amusement of the morning's chaos.

"Miss me so soon?" she taunted.

I huffed, pressing a hand to my forehead. "Come over."

A pause.

"Dorian?"

Another pause, followed by a wicked chuckle.

"I'll be there in twenty."

Manon never showed up unprepared.

She swept into my apartment with that effortless magnetism she carried everywhere. No cocktail dress or stilettos, yet somehow more devastating for her defiance of convention.

Her silk camisole caught the light in deep burgundy waves, barely-there straps revealing collarbones sharp enough to cut. She'd tucked it into buttery leather pants that curved along her hips like a second skin. A leather jacket hung from her shoulders, suggesting more than revealing.

Ballet flats. Cartier. Wealth that whispers, rather than shouts.

Dark hair fell in tousled waves, as if she'd rolled straight from someone else's bed.

I studied her, that familiar mix of envy and admiration rising in my chest.

She caught my gaze and smirked, tossing a small box and wine bottle onto my counter before shrugging off her jacket.

"Because," she said, "we missed your birthday celebration last night."

I rolled my eyes but warmth fluttered in my chest as I examined the bottle. A Bordeaux. An excellent vintage.

Manon noticed what mattered while feigning indifference.

She flipped open the cake box to reveal a dark chocolate confection topped with gold leaf. Without asking, she found wineglasses, uncorked the bottle, and poured two generous servings.

"The woman in the lobby," she said, swirling the crimson liquid before taking a sip.

I arched an eyebrow. "What about her?"

Manon settled against my counter, silk shifting against her skin as she moved. "You tell me. Unless you've started collecting assistants in expensive suits?"

I traced the stem of my glass. "She's waiting."

Her smile widened. "For what? Your autograph?"

"An answer."

"Well," she mused, "I expected you to spend your birthday with a billionaire." She lifted her glass. "Your standards have plummeted."

The wine spread warmth down my throat, rich and velvety.

Manon watched me, her expression too knowing. "What's stopping you? Fear he can't afford the good champagne?"

I exhaled. "You know why."

She tilted her head, studying me before leaning forward, her voice dropping. "Enlighten me. My mind-reading skills falter after two glasses."

"Manon."

"You wanted him." When I didn't respond, her tone sharpened. "You want him. Half the reason you wore that dress that makes you look like sin incarnate."

I had felt Dorian Wolker's name like electricity before seeing him. I'd gone to that party to discover what kind of man commanded such whispers.

Manon licked a smudge of chocolate from her lip. "So? Will you grace him with your presence, or should I tell him you've run off with me instead?"

I considered the question, rolling it over like wine on my tongue.

"Power play, Beatrix," she said. "Your favorite game."

I nodded. "Of course."

"And?"

My lips curved. "He works harder first."

A slow, approving smile spread across her face. "The ice queen returns from hibernation."

"He has power. Wealth. Gets what he wants." I straightened, decision made. "But I don't need his money. If he wants me, he earns me."

"And how will you make him dance to your tune?"

I reached for my phone and called the doorman. "Send her back up."

Moments later, precise footsteps echoed outside, followed by a crisp knock.

I opened the door to find the same woman, in her perfect pencil skirt and perfect silk blouse, hair cropped close to her scalp.

"Miss Winslow-Hale," she greeted me.

"I have a message for Mr. Wolker."

Understanding flickered in her eyes.

"Not tonight."

A barely perceptible nod. "As you wish."

After she left, Manon released a low whistle. "Cold. The man will freeze before he reaches you." She dragged her finger along the rim of her glass. "But nothing worth having comes without frostbite."

CHAPTER
Five

SIGNED, SEALED, WITHHELD

"**I** swear to God, Beatrix, if you wear anything boring tonight, I'll set this entire closet on fire."

Manon stood in the center of my bedroom, one hand on her hip, the other flicking impatiently through my wardrobe.

I sat on the edge of my bed, half-dressed, half-annoyed, watching her judge my entire existence with each unimpressed glance at my clothing options.

I sighed. "It's a book signing, Manon, not a seduction."

She whirled around, scandalized. "Are you kidding?!?"

Before I could protest, she turned back to the closet, yanking open a drawer where my lingerie was kept.

My very expensive, very underused lingerie.

She smirked. "Ah, *enfin*."

I groaned. "Manon…"

She held up a black lace bra and matching panties, delicate but devastatingly sheer.

She tossed them onto the bed and reached for another.

And another.

And another.

Soon, my bed was covered in a curated selection of the finest French lingerie, handpicked by a woman who lived by its philosophy.

She placed her hands on her hips, looking at me expectantly.

"Pick one."

I gave her a flat look. "No one is going to see it."

She scoffed. "You'll see it."

She pointed at the lace.

"This," she said, "is not only for men. Not only a tool for seduction."

She picked up a deep burgundy set, running her fingers over the lace.

"When you wear the right lingerie, you feel it," she continued. "It reminds you that you are a woman who should be adored, worshipped."

"By whom?"

She smirked. "By whoever is lucky enough to find out what's underneath."

I exhaled, picking up the black lace set she had first thrown on the bed.

Delicate. Devastating.

I stepped into the panties, fastening the bra into place.

Manon grinned. "Better."

She pulled out a sheer black slip dress.

"This."

"No."

"Yes."

"It's too..."

"It's perfect." She held it up against me, narrowing her eyes. "You haven't been fucked properly in months. If a man or woman doesn't take care of that tonight, I will personally see to it myself."

"Are you offering?"

Manon smirked. "I'm always offering."

I rolled my eyes, but I took the dress from her anyway.

She flopped onto my bed as I stepped into it, watching with far too much satisfaction as I let the fabric slip against my skin, clinging in all the right places.

Her smirk widened. "Now that," she declared, "is a woman who deserves to be worshipped."

I gave her a pointed look. "It's a book signing."

She stretched lazily, inspecting her nails. "And yet, somehow, by the end of the night, you'll turn it into an erotic thriller."

I huffed a laugh, shaking my head.

Manon lifted a brow. "You have this annoying, brilliant way of taking real life and making it fiction. Twisting it in a way people can't tell what's real."

I smirked, slipping on diamond earrings, brushing perfume over my pulse points. "It's a gift."

She grinned. "It's a weapon. And tonight," she tilted her head, eyes glinting, "I fully intend to ensure you get some inspiration."

I exhaled, smoothing my hands over my dress.

"I'll consider it."

Manon stood, looping an arm through mine.

"No need, *chérie*. I'll do the considering for you."

As I was about to set the perfume bottle down, she smirked.

"You know," she mused, "I recently learned something new."

"That's not surprising."

She leaned in, voice dripping with amusement. "Apparently, a little perfume on the edge of your anus does wonders."

I blinked. "I... uh... what?"

She sipped her wine, looking smug. "A French dom taught me last week."

I huffed a laugh. "Of course he did."

She shrugged. "I tried it. I liked it. I'm passing on the knowledge. Consider it my gift to you."

I gave her a pointed look. "And how does this help me at my book signing?"

She tilted her head. "Confidence, *chérie*. A woman should feel sexy everywhere."

I rolled my eyes. "You only want to see if I'll do it."

She smirked. "I already know you will."

And damn it, she wasn't wrong.

I let a single drop land at the edge, shivering as a slow, tingling burn spread through my body.

Manon grinned like the devil.

"Good, isn't it?"

I swallowed, clearing my throat. "It's... interesting."

She laughed, stretching out on my bed. "Oh, you'll thank me later."

I huffed, setting the perfume down and smoothing my dress into place.

Somehow, I wasn't so sure she was wrong.

I was mid-sentence, my voice smooth, controlled. The room hanging on my every words.

"'You like art, don't you?' he murmured against her ear, his fingers trailing down the exposed line of her spine."

The audience was still. Attentive.

"'Good. Because I'm about to make you part of it.'"

I turned the page.

I felt a shift in the air, a pull.

Weight settled between my legs before I looked up.

But when I did, I saw him.

Dorian.

Sitting toward the back.

Silent. Unassuming. Watching. Inevitable.

I swallowed.

The book in my hands suddenly felt too warm.

"'Put your knees on the steel, wide.'"

I kept reading, trying to control my breathing, to keep my voice steady.

The damp lace of my panties grew heavier, clinging to my skin, an unbearable heat pressing between my legs.

I pressed my thighs together, inadvertently making things worse.

I clenched my jaw, but it did nothing to stop it.

"'Lower,' he said. 'Let it press against you. Let it hold you open.'"

My body flooding, the lace growing stickier, the wet spot soaking deeper, threatening to show through.

I needed to steady myself, to breathe.

I lost my place.

Manon stood up, clapping, her voice bright, amused, effortless.

"Well, that's enough foreplay, isn't it?" she quipped, flashing her most dazzling, disarming grin.

The audience laughed, clapped along with her, the moment breaking and attention shifting.

I exhaled sharply, closing my book, using the motion to subtly press my thighs together, as if I could will away the deep, aching pulse between my legs.

I met Manon's gaze.

She always knew.

And she was enjoying this far too much.

I slipped into the bathroom, locking the door behind me, my breath still, uneven.

The lace of my panties had soaked through, and I knew if I sat too long in one place, it would leave a trace on the chair.

I turned on the faucet, splashing cold water onto my wrists, trying to steady myself.

I had done a damn good job holding it together after Manon's perfectly timed intervention. I reached under my dress, peeling my sticky panties down my legs, feeling the cool air hit my damp skin.

"B?" Manon's voice, light, amused. "You alive in there?"

I sighed, wiping myself down with a paper towel before opening the door.

Manon stepped inside without waiting for an invitation, eyes already glinting with mischief.

She took one look at the panties in my hand and let out a low whistle.

"Well," she mused, tilting her head, "someone had fun."

I rolled my eyes, about to toss them into the small bin beside the sink.

But Manon snatched them first.

She held them up between her fingers, inspecting the sheer, soaked fabric with a smirk.

"*Mon Dieu*," she said, bringing them to her nose and inhaling lightly.

I groaned. "Manon."

She grinned, unfazed. "No wonder you lost your place."

I reached to grab them back, but she danced away, tucking them into her clutch.

"You're going commando now," she said, as if it was a declaration.

I huffed a laugh, shaking my head. "You're unbelievable."

She winked. "You should thank me. If he's as dominant as they say, you're saving him the trouble of taking them off later."

I exhaled, smiling despite myself.

Manon had always been shamelessly free. It was one of the things I loved most about her.

Her expression shifted, sharpening.

"He's here," she said, in a murmur.

We both knew who she meant.

I nodded, licking my lips.

"And?" she prompted, tilting her head. "What do you want to do?"

I met her gaze and glanced down at the panties she had tucked away.

I lifted a brow. "I think you already have my answer."

Her lips curled.

She leaned against the counter, looking at me knowingly. "Are you sure?"

I let out a slow breath.

"I've thought long and hard about it," I murmured. "And I definitely want to give him a try."

Her smirk deepened.

"So..." she said, slipping her arm through mine, leading me toward the door, "let's make sure he knows it."

As we reached the exit, I paused.

"Wait," I said, glancing at her. "I still have books to sign."

Manon rolled her eyes, sighing dramatically. "He's not going anywhere."

I gave her a pointed look.

She smirked. "And if he is? I'll make sure he stays."

I narrowed my eyes. "How?"

Manon's lips curled. "You don't want to know."

I smiled, tilting my head as I met the next woman's gaze, my fingers lingering a second longer than necessary as I handed her book back.

Her breath hitched, her cheeks flushed pink, her eyes flicking between my lips and my eyes.

"I just finished your last book, and this one... I know it's going to be my favorite."

I parted my lips, letting my voice drop with a conspiratorial tone. "I hope it keeps you up at night."

Her eyes widened, and she gave a breathy laugh, gripping the book to her chest before scurrying away.

The next woman stepped forward, biting her lip, nervous, but eager.

"I, um..." She tucked a strand of hair behind her ear. "Your books are... incredibly inspiring."

I let my gaze drop to hers, slow, deliberate, tilting my head as if I was considering her words.

"Inspiring, how?"

She swallowed, pressing the book toward me. "They just... make me feel things."

I traced my pen over the cover before flicking my gaze up through my lashes.

"That's the point, isn't it?" I murmured, signing her name in an elegant, looping script.

I handed it back, my fingers grazing hers.

She sucked in a sharp breath, her eyes darkening, and I bit back a smirk.

"Enjoy it," I whispered, watching her shiver before she left.

Each fan was the same: wide eyes, flushed cheeks, nervous laughter.

And I gave them all what they needed.

A lingering glance.

A brush of my fingertips. A whisper of something short of scandalous.

It was a game.

And I played it well.

And the only player who mattered was getting closer.

Dorian waited patiently at the very back, apparently unbothered by the line.

The line moved.

One step closer.

Another woman, her voice breathy, her hands fidgeting.

"Your books make me feel so... *alive*."

I gave her a slow, knowing smile, dragging my teeth over my bottom lip.

"I hope they make you feel other things, too."

She blushed hard, eyes going wide, before letting out a nervous giggle.

Another step closer.

The lace of my panties was long gone, but the memory of them sticking to me still burned in my mind.

The line reached its last person.

He stepped forward, placing the book down in front of me with the same ease as every other fan before him.

I glanced at him with a small grin on my face as I did with other readers.

"To whom?"

"Dorian," he said, his voice smooth, effortless.

I took the book, opened the cover, and instead of his name, wrote my number.

I slid the book back across the table, but this time, I didn't let go immediately.

I let my fingers rest on it, keeping him there.

I leaned in, lips curved, voice low, dripping with something between promise and provocation.

"You can take me out to dinner," I murmured, soft but unwavering.

I tilted my head, eyes glinting.

"But only because I'll let you."

He took the book, holding my gaze for one unbearable, electric moment, turned, and left.

CHAPTER
Six

CONTROLLED BURN

The phone buzzed.

My agent.

I balanced the phone between my shoulder and ear as I flipped through my notes. "Hey, what's up?"

There was a pause before she said, "Your reading tonight is cancelled."

I stilled. "Cancelled?"

"Yeah. The bookstore called early this morning. Said they needed to reschedule."

I frowned. "Did they say why?"

"Nope. They asked if we could move it to a later date."

I exhaled, annoyed but curious. Bookstores didn't cancel readings last-minute. Something was off.

But before I could think about it too much, I tapped my screen and called Manon.

She answered on the second ring, her voice lazy, amused, as if she'd been expecting me.

"Let me guess," she drawled. "You're calling because of a new crisis."

I narrowed my eyes. "How do you know that?"

She laughed. "I didn't. But now I do."

I groaned. "Tonight's reading was cancelled. I don't like last-minute cancellations," I told her, tucking the phone between my shoulder and ear as I picked up a glass of water.

"*Non, chérie*," Manon said, amused. "You don't like when you're not the one making them."

I rolled my eyes. "It's odd. No explanation, no reason. The bookstore suddenly wanted to reschedule?"

"Oh, *mon amour*," she sighed dramatically. "Maybe the universe is simply telling you to relax for once. Come with me to the spa instead."

I sighed, walking toward the window. "I don't know…"

A knock at the door.

I paused.

Manon must have heard the hesitation in my silence. "B?"

"One sec," I murmured, still holding the phone to my ear as I padded toward the entrance.

The knock hadn't been loud or impatient. It was measured. Precise.

When I pulled the door open, my breath caught.

The woman standing before me radiated quiet authority: Her posture straight; her gaze cool; her presence one of calm efficiency laced with something... calculated.

She was dressed in a sharply tailored black blazer, the lapels crisp, the fabric hugging the lines of her waist. Beneath it, a high-necked ivory blouse lay smooth against her skin.

A fitted pencil skirt ended a fraction of an inch above the knee, accentuating long, toned legs wrapped in sheer black stockings. On her feet, Cartier ballet flats, their signature leather straps securing them around her ankles like a deliberate restraint.

She could have been delivering legal documents, or a court summons, or stepping into a boardroom to negotiate millions.

Instead, in her hands, she carried a silver tray.

Resting on top was a thick, expensive-looking envelope.

"Who is it?" Manon's voice crackled in my ear.

Still watching the woman, I murmured, "One of those messengers. Like the ones who delivered the artwork."

There was a brief silence.

"The hot ones?"

I rolled my eyes, but my lips curled. "Manon."

"I'm only asking."

I sighed, reaching for the envelope. The second my fingers lifted it, the woman lowered the tray, turned on her heel, and walked away.

Not a glance back.

Not a word spoken.

"B?" Manon's voice in my ear. "Why was she there?"

I stepped forward, watching as the woman reached the elevator at the end of the hall.

The doors slid open soundlessly.

She stepped inside.

The doors shut.

Gone.

"Beatrix," Manon snapped.

I exhaled sharply, closing the door behind me. "She gave me an envelope. Didn't say a word, handed it over, and left."

Manon perked up immediately. "Well? Open it."

I tore open the flap, my pulse quickening.

Inside, in familiar bold, controlled handwriting, were the words:

Dinner. Tonight. 8pm.

Manon, still waiting, finally huffed a laugh. "Well, well. He certainly has a signature move."

I let out a breath. "Precise words."

"Precise timing," she corrected.

I chewed my lip. "You think?"

"I think," she said, "that we won't be seeing each other tonight."

I smirked.

There was a shuffling sound on the other end of the line.

"Darlings, it was an absolute pleasure—I had such a lovely time. And you were both so very... accommodating." A small pause. "But I have a clothing emergency to attend to, so it's time for you to leave. Right now."

A soft laugh. A murmur of protest.

Manon's voice again, purring. "Come now, let's not make this difficult. We'll continue another time."

A low chuckle, the sound of movement. The rustle of fabric. A door opening, shutting, and Manon's voice back to me.

"I am absolutely coming over to make sure that when you see him, you make him melt."

I rolled my eyes, but my smile didn't fade.

"Fine," I said. "I'll see you soon."

I hung up and looked back down at the note.

8pm.

Of course.

Water cascaded down my body, steam curling around me as I rinsed the last of the suds from my skin.

I was finishing washing my hair when the phone buzzed on the bathroom counter.

I wiped a hand over my face and reached for it, answering with a breathy, "Yes?"

The doorman.

"Miss, your friend is here."

I blinked the water from my lashes, running a hand through my wet hair.

"Send her up," I said.

I hung up, grabbed a plush towel, and wrapped it around myself.

Moments later, a knock at the door.

I had little time to tie my damp hair into a loose knot before I swung it open.

Manon stood there, perfectly composed, impossibly elegant, already smirking.

Her gaze swept over me, unapologetic as she took in the towel, the damp skin beneath it.

"Well," she drawled, stepping inside with the ease of someone who belonged here. "I must say, it's nice to be welcomed this way."

I rolled my eyes, closing the door behind her.

"But," she continued, setting down her bag and turning toward me, "I don't think a shower will do today."

I lifted a brow. "Oh?"

She waved a dismissive hand. "No, no, no. A mere rinse won't be enough." She tugged at the towel.

It fell to the floor, pooling at my feet, leaving me completely bare before her.

She took a step back, eyes roving over my body with slow, deliberate precision.

"There's a lot of work to be done," she murmured, tapping her chin, her gaze flicking over my skin, my curves, my thighs.

I lifted a brow. "Excuse me?"

She smirked. "If you're going to be laid out for Dorian Wolker to devour, every part of you needs to be perfect."

She stopped in front of me, tilting her head.

Soft fingers ghosted over my collarbone, down my arms, tracing the subtle definition of muscle beneath my skin.

"We'll need to soften this."

She moved down to my waist, her touch feather-light, making my stomach flutter.

"And this... needs to be irresistible."

She took one more slow, sweeping look before grabbing my wrist and leading me toward the bathroom.

"The bath," she said decisively. "We start there."

Manon moved with effortless precision, her fingers skimming across the bottles and jars lining my bathroom shelves.

She plucked oils, perfumes, and salts, uncapping them one by one, inhaling their scent before selecting only the finest.

The sound of water filling the tub echoed softly as she added each ingredient with purpose, swirling the mixture with her hand until the scent bloomed into the air. Something deep, rich. Sensual, but soothing. A fragrance that melted tension while igniting something else entirely.

I leaned against the counter, watching her, still bare beneath her expert touch.

She smirked as she met my gaze.

"You'll thank me for this later," she murmured, running her hand through the water, watching the silken oils dissolve into it, turning it into a decadent invitation.

"Get in, *mon amour*. It's time to make you unforgettable."

The warm water lapped at my skin, scented with oils that sank into every inch of me, turning the bath into something between sanctuary and altar.

And I was the offering.

Manon worked with intent, moving through each step of the process with the same meticulous precision she applied to every aspect of her life.

And yet, my body wasn't cooperating.

It was the way she touched me—casual, practiced, but thorough.

The way her fingers threaded through my hair, massaging my scalp, sending a slow, indulgent wave of pleasure through me as she washed and brushed my strands.

The way she tilted my chin back, let the water run over me, cleansing, soothing.

I exhaled, sinking deeper into the bath.

I remembered her hands on me in a different way.

"You remember that night?" I murmured, voice lazy with nostalgia.

Manon stilled for a fraction of a second.

She resumed, dragging the comb through my hair with calm efficiency.

"We had many nights, *chérie*," she said. "You'll have to be more specific."

"The first one."

She paused, exhaling sharply.

"Beatrix. This is for Dorian. Not for us."

I nodded, forcing my thoughts back into the present.

She continued.

She cleaned my nipples, her movements efficient but precise, and I had to fight the urge to arch into it.

She slid lower, parting my thighs, gently wiping along the most sensitive places, inside and out.

My breath shuddered.

Manon paused.

"Are you going to start purring next?"

I groaned, covering my face.

She laughed. "Seriously, B. If you get this worked up now, he's going to break you before the main course."

I sighed, nodding.

By the time she had finished, my breath was uneven, my body taut with restraint.

She tapped my hip. "All fours."

I hesitated.

But obeyed.

She spread me apart, the sudden rush of cool air on my most vulnerable places making my breath catch.

Followed by—the enema.

I let out a low noise, feeling the heat rise again.

Manon sighed.

"B, if you make that sound again, I'm going to pull an ice cube tray from your freezer and bring it here."

I laughed breathlessly. "You wouldn't."

Manon smirked. "Try me."

By the time she was done, I was clean, ready, trembling—holding at the edge of control.

Manon rinsed her hands, standing back, watching me carefully.

Finally, she nodded.

"Good."

But she wasn't done.

She reached for the razor.

I stretched out my leg over the tub's edge, letting her glide the blade up my calf, my thigh, working with unshaken focus.

Her fingers brushed over my newly smooth skin, inspecting for perfection.

For the final touch, she nudged my legs apart, shifting lower.

The blade slid across my inner thighs, deliberate, practiced, erasing everything until everything looked just as she wanted—pristine, well-kept, enticing.

I swallowed hard.

She tilted her head, observing me.

"You're fighting it," she said softly.

I exhaled. "I know."

She smirked, tapping my thigh lightly.

"Good. You'll need to."

She rinsed the razor, drying her hands, standing back for one last look.

Her gaze dragged over my body, her work complete.

"This is for him," she reminded me, meeting my eyes.

Not for us.

Manon wrapped me in a soft towel, her touch unnaturally tender for someone who had spent the last half hour reminding me to control myself.

The thick cotton absorbed the last beads of water from my skin, her hands slow, methodical, as if she were handling something precious.

I let her.

I let her tilt my chin up to dry my throat, my collarbones; let her press the fabric down my arms, smoothing away the droplets that clung to me.

She took her time and stepped back.

"Lay down," she murmured, nodding toward the bed. "We're not finished yet."

I hesitated.

"I still need to oil you up."

I exhaled, too relaxed to argue, moving toward the bed and settling onto my back.

Manon moved with expert precision, lining up bottles of oil and cream beside her.

The first touch was deliberate.

She continued up my calves, my thighs, her touch never lingering too long in one place, sending a ripple of relaxation through me.

By the time she finished my legs, I was halfway to dreaming.

But she wasn't done.

"Turn over."

I obeyed without a word, letting my body sink deeper into the mattress.

Manon straddled me lightly, rubbing oil into my shoulders, down my spine, pressing into the knots along my back.

Somewhere between the long, slow strokes along my back, I drifted.

My breath slowed.

My body melted.

The relaxed sensation pulled me deeper and deeper into sleep.

I sunk back into awareness like a body submerged in warm water.

For a moment, I stayed still, my limbs weightless, my skin still scented with the oils Manon had rubbed into me.

A sleep like that—deep, uninterrupted, decadent—was rare.

As I stretched, my fingers brushed fabric.

Not sheets.

Something else.

I blinked awake, turning my head, and my breath caught.

The room had transformed.

My entire collection of lingerie, clothing, and footwear had been laid out in a meticulously curated display.

Babydolls, bralettes, bustiers lined up in a gradient of desire—soft, romantic lace beside bold, dominant leather.

A chain dress that was more metal than fabric. Stockings paired perfectly with garter belts.

Corsets and open-cup bras.

Thigh-high boots next to delicate pearl panties.

A vinyl dress that could ruin a man's restraint by existing.

And, standing in the center of it all, surveying her work like an artist before a masterpiece—Manon.

"Finally," she said as I sat up, her voice amused. "I was beginning to think you'd sleep through your date entirely."

I ran a hand through my hair, blinking at the sheer number of options before me.

"What the hell is all this?" I asked, still groggy.

Manon smirked, gesturing broadly. "Options, *chérie*. We need to decide how you want to be unwrapped tonight."

I laughed, still hazy from sleep. "You're ridiculous."

She ignored me, already moving toward the lingerie laid out on the bed.

"Now," she mused, tracing a finger over a sheer black set, "are we thinking soft temptation?"

Her hand drifted to a crimson lace bustier; bold, decadent, sinful.

"Or outright seduction?"

I bit my lip, considering.

She wasn't joking.

The layers, the colors, the texture of the fabric—all spoke before I did.

Manon tapped a finger against her lip. "What do you want him to think when he sees you?"

I smirked. "He's used to taking. I want him to *earn*."

Manon hummed in appreciation. "So we play with the balance."

I nodded, lifting the soft lace between my fingers. "He already wants me. We don't need to remind him of that."

Manon laughed, nodding. "No, we don't."

I set the lingerie down and turned back to her.

"He needs to earn it all."

Manon grinned.

"And what a pleasure that's going to be to watch."

She reached for a leather harness, raising a brow. "Too much?"

I smirked. "Not for the right occasion."

She laughed, tossing it onto a separate pile.

Manon lifted a chain garter, twisting it between her fingers. "The men who take don't think about whether they deserve it."

I smirked. "And I'm going to make sure he deserves it."

She picked up a black lace bustier, holding it up to me.

"This," she said, grinning wickedly, "with the pearl panties."

"Too easy."

Manon laughed, tossing it onto the bed.

She stepped back, tilting her head as she surveyed the curated selection of lace, leather, silk, and chains strewn across the room.

"We need something that works in two worlds," she mused, tapping a manicured finger against her lips.

"Something that makes him want to strip you in private—but keeps the rest of the world hungry, too."

I hummed, reaching for a sheer black blouse, a whisper of silk that would drape elegantly, teasing with the hint of what lay beneath.

Manon's eyes glinted with approval.

"That. With this." She plucked a high-waisted, fitted pencil skirt, the kind that clung like a second skin, hugging every curve.

I smirked, smoothing the fabric over my hips. "Class, with a touch of corruption."

Manon grinned. "YES!"

She paired it with lace lingerie that was more sin than modesty: a delicate cage bra, pearl panties, and a garter belt hidden under the skirt—a secret only I would know about.

The final touch? A blazer.

Sharply tailored, powerful. Masculine dominance wrapped over feminine seduction.

Manon stepped back, crossing her arms. "This gives him the best kind of torment."

"How so?" I asked, buttoning the blazer.

"Because," she purred, running a finger along the exposed dip of my cleavage, "it forces him to wait. To behave in public while knowing full well what's underneath."

I met her gaze, already picturing Dorian watching me in this.

The slow burn.

The power play.

The undeniable promise.

I exhaled, fastening the last button, before stepping into black, lace-up stilettos.

Manon's smirk turned smug.

"Oh, *chérie*," she said, voice rich with amusement. "He won't know what hit him."

Manon moved behind me, her fingers weaving through my hair, brushing, smoothing, styling.

Her touch was firm, practiced, but undeniably intimate.

I watched in the mirror as she gathered my hair, deciding on something sophisticated yet undone.

She pulled a few loose strands to frame my face, tilting my chin as she assessed her work.

"We want impact. Not excess," she murmured, lining my eyes with precision, painting my lips in a shade that was equal parts invitation and challenge.

Her voice was calm, steady, but suffered from an underlying charge.

I felt it in the way her fingers lingered as she traced the curve of my jaw, ensuring the blend was flawless.

The energy between us, thick, humming, a memory of every past moment we had shared.

Manon grabbed the bottle of perfume, tipping it at my pulse points.

Wrists.

Throat.

She leaned closer, voice dropping to a murmur.

"You could put a little here too," she said, tapping the curve of my hip.

Then, lower.

"Or here."

I shivered.

Manon laughed under her breath. "Breathe, *chérie*. You're supposed to be in control tonight."

I swallowed hard, meeting her gaze in the mirror.

She smirked, smoothing the lapels of my blazer, stepping back to admire our work.

Her eyes flicked over me, satisfaction clear in her expression.

"You look..." she trailed off, shaking her head.

"Devastating?"

Manon grinned wickedly.

"Dangerous."

The phone rang.

Manon and I both turned toward it, the sound slicing through the thick air of perfume and anticipation.

I reached for it, placing it on speaker.

"Miss Beatrix," the doorman's voice came through, efficient, professional. "Your car is here."

A thrill ran through me, excitement laced with something darker.

I met Manon's gaze in the mirror.

She gave me one last slow look, eyes flicking from my sharpened jawline to the curve of my legs, the way the fabric clung and commanded.

"You're ready."

I turned to her, placing a soft kiss on her lips, a brief touch, a silent thank you.

Manon huffed in amusement, but pulled back, shaking her head.

"B, you cannot ruin my work before it even reaches Dorian."

I laughed, adjusting the collar of my blazer.

I looked around the room.

The battlefield of our preparation.

Lingerie draped over chairs. Makeup brushes scattered across the vanity. Open perfume bottles still filling the air with whispers of seduction.

I sighed. "I made a mess."

Manon smirked. "I'll clean up. You go conquer."

I turned back to her, eyes narrowing. "You don't have to."

She waved a dismissive hand. "Go. I'll tidy up before heading to the spa."

I gave her one last smirk, and grabbed my clutch, stepping toward the door.

We left the apartment together, the air shifting the second we stepped into the hallway.

As I moved through the building, I felt the shift around me.

Every man I passed stared.

There was electricity crackling in the air, a hum of awareness, desire, and something dangerously close to reverence.

I didn't acknowledge them.

Didn't need to.

Manon, walking beside me, chuckled under her breath.

She waited until we reached the curb, until the car door was open and I was about to step inside, before she leaned in and whispered against my ear.

"Every man wants you tonight, B."

She pulled back, grinning knowingly.

"Use it."

I held her gaze for a long beat.

I stepped into the car, the door closing behind me.

CHAPTER
Seven

DINNER TERMS

The city lights blurred past the tinted windows, golden streaks against the dark velvet of the evening.

The hum of the car engine was smooth, steady, but my thoughts were anything but.

As the weight of the moment settled around me, I realized—

I hadn't properly thanked Manon.

Not for the meticulous care, the expert hands, the unwavering patience as she indulged my need to control this moment.

I pulled out my phone and dialed.

She answered on the second ring, voice already amused.

"Miss me already?"

I smirked. "You know, I don't think I actually thanked you."

A pause, followed by a mock gasp.

"*Mon Dieu*! Beatrix forgetting her manners? Call the press."

I rolled my eyes, but I could hear the genuine warmth beneath the teasing.

"This is what friends are for," she continued. "Besides, I still haven't gotten you laid recently, which I consider a personal failing."

I laughed, shaking my head.

"You're ridiculous."

She hummed in agreement. "Yes, but I'm also right."

I sighed, staring out at the city.

I murmured, "Do you think I'm experienced enough for a man like him?"

Manon scoffed.

"Beatrix."

"I'm serious."

"Oh, *chérie*," she purred, pure mischief in her voice, "do you need me to remind you of our adventures after college?"

I groaned. "God, please don't."

"Oh, but I must."

I could hear the smirk in her voice.

She launched into a gleeful recounting of our more... decadent adventures.

"Remember the Italian sculptor?" she said. "The one who swore he could carve marble better after he'd spent a night between our thighs?"

I covered my face with one hand.

"Manon—"

"Or the countess in Vienna?" she went on, unfazed. "She had a champagne kink, remember? Wanted to drink from the most delicate of glasses—"

I groaned again. "Enough."

But she wasn't done.

"What about that duke's son in Prague? You know, the one who nearly cried when you—"

"Manon!" I yelped, laughing despite myself.

She laughed, wicked and free.

My face was hot, my stomach hurting from the ridiculousness of it all.

Without missing a beat, she sighed dramatically.

"Ah, those were the days. When men begged and women purred, and the world was ours for the taking."

I rolled my eyes. "It still is."

Manon hummed in agreement.

"So tell me, *ma belle*, are you really worried about handling one man, after everything we've done?"

I hesitated. "Dorian is..."

"Different?" she guessed.

I exhaled. "Yes."

Her voice softened.

"That's for you to decide," she said. "That's the fun of it."

I exhaled, watching the lights flicker across the car's interior.

"So *enjoy* it, Beatrix."

Her voice was lighter now, playful. "Make him sweat. Make him beg. Make him work for it. But most of all—"

I smiled, already knowing what she was about to say. "Make it fun."

A smile curled at my lips as I tilted my head back against the seat, exhaling slow and steady.

She was right, of course. She always was.

The question was no longer whether I was experienced enough for Dorian Wolker.

It was whether he was ready for *me*.

The car slowed, the transition as smooth as velvet.

Outside, no flashing signs, no obvious entrance. A sanctuary for those who belonged.

The moment the car rolled to a stop, the valet service moved seamlessly, my door swinging open without hesitation.

Beyond the door was not a lobby. Not a street.

A private elevator, waiting.

No waiting lists. No crowds.

No mistakes.

I stepped inside, the doors gliding closed with a whisper, and the ascent began.

The elevator was sleek, mirrored, the kind of design that spoke of opulence without needing to prove itself.

The moment it reached the top, it opened onto a red carpet, and the entire city of Manhattan stretched out before me.

My breath didn't hitch—not visibly, anyway.

But the effect was undeniable.

The restaurant was as exclusive as they claimed.

Normally, it handled hundreds of guests per night, perched atop one of the tallest buildings in the city.

Tonight, however, it was half-empty.

Not understaffed. Not underbooked.

Simply... emptied.

The atmosphere was even more hushed than usual, the quiet hum of conversation feeling strategic rather than natural.

I didn't have to ask why.

Dorian had ensured fewer eyes were on me tonight.

The host approached—a tall, broad-shouldered man, sharp in his suit, exuding a quiet authority.

He inclined his head. "Miss Beatrix."

He knew my name. Of course he did.

He gestured toward the heart of the restaurant, but as he led me forward, I realized—we weren't going toward the usual private alcoves.

No.

We were going higher.

The table above all others.

A single, raised platform overlooking the entirety of the room.

A booth of black velvet, perched like a throne.

It was set with exquisite simplicity—a single candle, fine crystal, the city a vast expanse beyond the glass.

But as I slid into the seat, I noticed something else.

I could see everything.

The entire restaurant unfolded beneath me—a sea of power players who had no idea they were being watched. The glittering sprawl of the city stretched beyond the walls, a dizzying view of ambition and excess.

But no one could see me.

The placement was intentional.

A ghost table.

One that allowed me to observe but remain unseen.

His table.

His design.

The host pulled out my chair, but before I could ask, he spoke smoothly. "Your date has asked that you wait here for his arrival."

A slow, deliberate power play.

I smirked but said nothing, lowering myself into the seat with practiced ease.

The host set down a crystal glass of deep red wine.

"The finest in our collection," he murmured, before stepping away.

I lifted the glass, taking a slow sip.

Alone.

Waiting.

With the expanse of the city before me—

And the emptiness beside me where Dorian should be.

The candle flickered. The city glowed.

And I waited.

Minutes slipped by, the edges of time softening, stretching, lengthening.

Dorian was not here.

The wait was deliberate—a power move in the most excruciating form.

I could feel it working.

Not in frustration. Not in impatience.

In something far more dangerous.

Arousal.

The longer I sat there, the more I felt the slow build of heat in my body, the awareness sinking into my skin.

The anticipation was turning against me, twisting into something visceral.

I let my gaze drift past the restaurant's glass walls, toward the glittering skyline that stretched endlessly before me.

How many people were fucking right now?

How many bodies were tangled in sheets, pressing against windows, giving into pleasure with the city sprawled beneath them?

Somewhere, in one of those towers, a woman was gasping against silk.

Somewhere, a man was pressing a lover against a penthouse window.

Somewhere, someone was waiting, as I was—aching, restless, desperate to be touched.

I shifted in my seat.

Beneath me, the restaurant continued to empty.

The subtle murmur of conversations faded. A handful of guests remained, but I watched as servers approached them with quiet discretion, reminding them it was time to leave.

Not a single person questioned it.

Not here.

Not in a place where money and power dictated everything.

I exhaled, dragging my nails gently over the linen tablecloth.

Still, no Dorian.

The clock inched toward nine.

I reached for my phone, my fingers brushing against it before curling away.

No.

Picking it up would mean acknowledging the wait.

Acknowledging that it was getting to me.

I kept my hands still, my back straight, my posture regal.

But between my thighs, I was wet.

The slow, pooling kind.

The kind that came from wanting and not receiving.

From patience fraying at the edges.

From knowing that when he finally did arrive, I would be ready.

I let out a slow breath.

Then, finally, I picked up my phone, opening my emails with effortless grace.

Not to check.

Not to distract.

But to make it look like this was nothing.

That my body wasn't betraying me.

That my thighs weren't slick, that I wasn't shifting to ease the ache.

That I wasn't already halfway to surrender.

I inhaled deeply.

And breathed myself back into control.

I had meant to skim the emails, feign indifference, but the moment my eyes landed on the subject line, I paused.

A name.

The kind that carried weight. That "mattered."

I clicked and read, the words pulling me in, sentence by sentence, the critic's praise unfolding like a carefully layered seduction.

"Beatrix's latest work is not merely erotica—it is a redefinition of sensual literature. A masterclass in prose that does not titillate for the sake of titillation, but wields desire as a narrative force, shaping character, shaping conflict, shaping art itself."

I swallowed, my pulse quickening.

"For decades, we have dismissed erotica as lesser literature, yet Beatrix has ripped the veil from our assumptions. If there is justice, this book will sweep every major literary award this year, marking a generational shift."

"Beatrix is not just a writer to watch—she is the writer of her generation."

It made me flush.

Heat crawled up my neck, not from arousal this time, but from something dangerously close to reverence.

The thought of being read like this. Understood. *Seen*.

And for the first time that night, it wasn't Dorian's name sending shivers through me.

It was my own.

I let the screen dim, my hands warm, my skin buzzing from the sheer weight of it.

And that's when he appeared.

Unhurried. Unbothered.

Dorian.

My eyes flicked up, and there he was—tall, composed, moving toward me with a kind of lethal grace.

As if the wait had been nothing.

As if time itself bent to him, not the other way around.

I didn't gasp.

Didn't startle.

But my fingers curled against the tablecloth.

Because suddenly, the heat burning beneath my skin had nothing to do with the review.

CHAPTER
Eight

POLITE DEFIANCE

Dorian moved as if he had all the time in the world. Unhurried, deliberate.

Below us, the restaurant—normally a sanctuary for whispered power plays and indulgent decadence—was deserted.

Not slowing down.

Not emptying naturally.

Cleared.

Only him.

Only me.

And a small bell that had appeared at my table while I had been too distracted—too flushed, too wet, too consumed by my own praise—to notice.

I let out a slow breath, watching him take his seat.

No apology. No explanation.

Dorian's gaze dragged over me, measuring, taking, understanding.

A silent possession.

His voice, when it finally came, was silk spun around steel.

"I hope you didn't wait too long."

A cruel indulgence because he knew, to the second, how long he had made me wait.

One hour of mounting tension.

Sixty minutes of my body unraveling, softening, warming, opening.

I let him have the silence, watching him back, watching the way the candlelight flickered over the sharp carve of his jaw, the precise tailoring of his suit.

I let my lips curl, my fingers trailing along the stem of my wine glass.

"I kept myself entertained."

I took him in, meeting his gaze, unblinking.

And what I saw was a man who exercised control over every inch of his existence.

The way he sat—composed, at ease, but still in command.

The way his body moved, chiseled to precision, powerful without wasted effort.

To make sure that whoever looked at him understood without the shred of a doubt who was in charge.

And yet—

Not me.

Not yet.

Because he had made a mistake.

A calculated one, perhaps, but a mistake nonetheless.

He had ensured that I was seated, contained, my body hidden.

That the meticulous preparation I had undergone—the lingerie, the garters, the scent that he would soon crave—remained concealed.

That he could see my face, my expression, my pleasure.

But not all of me.

That was by his design.

An attempt to rob me of the initial power, to force me to reveal myself on his terms.

To make me wait—again.

My smile didn't waver because if he thought he was the only one who knew how to play this game, he still had so much to learn.

His fingers grazed the bell, a movement so light it was almost dismissive.

The response was immediate.

The chef, a man whose name was spoken in hushed reverence among the elite, a culinary god known for crafting dishes that were as much art as they were indulgence, appeared.

And he had come, summoned like a mere servant.

The chef bowed his head, his voice laced with deep, earnest gratitude.

"Mr. Wolker, it is an honor."

He didn't say welcome.

Because this wasn't about hospitality.

It was about privilege.

About Dorian's presence itself being a gift.

"I have prepared something special for you," the chef continued, his voice measured, carefully controlled. "Based on the exciting requirements communicated by your trainer and dietitian."

Dorian said nothing, merely nodding in acknowledgment.

The chef turned to me then, his demeanor still respectful but shifting toward charm.

And in that single second, before the words could even leave his mouth—

Dorian glared.

The shift in atmosphere was palpable.

Cold. Absolute.

The chef caught himself, swallowed whatever he had been about to say, lowered his gaze, and retreated into quiet compliance.

Dorian's voice cut through the stillness.

Low. Commanding.

"Stand up."

The words were not a suggestion.

The tension in the air became razor thin.

For a beat, I froze.

He expected me to obey.

Here. Now. In the middle of an empty restaurant, under the gaze of a man who had prepared a meal worthy of kings.

Shock flickered through me. But so did something else.

Hot. Sharp. Dangerous.

A shiver ran down my spine, the ache between my legs tightening.

I didn't move.

Not yet.

I held his gaze, deliberately delaying my response, watching for a crack in his resolve.

Would he back down?

Seconds stretched—awkward now, drawn taut with an unspoken struggle.

But I could feel it, spreading through me, wet and wanting.

If I didn't move now, I would come right here, against the banquette, humiliatingly obvious.

And that would be far worse than standing.

So I did.

Measured.

On my own terms.

Dorian's eyes dragged over me, unblinking.

He took his time, absorbing every detail—the cut of my clothing, the way the fabric clung to what he couldn't yet see.

"Not enough."

My breath hitched.

His tone didn't change.

Didn't rise.

He lifted a single finger.

"On the table."

The chef stiffened, his posture suddenly awkward, caught between reverence and discomfort.

The only sound was the candle flickering, the wine in my untouched glass settling in delicate ripples.

I didn't move.

But my thighs pressed together.

Because this wasn't about seduction anymore.

It was about my submission.

A slow-burn seduction of dominance.

And my body already knew its answer.

The silence between us stretched, thick with tension.

The candlelight flickered, casting elongated shadows across Dorian's sharp features, the golden glow licking at his jawline like an artist's final brushstroke.

His eyes didn't waver.

Neither did mine.

I turned to the chef, who stood frozen in place, caught in the strangeness of the moment.

"Would you be so kind?" I murmured, my voice smooth, deliberate.

The chef hesitated.

His hands found my waist, steady but careful not to linger too long.

Not with Dorian watching.

I placed my foot onto the banquette, feeling the way my stiletto heels wobbled against the cushion.

The fabric shifted beneath me, the precariousness of my position adding a new, sharp thrill.

Then, I lifted one leg onto the table.

As I did, the edge of my thigh grazed Dorian's face.

A whisper of contact.

A brief, electric moment where I felt his breath against my skin.

Heat curled low in my belly.

I stepped up fully, placing the other leg onto the table, rising, straightening—

Standing above all.

From this vantage point, the entire city stretched below me.

The skyline, a dazzling sprawl of ambition and indulgence.

I felt powerful.

Elevated.

A goddess on a pedestal.

And yet—

I was only here because he told me to be.

The realization sank deep, threading through the arousal already simmering inside me.

Because no matter how exalted I felt, the truth remained:

I was standing where he wanted me.

Where he placed me.

Power and submission—two sides of the same exquisite coin.

I looked down at him, my breath steady, my chin lifted.

He didn't move immediately.

He simply looked.

Then, with the same deliberate ease that had defined every movement of his tonight, he pulled out his phone.

And took a picture.

Of my feet, the delicate curve of my arch in my strapped heels, the sharp contrast of black leather against my skin.

Of my legs, lingering on the exposed length of my thighs, and the space between them.

I inhaled sharply, heat flooding through me.

Click.

Another angle.

Click.

The weight of his gaze was one thing.

The permanence of his camera capturing me—claiming me—was something else entirely.

"Turn around."

My pulse skipped.

A command, not a request.

I lingered just long enough to remind him I was still my own.

Then, I obeyed.

Turning, fully aware of what I was revealing.

The back of my dress dipped low, dangerously close to indecency, the silk framing the ghostly lines of my concealed lingerie.

He took more pictures.

Of the curve of my spine.

Of the way the fabric traced my ass.

Click. Click. Click.

The air in the restaurant had changed.

The chef, still standing awkwardly nearby, was attempting to control his breath.

Finally, Dorian lowered the phone, exuding satisfaction as he turned toward him.

"I've sent all the images to my diet and fitness team," he said casually.

The words should have sounded absurd.

Instead, they landed with a brutal, calculated weight.

"They should have everything they need to help you craft the perfect meal for the two of us," he continued, slipping his phone back into his pocket.

Then, after a pause—

"Not as good as a full assessment, but it'll do for today."

The chef, visibly relieved, nodded hurriedly, taking the chance to disengage without confrontation without hesitation.

And still—I stood there, waiting, my body burning under Dorian's scrutiny.

I had expected control.

I had prepared for power.

But I hadn't expected *this*.

Dorian sat there, completely at ease, watching me as though I had already surrendered; as if it had never been a question.

The first click of his camera had sent a thrill down my spine, a whispered acknowledgment of the unspoken tension between us.

The second had made me damp.

By the third, I was fully aware of what he was doing.

And yet—he never asked.

Not once.

Not for permission. Not for consent.

He took.

Possession without warning. Without invitation.

I should have said something.

Should have challenged him.

But I didn't.

Because in that moment, I was too busy grappling with something I had never felt before.

Not submission. Nor surrender.

Something closer to violation—but one that *I* had let happen.

I stood on the table, silk whispering against my skin, the slit of my dress revealing hints of lace and garter.

He had taken pictures. Of my feet, my legs, between my thighs. And more.

An assertion that he would take whatever he wanted.

And when he had sent those pictures to his diet and fitness team, when he had said it wasn't as good as a full assessment but that it would do for today—

I had been with dominant men before. Men who mistook violence for power. Who took with force, who thought control meant brutality.

I had always known how to turn that against them— how to dominate them emotionally, mentally, how to make them need me more than I needed them.

This was different.

Dorian Wolker wasn't trying to break me through force.

He was simply claiming me as if it were inevitable.

And I had no idea how to turn the game in my favor.

I let my eyes flicker down to him, breathing controlled, face unreadable.

He was the most dominant man I had ever met.

The air between us was thick, the weight of what had happened pressing down on my skin like an unspoken demand.

I could still hear the soft clicks of his camera in my mind, the memory of his voice—so smooth, so sure—telling the chef he had enough information to craft my perfect meal.

I had let it happen; let him take.

It was time to take something back.

I lowered myself to my knees, the silk of my dress pooling around me, my thighs spreading enough to tempt, to tease, to make him want to reach out and close the space between us.

But not enough to let him have it.

Not yet.

Dorian had put his phone away.

No more pictures. No more documentation.

This moment belonged only to me.

His gaze sharpened. He wasn't unaffected.

My first victory.

I let the moment stretch, watching him, waiting.

Then, with a flicker of movement so smooth, so controlled, I shifted—agile, effortless.

Now, I was sitting on the table, my legs draped in the way that demanded his attention.

I didn't hesitate.

Didn't second-guess.

I lifted my foot and placed my stiletto on his crotch.

It was deliberate. Precise.

Not crushing, not forceful.

But a whisper of pressure, enough to feel the shape of him rise beneath the fine wool of his trousers.

And God, he reacted.

A sharp twitch beneath me.

A single exhale through his nose, so controlled, but not quite.

I could feel him hardening under my heel.

He didn't break his posture, didn't let a single shift in his expression betray what was happening.

But his body didn't lie.

I pressed a little more.

Enough to feel the thickening heat beneath the sole of my shoe.

A test.

And a confirmation.

I lifted myself, leaning forward, shifting closer.

My dress slid dangerously high, the slit parting further as I moved.

His gaze followed the motion, his breath steady, but tight.

I slid my knee against his stomach, inch by inch.

His suit was smooth, the expensive fabric cool against my bare skin.

My breasts met his face, brushing against his lips as I leaned in.

Soft lace. Bare heat beneath.

His breath hitched, warm against my skin, spreading over the sensitive flesh of my breasts.

I could feel it.

The way his chest rose a little too sharply.

The way his fingers flexed, fighting the instinct to grab.

I arched my back a touch more, letting the curve of my breasts fully press against his mouth.

A tease. A temptation.

Then, higher still.

I moved with agonizing slowness, my collarbone skimming the stubble of his jaw.

My lips inches from his.

I could feel the tension coiling inside him, the way he was fully hard beneath my heel now, the rigid heat straining against his trousers.

His breathing was deep, measured.

But I could tell—if I pressed my mouth to his, if I so much as parted my lips against his own—

He would lose himself.

I held there, hovering.

Close enough that I could taste his breath, feel the heat radiating from his skin.

He didn't move.

Didn't take.

Didn't claim.

But he wanted to.

Desperately.

And that was my second victory.

Before he could react—before he could give in to what I knew was burning inside him—

I rolled off him, moving as fluidly as I had started, slipping back into my seat.

Settling as if nothing had happened.

Like it had been nothing at all.

I reached for a napkin, smoothing it over my lap with calculated ease.

Then, finally, I lifted my gaze.

My voice was casual, amused.

"So," I murmured, my lips curling at the edges. "What do you think the food will be?"

Dorian's fingers brushed the rim of his wine glass, the movement slow, teasing, as if tracing the outline of a thought he wasn't quite ready to say.

I watched his lips part, the slightest curl at the corner, and already, my body reacted.

Our conversation a prepared meal plated in words instead of flesh.

"An interesting start," he murmured, his voice dipping low enough to settle in the pit of my stomach. "A taste that lingers, plays on the tongue. But the best meals? They don't rush to be consumed."

I traced the stem of my glass, mirroring the movement of his fingers on his own.

I wondered if he imagined my fingers on him.

I knew I was imagining his on me.

"Some flavors," I replied, tilting my chin, "are meant to be savored."

His eyes darkened.

Oh yes, he felt it.

The tension, the pull.

The ache building between us.

"I agree," he said smoothly, lifting his glass, taking a slow sip, dragging it out.

My eyes flicked to the movement of his throat as he swallowed.

Unfair.

Unfair how something so small could make me feel this tight, this wet.

"But tell me, Beatrix," he continued, setting his glass down with calculated ease, "how long can something be teased before it begs to be devoured?"

My breath caught.

The pulse between my legs throbbed, answering for me.

I let my lips curve into something playful, tilting my head. "That depends," I said lightly, trailing my fingers up my own wrist, my touch featherlight, making my skin tingle. "On whether the one doing the teasing has the patience to handle the begging."

The tension coiled sharper.

His hand curled into a loose fist against the table, as if he were holding himself back.

I knew what he wanted.

What he was imagining right now.

Me, beneath him.

Or perhaps seated as I was, legs spread, lips parted, waiting for his next move.

Dorian inhaled, his restraint so tight, so painfully obvious.

"Patience," he mused, his voice dipping lower, smoothing over me like warm honey. "A virtue. One I've mastered."

He studied me, eyes reminding me how much of me was already his.

Even if I wouldn't admit it.

"But some things," he murmured, "shouldn't be left too long. They become... unbearably soft."

Fuck.

A sharp pulse shot through me, hot and damp, pooling at the very core of me.

I crossed my legs, knowing he saw it.

"I imagine," I said carefully, forcing air back into my lungs, "some things are better when they fall apart in the right hands."

His fingers twitched.

His jaw flexed.

And under the table—he was so hard now.

I didn't have to see it.

I felt it.

I knew.

I let the silence stretch, letting him stew in it, letting him throb against his own control.

Then, I lifted my glass, tilting it toward him in a silent toast.

"To restraint."

Dorian exhaled through his nose, slow, measured.

His fingers tapped the table once—a small warning, a quiet promise.

When he finally spoke, his voice was dark, knowing.

"You can take all the time you need."

A slow smile spread over his lips.

"But when you give in—"

A flick of his fingers, dismissive.

"I don't do small bites."

Heat rushed through me, heady and violent.

I clenched my thighs, relieving the ache.

I had won this round.

But he had already set up his opening for the next.

The conversation had simmered, steeped in tension, each word a taste, a tease, a test.

But the night didn't end in surrender.

Instead, it unfolded course by course, indulgence by indulgence.

The meal before us was opulent, a decadent display of Dorian's world—flawless execution, perfect presentation, indulgence without excess.

Every bite was rich, layered, balanced—a reflection of him, of this night, of the way he played with restraint and satisfaction.

I watched him as we ate, savoring the slow burn of what wasn't happening.

Despite the tension, despite the undeniable need curling between us, he didn't push.

There were no more demands.

No more unspoken commands.

Just... time.

Conversation.

The dance of two minds who knew the inevitable was coming, but weren't ready to rush to the final act.

When the plates were cleared, and the last sip of wine had been tasted, he didn't press for more.

He simply stood, offering his hand, leading me out into the night.

The city air was cool, a sharp contrast to the heat still simmering in my skin.

We stopped beside the waiting car, the moment stretching a little too long.

He leaned in.

Not to claim, not to take.

A soft brush of his lips against my cheek.

A whisper of touch, a promise instead of a demand.

When he pulled back, he studied me for a moment. "May I call on you again?"

"I'd like that too."

His lips curved—satisfied, but not triumphant.

He opened the car door, watching as I slid inside.

As the car pulled away, I stared out at the city lights, still feeling the ghost of his breath against my skin.

CHAPTER
Nine

READING ROOM

I woke late, tangled in silk sheets, my body still humming with unspent energy.

It was nearly noon when my phone buzzed.

I didn't have to check the screen.

Manon.

I answered, already bracing.

Her voice came through, bright, eager, relentless.

"Tell. Me. Everything."

Manon's voice was incredulous, her laughter bubbling through the phone like champagne.

"Wait, wait, wait. Are you telling me that after all that—all that tension, all that build-up, all those stolen glances and whispered innuendos—he didn't take you?"

I sighed, stretching beneath my sheets, still drenched in the memory of last night.

"Not in the way you mean," I said, voice still sleep-heavy, but the implication unmistakable.

Manon made a strangled sound of disbelief.

"What the fuck, Beatrix? You mean to tell me that you went through an entire meal of power play and heated glances, you strutted in that absolutely obscene dress, you teased him until he was probably harder than steel, and you walked away without even so much as a goodnight fuck?"

I laughed, the absurdity of it hitting me now in the daylight. "It was a choice."

Manon groaned. "A terrible one."

"It was strategic," I corrected. "The best games don't end too soon."

"I bet your sheets disagree."

I flushed, shifting against them, the slick remnants of my arousal from last night still clinging to my thighs.

Manon must have sensed my hesitation.

"You were soaked, weren't you?"

I bit my lip. "Drenched."

A long pause. Then, a slow, wicked laugh.

"And yet… you didn't even touch yourself, did you?"

I exhaled heavily, rubbing my face. "I was too spent."

Manon tutted loudly, the sound exaggerated.

"Unacceptable. I simply cannot allow my best friend to suffer like this. Beatrix, you need to call me back—on video. Immediately."

I rolled my eyes. "Why? So you can lecture me in high definition?"

"No," she said primly. "So I can assign you a task. Now, get up and go look at your toy drawer."

I groaned. "Manon—"

"No arguing. Go. Now."

Sighing, I rolled out of bed, padding across my room, pulling open the drawer that Manon had single-handedly filled over the years.

It was a veritable arsenal of pleasure, all meticulously organized, each one a gift from my scandalous, well-meaning friend.

"Which one am I supposed to use?" I asked, eyeing the collection.

"That depends." I could practically hear the smirk in her voice. "How desperate are you?"

I narrowed my eyes at the screen. "You're evil."

"And you're a pent-up mess." She hummed, considering. "Pick the one you think will get the job done. Go take a long, hot bath and handle your situation."

I sighed, already feeling the heat curling low again.

She was right.

I needed this.

"Fine. I'll call you later."

"After."

I laughed, hanging up.

It was going to be a very, very relaxing morning.

I hung up with Manon, shaking my head at her persistence.

But she wasn't wrong.

My body wasn't satisfied.

Not even close.

The tension from last night still coiled inside me, a slow, smoldering heat, refusing to be ignored.

I stretched against the sheets, feeling the lingering slickness between my thighs, a reminder of how far I had let things go without relief.

That wouldn't do.

Not today.

Not when my mind was still painted with images of Dorian.

I moved to my nightstand, pulling open the drawer where Manon had stocked me with every imaginable tool for pleasure.

My fingers traced over the collection before stopping on one particular device.

A connected toy.

A dangerous one.

The company had approached me last year, asking permission to sync their technology with my stories—to translate my filthiest words into something felt.

I had agreed, out of curiosity.

What I hadn't expected was that some of the stories they selected were old, unrealized fantasies—things I had once written for myself, for my own secret indulgence.

Things I had never actually experienced.

I scrolled through the selections, my pulse quickening.

Then I found it.

An old piece—one I had forgotten about until now.

A man taking all three of my holes, stretching me, claiming me, marking me until I couldn't remember where I ended and he began.

My thighs pressed together involuntarily.

I had written this fantasy before I truly understood my own desires; before I knew how much control over the dynamic mattered to me.

Now, though?

Now, I was willing to surrender—when the right man demanded it.

With a slow exhale, I connected the toy, feeling the first gentle hum between my legs.

My breath hitched.

Then, the pulses began, matching the rhythm of the story.

The first touch was light, teasing.

Then deeper.

Then again.

The simulation had me bent over, ass slick and ready, my body taking two at once, spreading wider with each thrust.

I moaned, my hips rocking against the toy, letting it push deeper, working in perfect rhythm with the filthy words whispered into my ears.

My mind blurred.

The faceless dominant in my story had a form now.

A voice. A presence. A name.

Dorian.

Dorian pressing me down, forcing me open.

Dorian's breath at my ear, whispering how wrecked I was going to be when he was done.

My breath shuddered, my body trembling as the toy moved between my slick folds, pressing deeper into my ass, stretching me in sync with the scene.

I was so close—

I remembered not liking how I had written the ending.

It hadn't gone far enough.

It hadn't satisfied me.

With a frustrated moan, I reached for my phone, trying to adjust the settings, my fingers slick with arousal as I struggled to swipe.

The screen wouldn't register my touch.

I huffed, wiping my hand against my thigh, still struggling to gain control.

A notification popped up.

My breath froze in my chest.

The name on the screen made my pulse slam against my ribs.

Dorian Wolker.

My eyes flicked to the message, the words burning into my vision.

"Last night was fun. If interested in more, check email."

The toy buzzed inside me, still pulsing, still playing to the rhythm of my unfinished fantasy.

But now, all I could think about was him.

The real him.

His hands. His voice. His control.

Heat licked through me, the message slicing through my restraint like a blade.

My walls clenched hard, the pleasure spiraling, building, tipping over the edge.

My hips jerked, my body seizing as the orgasm hit me like a shockwave, sudden and violent.

I arched, a ragged moan slipping past my lips as wave after wave crashed through me.

My legs shook, my skin burned, the release so intense I nearly blacked out.

Body still trembling, spent, ruined.

And yet—

I was already aching for more.

CHAPTER
Ten

EYES UNSAID

My pulse still thrummed, body shaking from the aftershocks of release, but my mind was sharp again, snapping back to reality.

Dorian had told me to check my email.

Still catching my breath, I wiped my fingers clean against the edge of a towel, tapping the app open with something between anticipation and impatience.

The first email at the top was a reschedule notice for last night's reading.

I skimmed it quickly, expecting some vague excuse about scheduling conflicts or unforeseen circumstances.

Instead, something caught my eye.

The new date.

It had been moved to a night when I had nothing else on my calendar.

That appeared intentional.

Before I could dwell on it, my phone buzzed—my agent calling.

I answered, already assuming the reason.

"Let me guess. You saw the review?" I said, still staring at my inbox.

My agent laughed, the sound brimming with satisfaction. "Of course I did. And so did the entire literary world. Congratulations, darling—you've breached out of erotica. You're being hailed as a generational talent."

I exhaled, rolling onto my side, the praise washing over me, hot and slow.

I'd been called many things before—controversial, provocative, indulgent.

But this?

This was different.

The critic had called it a revolution.

A turning point in literary eroticism.

Something that would bridge the gap between high art and desire.

Something that had never been done before.

I should have been giddy. Thrilled. Buzzing.

And I was.

But beneath that satisfaction was something else.

A nagging, simmering hunger that the review didn't touch.

Not like Dorian had.

Not compared to last night.

I shook the thought away as my agent kept talking.

"And there's already buzz about awards season. If this book makes it into the shortlist for literary prizes..."

I interrupted her, smirking. "If they can handle it."

She laughed. "They won't have a choice."

There was a pause, a rustling of papers.

Then—

"Oh, right. I was actually calling about something else. The bookstore reached out with a request to reschedule last night's event. Are you free that night?"

I stilled.

The email had said the event was already set. Announced.

I could feel his power in that.

Dorian had arranged it. Pulled strings without asking, my agent unaware.

I hesitated.

I didn't like the idea of giving him the satisfaction of my easy compliance.

Not after how he had made me wait, made me *want*.

But this?

This was a small, innocuous gesture.

One that would keep him wanting more.

I smiled, letting the game continue.

"Yeah, I'm free. Let's do it."

"Perfect. I'll confirm now."

She hung up before I could ask anything else.

I checked my messages, but nothing from Dorian.

Still frowning, I went back to my inbox.

The next few emails were congratulations from fellow writers, a mix of jealousy and genuine support about the glowing review.

They floated as shadows as I kept looking.

There were event invitations, requests for collaborations from magazines and publishers.

Some were from businesses, offering sponsorship deals, brand partnerships, and high-profile partnerships in general.

Some were investment proposals, offers to collaborate on luxury ventures, invitations to join exclusive circles of influence.

My name had value beyond literary circles now.

I kept scrolling.

And scrolling.

Nothing.

No email from him.

My stomach tightened, the mix of confusion and frustration twisting through me.

Had he meant something else?

Had he sent it to another account?

Or—was this another one of his games?

I exhaled sharply, clicking my phone off, the empty inbox mocking me in the silence.

I pushed aside my frustration at the empty inbox, forcing myself to refocus. If he wanted me to chase him, he'd have to wait.

I returned to my emails, sorting through invitations, proposals, and congratulatory messages.

Each reply had to be precise—flirtation as strategy, power as seduction.

To a well-known fashion brand:

Tempting. But I don't only wear beauty—I make it unforgettable. If we're crafting desire, I'm intrigued. My assistant will make sure you keep me wanting more.

To a high-profile publisher:

Intellectual foreplay is delightful, but I do hope this won't be a dry affair. I need a little indulgence with my literature. My assistant will ensure I'm properly... enticed.

To an art collector:

Seduction is in the mystery, the hint of what's out of reach. Are we merely teasing or inviting obsession? Let's find out.

To a business executive:

I never give away influence—I let men earn it. If this is another pitch, I'll pass. If it's a game worth playing, my assistant will arrange the stakes.

To an investment group:

It's not only my name you're after—you're asking for my presence. And that comes at a cost. My assistant will see if you can afford it.

Each answer was bait, not surrender.

I let them think I was intrigued—never eager. Always setting the tone.

Then something caught my eye.

A contract proposal.

The subject line: *Per our discussion last night—terms enclosed.*

I hadn't discussed any partnerships.

I opened it.

The email was clinical.

Please find attached the preliminary contract per our conversation at the event. The terms reflect the agreement as discussed. We look forward to your response.

No warmth. No elaboration.

I clicked the attachment.

The LLC name was unfamiliar.

I read it again.

A reference to a character in one of my books.

A man who acquired power through veiled moves and quiet control.

A slow smile curled my lips.

I opened the attachment and scanned the document.

The further I read, the more I realized what this was.

It was detailed. Meticulous. Controlling.

A precise regimen—training, sleeping, eating. Each moment accounted for.

Sex acts—explicitly detailed.

Limits—established, yet designed to be tested.

Submission—not in moments, but in essence.

Dorian in charge of everything.

The structure of my days, the permissions I'd need to seek.

How I would be disciplined and rewarded.

Absolute, consuming, undeniable control.

I traced a fingertip over the words, my pulse quickening.

Some parts... intrigued me. Deeply.

The idea of being tamed, shaped, broken in all the ways that turned surrender into a work of art.

A sharp rising hunger rose through me.

I swallowed hard, pressing my thighs together.

There were the parts that made something in me resist.

The contract didn't ask for my submission.

It demanded it.

There was no room for negotiation. No room for the quiet power I was used to wielding even in submission.

Complete surrender.

I had played these games before. I had submitted, but only to the extent that I chose to.

This contract asked for more.

It wanted everything.

The phone rang twice before Manon answered.

"*Ma chérie*, tell me you finally came to your senses and gave yourself a proper orgasm this morning."

I rolled my eyes, even as my lips curled into a smirk. "I have something better for you."

"I'm listening."

"I need your help... crafting a response."

There was a pause. Then a knowing hum. "To whom and about what?"

I hesitated.

"Oh. Oh, this is going to be fun."

I opened up the contract again, flipping through the pages.

"He sent me something."

"More artwork?"

I glanced over the section on discipline. My pulse skipped.

"A contract."

Manon's laugh was wicked. "Oh, B. You do attract the best kind of trouble."

I leaned back against my chair, exhaling. "It's detailed. Very... precise. Very him."

"And?"

"And some of it, I like."

"And the rest?"

I tapped a red fingernail against the page. "It requires full surrender."

Manon's breath hitched. "That's not your game."

"No."

"You don't give control. You let men believe they take it."

I smiled.

There was a beat of silence, then Manon purred, "So. How shall we make him work for it?"

I grinned. "That's where you come in."

Manon hummed thoughtfully. "If he wants your submission, he'll have to earn it. And if he doesn't know that yet, well—he will soon."

I laughed, my body still thrumming from the residual arousal the contract had stirred in me.

"I'm coming over," Manon said suddenly. "We should read this together before we craft a response. After all, two minds—and two very dirty imaginations—are better than one."

I smirked, stretching out on my bed, still feeling the lingering heat between my legs.

"Make it fast," I murmured. "I might need another bath after this."

Part 2

POWER GRAMMAR

CHAPTER
Eleven

RED INK

I stepped into the shower, letting the hot water slide over my skin, washing away the lingering tension—and the undeniable arousal—that Dorian's contract had stirred in me.

The heat did little to cool me down.

I lathered up, hands moving slower than necessary, my thoughts lingering over certain clauses, certain demands.

Would I let him dictate my meals? My schedule?

Would I let him punish me? Would I—

I exhaled sharply and turned the water to cold.

The sudden shock made me gasp, snapping me back into control.

No. I wasn't going to let myself fall into this too easily.

Dorian was a man used to getting what he wanted.

But I wasn't something to be owned.

The intercom buzzed as I stepped out, the sound
startling in the steamy quiet of my bathroom.

I wrapped a towel around myself and pressed the
button.

"Miss Beatrix, your guest has arrived."

I smirked. Manon never wasted time.

"Send her up."

I had a flicker of time to tighten the knot on my
towel before the knock came.

Opening the door, I found Manon leaning casually against the frame, one eyebrow arched as she swept a
knowing glance over me.

"If I didn't know better, I'd think you were trying to
seduce me, *ma chérie.*"

I rolled my eyes, but smirked.

"This is becoming a habit, isn't it?"

She stepped inside, heels clicking against the floor
as she gave me a slow once-over. "First, you answer the
door in a towel, now you do it again? Should I start assuming this is how you like to greet me?"

I laughed. "Should I assume you're keeping track?"

Manon shrugged dramatically. "I have to say, if this
is your way of coming on to me, I appreciate the com-
mitment to a theme."

I leaned in, voice low, teasing. "Oh, darling. If I
wanted you, you'd already be in my bed."

Manon grinned. "Touché."

She brushed past me, tossing her coat over the nearest chair before turning back with an expectant look. "Now, put something on. We have work to do. This contract of yours isn't going to rewrite itself."

I sighed, glancing toward the bedroom.

The towel clung a little too perfectly.

Manon followed my gaze and smirked. "Unless, of course, you're planning to negotiate this naked. Which, I'll admit, could be a power move."

"Tempting," I said dryly, "but I'd rather have some armor for this."

"Good girl," she murmured, sinking into my couch as I disappeared into my room. "*Dépêche-toi*! I want to see what our dear Dorian thinks he can get away with."

I emerged from the bedroom, damp hair falling over my shoulders, wearing nothing but a tight white T-shirt and jeans. Bare, comfortable, but still deliberately effortless.

Manon gave only a flicker of attention to my outfit—her attention locked onto the printout of Dorian's contract.

"'The submissive shall adhere to a structured training schedule designed to enhance physical endurance, mental discipline, and obedience.'" She paused, giving me a slow, knowing smirk. "Obedience? He really thinks he's getting that from you?"

I leaned against the counter, arms crossed, smirking back. "Wishful thinking."

"Adorable." She flicked to another page, reading further. "'The Dominant will oversee all aspects of the submissive's routine, including but not limited to dietary intake, exercise regimen, and appropriate social engagements.'"

She raised an eyebrow. "So, he wants to control your diet, tell you when to work out, *and* decide who you can see?"

"Men have tried for less."

Manon snorted. "And where are they now?"

"Scattered across three continents, still wondering what went wrong."

She let out a laugh, flipping further. "'The submissive will undergo regular evaluations to ensure compliance and receptivity to training methods.'"

She turned to me with an exaggerated expression. "Are you signing up for a sex internship?"

I groaned, rubbing my temples. "I hadn't gotten to that part yet."

She waved the paper. "*Mon dieu*, Beatrix, are we dealing with a corporate acquisition or a submission contract?"

I scanned ahead and—oh.

A slow heat curled through my stomach as my eyes trailed over a particular clause.

Before I could comment, Manon let out a dramatic gasp.

"Wait. 'The submissive will be required to undergo sexual measurements to ensure optimal compatibility with the Dominant's needs.'"

She turned to me, delighted. "Sexual. Measurements."

I bit my lip, trying not to smile. "That's... new."

Manon collapsed onto the couch beside me, cackling. "*Ma chérie*, he wants to measure your holes."

I covered my face, laughing despite myself.

She nudged me. "So, tell me. Did he send measuring tape with the contract, or are we waiting for a tailor to show up with a clipboard?"

I peeked at her from behind my fingers. "I assume he has his own... methods."

Manon grinned wickedly. "Oh, I bet he does."

I exhaled, but my thighs pressed together involuntarily. I could already picture it—Dorian, deliberate and focused, touching, testing, taking his time.

The thought sent a pulse of heat between my legs.

Manon was still reading, her amusement shifting to something else.

She sucked in a breath. "Oh. *This*. 'The submissive is expected to anticipate the Dominant's needs and act accordingly, even in the absence of explicit instruction.'"

She tapped the paper, her voice lower now. "Mmm. I like that one."

I hummed, pretending not to notice the way she squeezed her thighs together.

She kept going, but her tone had changed. Less playful. More measured.

More... heated, as I was.

My own body betrayed me at certain clauses. Some of the expectations, the unrelenting control, the precision of his rules—they shouldn't have turned me on, but they did.

And Manon, still pacing, was not unaffected either.

By the time she reached the final clauses, there was a noticeable tension in the air.

Manon stopped.

Took a slow, steady breath.

Then, with no small amount of amusement, she turned to me.

"I need a little space."

I smiled, legs still crossed, resisting my own growing need. "Oh?"

She smirked, stretching her arms above her head like a cat. "Unless, of course, you'd prefer to stay and watch. But, I should warn you—I need to finish myself off."

I laughed, but I also understood.

This contract—this ridiculous, consuming contract—had done something to both of us.

I tilted my head, smirking. "Enjoy yourself, then."

Manon winked. "Oh, I intend to."

And with that, she disappeared into the bathroom, leaving me alone with my own pounding, aching need.

I was about to sit back down when I heard it—

Loud, unrestrained moans.

Manon wasn't holding back.

A long, drawn-out cry of pleasure, her voice thick with surrender.

Then, the shower turned on.

A few minutes later, the door swung open, and Manon emerged, freshly showered, wearing only a Cheshire cat smile.

She stretched, her bare skin still damp, then flopped onto my bed like she owned the place.

"That was amazing."

"Glad to know Dorian's contract was that stimulating for you."

She grinned, stretching her arms above her head. "Mmm. I'll admit, I didn't expect to enjoy certain parts quite so much."

Then she sighed dramatically. "But now, I need new clothes. My previous ones... didn't survive."

I snorted. "You're a menace."

She grinned wider. "And yet, you let me into your closet anyway."

She slid off the bed, completely at ease with her nakedness, and disappeared into my walk-in closet, muttering in French about the state of my lingerie collection.

I rolled my eyes.

Manon had told me more times than I could count about the importance of good lingerie.

It wasn't about how it looked—it was about how it made you feel.

And every time she had this conversation with me, it was with the same mild disapproval, like a teacher disappointed in a student's half-effort.

"You dress exquisitely, *ma chérie*, but underneath? *Tsk*. You're still too focused on 'good enough.'"

I could hear her rifling through my drawers, sighing at my choices.

"Beatrix, really? You could do so much better."

I leaned against the doorway. "Are we having this conversation again?"

She emerged from behind a rack of dresses, holding up a sheer lace set, dramatically shaking her head.

"You should already know better."

I laughed, watching as she sorted through my most delicate pieces, critiquing, selecting.

"I put effort into my lingerie."

She lifted a single eyebrow. "Do you?"

I crossed my arms, amused. "You think I don't?"

She sighed, exasperated. "You put enough in to be tempting, enough to be alluring. But where's the indulgence? The self-worship? The devotion to the art of it?"

I smirked. "You make it sound like a religion."

Manon grinned. "For French women, it might as well be."

She turned back to the drawers, pulling out options and dismissing them as quickly.

"Good lingerie isn't only about seduction. It's about confidence. It's about what you know you're wearing, even if no one else sees it. It shapes how you carry yourself. How you move. It makes you untouchable."

She finally settled on a black lace set, the kind that hugged every curve while still leaving plenty to the imagination.

Then, she grabbed something comfortable but effortlessly sexy to throw over it—a sleek fitted top, high-waisted trousers, the kind of look that hinted at danger while remaining deceptively casual.

She dressed quickly, efficiently, emerging from the closet looking completely composed—as if she hadn't spent the last ten minutes naked, discussing the finer points of lingerie while sifting through my wardrobe.

There was no way to tell what she had chosen to wear underneath.

No one would be the wiser.

I took her in, tilting my head. "I never would've paired that together. But it looks hot."

Manon smirked. "Glad to know I can still be your fashion consultant, *ma chérie*. Someone has to save you from yourself."

Manon sank into the couch beside me, one leg folded under her as she skimmed the contract again. Her usual air of playful amusement had settled into something sharper—focused, strategic.

She tapped a red-lacquered nail against the page, tilting her head. "Alright, *ma chérie*. Let's decide what the big bad wolf can and cannot have."

I smirked, catching the pen she tossed me. "He's used to absolute control."

"And you," Manon said with a knowing look, "are used to making men think they have it."

She grinned, flipping through the contract. "The most obvious non-negotiable—he needs to understand that for everything, at every step, he has to ask for your consent."

I nodded. "Explicitly stated. No assumptions."

She circled the section, her strokes decisive. "And none of this fantasy where he dictates your life outside the bedroom. You like control games? Great. But only when you allow it."

I twirled the pen between my fingers. "I'll allow the illusion of power where it serves me."

She laughed. "Now you're thinking like a proper queen."

We continued through the document, negotiating clauses, adjusting language.

My fingers tightened around the pen.

Manon, still flipping through, didn't notice the way my expression cooled.

"This clause about not seeing certain people is offensive."

She stilled.

I met her gaze. "Did he really think he could dictate when we see each other? How often? Under what circumstances?"

I exhaled, running my pen brutally through the entire section.

"This is a deal-breaker. You and I see each other anytime, anywhere. Non-negotiable."

For a long moment, she didn't speak.

"*Ma chérie...* you do love me, don't you?" she said, teasing.

I scoffed, but my lips twitched. "It took you this long to figure that out?"

She cleared her throat, regaining her usual bravado. "Well, I approve of this particular power move."

"As if there was ever a world in which I'd let a man dictate my friendships."

She clutched her heart dramatically. "And they say romance is dead."

I rolled my eyes, nudging her shoulder before moving on.

"Okay. The dietary restrictions?"

Manon groaned. "Ugh. No man should ever be involved in meal planning. Hard pass."

I chuckled. "He can make suggestions. But I eat what I want."

She marked it up. "Training regimen?"

I tapped the pen against my lip, considering. "Some structure is fine. I like discipline. But not as a rule. If I wake up and don't want to train, I won't."

Manon smirked. "You're keeping him on his toes already."

We went through every line, paring it down, reshaping the terms into something that suited me.

The final version left no room for misinterpretation.

Dorian would get control—but only what I permitted him to have.

And the clause about Manon? Gone. Without discussion. Without compromise.

Manon stretched, tossing the pen onto the table with a satisfied sigh.

"I hope he enjoys this little power check."

I smirked. "Oh, he will. He just doesn't know it yet."

Manon stretched, tossing the pen onto the table with a satisfied sigh. "Alright, *ma chérie*. That was fun. But now, we need to make sure this is airtight."

I frowned. "You think I need a lawyer to finalize the language?"

She gave me a pointed look. "Oh, I know you do. If he's treating this like a business deal, then so should you."

I leaned back against the couch. "The one I have doesn't go as hard into this kind of stuff."

Manon smirked. "No problem. I know someone."

Before I could ask, she was already pulling out her phone, dialing.

I expected her to call some high-profile, dominatrix-friendly attorney. Maybe someone who had handled a handful of NDAs for celebrities with particular tastes.

Instead, she uttered a name that made me sit up.

The man she was calling wasn't some obscure legal figure in underground circles. He was one of the top corporate lawyers in America.

A man whose name alone could send chills down the spines of CEOs.

Not someone known for negotiating BDSM contracts.

And yet—

He picked up immediately.

"Manon." His voice was smooth, controlled—polished, the kind of tone that belonged to a man who owned rooms and orchestrated empires.

But there was an edge of something else.

Something submissive.

Something that only existed when he was speaking to her.

"To what do I owe the pleasure?" he asked.

Manon smiled, indulgent, in no rush to answer. She let the silence stretch long enough before finally murmuring, "Now, *cher*, do you really need me to tell you that?"

I could hear his breath hitch over the phone.

Then, composed but a fraction slower than before—

"What kind of business?"

Manon's eyes glittered as she reclined against the couch, tapping a lazy finger against her thigh.

"One that requires extreme discretion."

A sharp exhale. Then, a slight chuckle, forced. "Is that so?"

Manon dragged her nail along the rim of her phone, like she could touch him through it

"Mmhmm. I need someone who understands the importance of keeping things... contained."

There was a beat of silence.

"I assume you'll want it handled immediately."

Manon's smile deepened. "You assume correctly."

"Send it over. I'll take care of it. Personally."

"Oh, *cher*, I would expect nothing less."

His breath hitched again.

Manon tilted her head, as if deciding whether she wanted to push further, to tease him a little more.

She must have decided against it—because a moment later, she simply said, "I'll be waiting."

Without another word, she hung up.

I crossed my arms, amused. "So. You have America's most ruthless corporate lawyer taking time out of his schedule to handle my contract?"

Manon grinned wickedly. "He owes me. And besides"—she leaned in, conspiratorial—"I think he enjoys doing what I tell him to."

I shook my head, laughing. "You really do have everyone eating out of your hand, don't you?"

She shrugged, unbothered. "I don't see the point in having power if you don't use it."

I smirked, reaching for the glass of water beside me, taking a slow sip. "I'll drink to that."

Manon's eyes flicked to the glass. She let out a low, amused laugh.

"Ah, *bien sûr*. Already staying properly hydrated. Look at you, Beatrix—completely in compliance with the contract before it's even signed."

I almost choked on my water, laughing. "You know, I do like to be ahead of the curve."

Manon's lips curved wickedly. "Mmm, funny—so does Dorian's head, from what I hear. And your curves, well... the two are meant to meet."

I rolled my eyes, though I couldn't stop the smirk from spreading across my lips. "You're impossible."

She winked. "And yet, you adore me."

Then, as if remembering something, she turned to me. "By the way, there's a jewelry auction coming up. We should go."

"You want more diamonds? Haven't you already conquered every Cartier vault in Paris?"

Manon grinned, unrepentant. "Indulgence, *ma chérie*. Plus, you never know who we might see."

I tilted my head, intrigued. "Go on."

She smirked, mysterious and knowing. "I have a feeling it will be interesting."

And with Manon, that usually meant trouble.

CHAPTER Twelve

FINE PRINT

It had been two weeks since I'd sent my redlined response to Dorian's contract.

Two weeks of silence from him.

I knew it had been received. Manon's lawyer had made certain of one thing: Dorian Wolker only had power over me when I chose to give it.

I had other distractions.

My book had exploded beyond expectation—interviews, panels, critics arguing whether I was a feminist writer or a provocateur.

They were talking about me.

Meanwhile, Manon's star was also burning at an all-time high.

She had sprinted past supermodel into fashion icon— designers chasing her approval instead of the reverse.

And, naturally, that annoyed her mother to no end.

"I keep telling her I could have been a lawyer like my brother, but no. She'd rather be scandalized by the fact that her daughter is a cultural phenomenon," Manon said, twirling her champagne flute between her fingers as we walked toward the auction entrance.

I smirked. "She must be livid."

"She sent me a three-page letter last week about 'proper careers,'" Manon sighed dramatically. "I framed it. It's now hanging in my dressing room."

I laughed, but before we entered, Manon tugged at my arm. "Let's freshen up first. I need to make sure my lipstick is still capable of causing a scandal."

I grinned and followed her into the marble-lined restroom.

We had stepped into the restroom when the air shifted.

A presence entered the room, and I didn't have to turn to know who it was.

Manon's mother.

Draped in deep burgundy Saint Laurent, her diamonds precise, her posture unbreakable.

The disapproval in her eyes felt permanent, carved into marble generations old.

"Manon."

One word. A blade.

"*Maman.*"

A slow, deliberate glance at Manon's reflection. "Dressed to cause a scandal again, I see. As you always seem to be in auction rooms."

Manon smirked. "You've always taught me it's important to have consistency."

Her mother's lips pressed into a thin line. "And yet, you insist on embarrassing our name. First as a model, now as... an icon, if the press is to be believed."

Manon applied another swipe of lipstick, unbothered. "I'm glad to see you read the press. I wasn't sure you acknowledged my existence anymore."

Her mother's jaw tightened. "The world already knows your power, Manon. You do not need to beg for their attention."

That was when I stepped in. "She isn't begging for anything. She's taking what she wants. Which, last I checked, is the entire foundation of your world."

Manon's mother turned her sharp gaze to me and laughed, a hint of disgust layered deep in her throat.

"Ah, Beatrix. The harlot in print."

"I prefer 'literary harlot.' It has a better ring to it."

She tilted her head, examining me. "You encourage her worst impulses. And worse, you let her think this kind of life is power. But fame is a disease, Beatrix. Power does not come from exposure. It comes from discretion. Something our family has held for generations."

Manon rolled her eyes. "And I'm a stain on it, I know."

Her mother's expression didn't shift.

Then, finally, she turned to the mirror, adjusting the diamond choker at her throat.

"Your father wanted me to tell you I shall be bidding tonight to take those French possessions back to the homeland, where they belong. Not in the hands of..."

She turned, assessing me, her gaze sweeping over me with disdain so precise, it could cut glass.

Then she gave a small, dismissive wave of her fingers. "...Whatever this is. Do try not to embarrass us."

And with that, she turned and left.

The door shut with an echoing finality.

Silence settled between us.

Then, Manon sighed dramatically. "She's in rare form tonight."

"That wasn't rare. That was a goddamn art piece in controlled cruelty."

Manon shrugged, but her lips twitched. "She's mad that I exist loudly. And that we're still friends."

I looped my arm through hers. "Then let's make sure she hears you tonight."

She grinned. "Oh, *mon dieu*, yes. Let's."

And with that, we swept out of the bathroom and into the auction hall, ready to make some noise.

Manon's mother had been one thing. Bumping into *mine* was another.

She stood at the entrance of the auction hall, wearing an ivory Chanel suit, pearls at her throat, her hair swept into a sleek, severe chignon.

She was speaking to another woman—another social force in this room—but the moment her eyes landed on me, her conversation halted.

Manon leaned in and whispered, amused, "I think she spotted her feral child."

I glanced sideways. "I think she's debating whether she should acknowledge me at all."

She did.

With a single step forward, she examined me—assessing, cool.

Then, finally, approving.

Not of me.

Of what I had become.

"You've done well for yourself," she said smoothly, as if it had been inevitable.

"I have."

"I don't care for the... subject matter. But the New York Times seems to believe it has merit. And I suppose that means something."

Manon snorted.

"You always did trust their opinion more than mine."

"A reputable publication, at least."

Manon tilted her head, amused. "Ah, so literary erotica is fine—as long as the right critics approve?"

Mother's gaze flickered to Manon.

Then, finally, she sighed. "I suppose some things are out of my control."

A glance toward the auction hall. "Well. I must go in. I'll see you inside."

I let out a slow exhale.

Manon was grinning like a cat.

"That was incredible."

I rolled my eyes. "Glad you enjoyed it."

She looped her arm through mine. "Are you kidding? I live for that kind of irony."

As I settled into my seat, I traced a lazy fingertip over the embossed cover of the auction catalog before flipping it open. The room hummed with quiet anticipation, the kind that only the ultra-wealthy could muster; the calm before a financial storm.

Manon leaned in beside me, flipping a few pages with effortless grace until her perfectly manicured nails landed on the star of the auction: The Luxuria Collar.

Obscene in its perfection—platinum and black rhodium embracing a blood-red Burmese ruby, surrounded by impossible diamonds. Jewelry masqurerading as restraint.

The centerpiece, the impossibly rare, 100-carat blood-red Burmese Mogok Ruby.

Rumors said it marked its owners.

I shifted in my seat.

Manon, ever perceptive, smirked.

"It's obscene, isn't it?" she mused, her voice low, knowing.

"Obscenity has never been so well-dressed."

Manon laughed softly before trailing a finger over the page. "Look at these stones."

Blue, pink, and red diamonds, emeralds... Each one rarer than the last, more impossible, more indulgent.

Not to mention the closure.

I swallowed.

A 5-carat alexandrite gemstone, shifting in hue from deep forbidden green to a wicked, bruised plum-red under candlelight.

It locked into place with a secret mechanism, the key designed to be worn as a ring—an unspoken promise of possession.

Manon hummed, tapping the page, her eyes gleaming with amusement. "Maman is going to want this."

I scoffed. "She'd lock you in it."

Manon smirked. "She'd try. But let's be honest—it's far more likely that Dorian would lock *you* in it."

A prickle of heat curled in my stomach, my gaze flicking down to the picture of the collar on the cover of the auction catalog. A symbol of wealth, power, and possession—and it was here, now, in front of me.

Manon's smirk grew as she watched me stare at it. "What, no witty retort? Don't tell me the thought turns you on?"

I rolled my eyes, but didn't deny it.

Instead, I exhaled, shaking my head. "We're not bidding on this."

Manon nodded. "Of course not."

Even she had her limits.

"Are you actually going to be responsible tonight?"

Manon placed a delicate hand over her chest, feigning offense. "I am the picture of responsibility."

She laughed, flipping a page in the catalog. "Fine. Tonight, I'm being... frugal. I'm not bidding more than one million on any single item."

I blinked. "That's restraint?"

"I've watched you. Turns out restraint is its own kind of power. I thought I'd try it."

I exhaled, shaking my head. "My love, that isn't self-control."

"Oh, I know." She winked. "But it's a start."

The auctioneer took his place, the soft murmur of conversation fading into an expectant hush.

The first few lots moved quickly—exquisite antiques, rare *objet d'art*, pieces of history changing hands with the simple flick of a paddle. Manon and I observed in silence, catalogs in hand, wine untouched.

Then, something became clear.

Every time a French-made piece came up, Manon's mother acquired it.

At first, she faced competition. Other bidders, including mother, placed aggressive bids. But the longer the auction went on, the more people fell away.

No one wanted to challenge her.

Her family name had built empires in France, and she was ensuring that everything of value returned to the homeland.

Manon made a soft, unimpressed noise. "She's buying France back one auction at a time."

I smirked. "Your inheritance at work."

Manon exhaled, flipping the page. "More like my inheritance disappearing."

Then, the pattern broke.

A striking, modernist American-made piece—sleek, unexpected, a deviation from the usual European fare.

The starting bid: $50,000.

Manon perked up. "That's the one I want."

"At least it's not French."

She grinned. "That guarantees dear *maman* won't bid on it."

A few bidders entered the fray. Paddles rose. The price climbed.

$60,000.

$70,000.

$80,000.

Manon raised her paddle, unfazed.

A pause. Manon was about to win it. The auctioneer lifted his hammer, only to be interrupted by—

A new bid.

Until now, Manon's mother had only bid on French-made pieces. This was a deliberate move. A challenge.

Manon's eyes sharpened.

The bidding continued. One by one, the competitors dropped out.

The price rose beyond reason.

$100,000.

$200,000.

$500,000.

I leaned in. "Manon. This isn't worth it."

She ignored me.

Her mother bid $900,000.

I grabbed Manon's wrist. "You said you wouldn't bid over a million."

The auctioneer was about to grant her mother the win.

Then—a sharp lift of Manon's paddle.

"One million."

The room gasped.

Her mother's paddle rose immediately.

"One point one."

Manon turned. Looked at her.

Then smiled.

A slow, deliberate curve of her lips.

I squeezed her arm. "You said you wouldn't bid over a million."

She turned to me, satisfaction gleaming in her gaze.

"I didn't."

I blinked.

The auctioneer's hammer fell.

Manon's mother had won.

Beside me, Manon was the one who looked victorious.

She leaned back in her seat, her smirk positively feline, sipping her wine like this had been a game, and she had played the perfect move.

Across the room, her mother sat all too composed.

Perfectly composed.

Only the tightness of her jaw betrayed her.

Manon, utterly unbothered, turned to me, lifting her glass. "To self-control."

I exhaled, shaking my head. "You're insufferable."

She laughed, unrepentant. "Oh, I know."

The silence in the room thickened as the auctioneer made his final preamble.

The Luxuria Collar sat displayed in its velvet-lined case, a gleaming testament to power, possession, and indulgence.

Manon leaned in, her voice a lazy purr of amusement. "Tell me that doesn't look like a bondage collar."

Her lips curled. "Now the real question is—who in this room is going to buy it for their submissive?"

She let her gaze drift, scanning the glittering guests, her eyes alight with mischief.

"Gérard, perhaps? He likes control, but I wonder... maybe he'd rather be the one wearing it?"

I bit back a laugh. "You think he likes to be led around on a leash?"

Manon smirked. "The man owns a yacht named *Obedience*. What does that tell you?"

The auctioneer's voice cut through the anticipation.

"Ladies and gentlemen, as you all know, this masterpiece was crafted in France. A symbol of its nation's unrivaled artisanship. As such, we anticipate great interest in ensuring it returns to the homeland."

Manon and I exchanged a look.

We already knew what was about to happen.

The auctioneer continued.

"Due to the nature and history of this piece, all bidding will be conducted anonymously."

Manon whispered "They really understand the assignment, don't they?"

I smirked. "Let's see who takes the bait."

The first bid came through immediately.

"$100 million."

Manon inhaled. "Oh, someone wants it badly."

I let my eyes drift across the hall. "Whoever it is, they don't want any competition at the start."

I glanced at the auctioneer's assistant. A phone bidder was on the line.

"$250 million."

I whispered, "That one came through the phones."

Manon's nails drummed against the table. "Shall we take bets on which of our past lovers might be on the other end?"

I smirked. "The Duke?"

She rolled her eyes. "Oh, please. He'd put it on a sculpture instead of a person."

The price climbed.

"$300 million."

Manon let out a soft whistle. "That narrows the field significantly."

I felt it, then; the weight of something unspoken.

Manon's gaze flickered to her mother.

I followed suit.

She had not yet bid.

But I could see it, the sharp calculation in her eyes.

She wasn't only here to buy back French-made pieces.

She was here to win.

And she never lost.

The room stopped pretending this was a normal auction.

The two forces left standing were: Manon's mother. A woman who, until tonight, had never lost a fight in her life and had no intention of starting now; and an unknown phone bidder. A shadow in the auction, an unseen force challenging a woman who had never been challenged before.

I leaned toward Manon, my heart hammering. "I think it's him."

Her gaze flicked to me, sharp.

"$550 million," the auctioneer called.

I swallowed. "Dorian."

Manon laughed. Hard.

The auctioneer looked at her, his face a sharp rebuke.

"$600 million."

I exhaled. "You don't think he'd do it?"

Manon regarded me with genuine curiosity. "He may be rich, but Beatrix, *maman* is..."

She trailed off.

We both looked at her mother.

Every time the price jumped, she had taken a little longer to answer.

Not because she couldn't afford it.

Because she was calculating.

Manon leaned in, voice low. "Do you really think he's capable of beating her?"

I wasn't sure.

Manon's lips curled, reading my silence. "Even he has his limits. Going against her is insanity. She is not the kind of person who doesn't get what she wants."

Her mother placed another bid.

Manon exhaled. "And she looks angry. Really angry. After what I did tonight, she is not losing this. She won't let it happen."

I glanced at her mother again.

She was controlled, but beneath it, she was fuming.

Manon nudged my thigh with her knee. "I know what you're thinking."

I tore my gaze away. "And?"

She smirked. "I think you *like* the idea of him fighting for you."

I flushed.

Manon laughed again. "You're soaking, aren't you?"

"$750 million."

I took a slow, steady breath.

"$800 million."

Manon's mirth faded a bit. "Whoever this is, they're serious."

Her mother hesitated.

A fraction of a second.

Then she bid.

"$850 million."

A murmur swept through the room.

People were getting nervous.

I kept my eyes on the auctioneer's assistant, the one handling the phone bidder.

"One billion."

The room gasped.

A stunned pause.

Even Manon froze.

The auctioneer struggled to keep his composure.

Every eye in the room turned to Manon's mother.

She had a bid ready.

Her finger hovered over the enter button.

Manon squeezed my knee. "Watch."

Seconds dragged.

"$1 billion, going once," the auctioneer said, his eyes pleading with Manon's mother to let the game continue.

The whole room focused on Manon's mother.

"Going twice."

Murmurs floating through the room, a mix of astonishment she was not going all in.

"Sold. One billion dollar. A new auction record for jewelry."

The audience clapped, a mix of shock and excitement at witnessing what everyone believed was an auction for the history books.

No one, except for Manon and I, noticed how Manon's mother's shoulders dropped.

A flicker of defeat.

Then she sat straighter, looking unbothered.

Manon's eyes gleamed, savoring every second.

"I have never seen maman beaten twice in one night. This is... almost better than sex."

I stared at her.

She narrowed her eyes. "I said almost."
I didn't blink.
She huffed. "Oh, don't look at me like that."
But there was a new flush in her cheeks.
And her fingers?
Still gripping my knee.

CHAPTER
Thirteen

TERMS & CONDITIONS

Time moved, as it always did, dragging me along with it.

My book dominated the charts, a permanent fixture on the bestseller lists.

The mainstream media couldn't get enough of me. I was the authority on sex, power, and seduction. Morning shows, late-night panels, feature interviews.

They talked about my work as though I had unlocked some great cultural shift, and perhaps I had.

I had moved beyond erotica. I was literature.

Manon, meanwhile, had set the fashion world on fire.

She had been named the new face and body of Agent Provocateur—a brand that didn't only embrace sexuality, but weaponized it.

A *British* brand.

Not French. Not Chanel. Not Dior. Not something her mother could proudly claim as an extension of the family legacy.

No. It was lingerie, seduction, and rebellion made into fashion.

A direct fuck you to the expectations placed upon her.

The industry was obsessed. The campaign was everywhere.

Her mother was seething.

But for all the success, for all the power moves we played...

Dorian hadn't answered.

No text. No email. No acknowledgment of the redlined contract I had sent back *weeks* ago.

And I hated that it bothered me.

So I threw myself into discipline. Control. Strength.

Manon and I did yoga with an exclusive instructor, someone who catered only to the most elite.

I pushed myself harder, stretching deeper, tightening every inch of my body.

Manon, meanwhile, was entirely amused.

"Maybe you scared him away," she mused lazily, stretching like a cat beside me, her body sinuous and inviting, teasing both me and our instructor with the ease of a woman who understood the full force of her sexuality.

I exhaled, pushing further into the pose. "Please."

She smirked. "B, you sent him a contract that told him in no uncertain terms that you're in control. He's used to women signing themselves away. You? You made him beg for every step."

I held my pose. "Or maybe he's playing a longer game."

Manon's eyes gleamed. "Are you sure? Or are you hoping?"

"If he answers before the month is over, you take me to La Perla's private couture salon in Paris and buy me any piece I want."

Manon's smirk widened. "And if he doesn't?"

I hesitated.

She leaned in, voice a sultry whisper, her breath warm against my cheek. "Then you do a private photo-shoot for me. One where I get to direct, and you have to wear whatever I tell you."

I narrowed my eyes. Manon in charge of a photo-shoot meant she would push boundaries.

"Something reasonable," I countered.

She grinned, teeth flashing. "B, you know me better than that."

I sighed. "Fine. Deal."

Her smile turned triumphant. "Perfect."

Across the room, our instructor watched us, his gaze moving between us, lingering a little too long on the curves of Manon's body, the stretch of my own.

Manon noticed.

Of course she did.

"What do you think?" she said, turning toward him, her voice slow, measured. "About us?"

He raised an eyebrow. "About?"

Manon gestured to me, then herself. "Our dear Beatrix is very tense."

The instructor was professional, stepping forward, adjusting my pose with the lightest touch, but his fingertips lingered half a second longer than necessary.

"You carry a lot of tension here," he murmured, his voice smooth, almost hypnotic.

Manon smirked. "See? She needs more than yoga to loosen up. Perhaps the three of us should explore... other methods of relaxation."

I huffed, indignant.

"Manon."

She grinned, entirely unrepentant.

"What?" she said sweetly. "It's a genuine offer."

I rolled my eyes. "Not everything is about sex."

She tilted her head. "Not everything, but this"—she gestured between the three of us—"feels like it could be."

The instructor's hands were suddenly firmer, more present. Less detached. He was listening.

I sighed. "I haven't gotten laid recently."

Manon feigned shock. "B, you're admitting it?"

I exhaled, my resistance weakening. "Fine. Maybe you're right. For one night, it could be fun."

The instructor's gaze flickered between us, his professionalism slipping.

Manon smirked.

CHAPTER Fourteen

GENTLE CORRECTIONS

I woke to the slow vibration of my phone, its insistent hum threading through the delicious haze of spent pleasure.

The penthouse suite was bathed in soft morning light, the floor-to-ceiling windows framing the Manhattan skyline like a masterpiece. The room reeked of indulgence—lace and leather tangled on the marble floor, restraints half-fastened, dildos abandoned mid-experimentation. The bedside tables were cluttered with empty bottles of vintage champagne and whiskey, the air thick with the scent of sweat, sex, and spilled liquor. A scene of glorious, unapologetic excess.

I blinked against the brightness, my phone still pulsing against the silk sheets. A message.

From him.

Manon stirred beside me, naked and radiant, stretching like a satisfied feline, her skin gleaming in the golden light. The suite, nestled at the top of one of the most exclusive hotels in the city, was her home for now—her idea of permanence was as fluid as her whims.

A low groan rumbled from the other side of the bed—the yoga instructor, his muscled arm draped lazily over my waist. I had forgotten he was even there.

I turned to Manon, my voice hushed but charged. "He messaged me."

She yawned, arching her back in a slow, luxurious stretch, then turned with a lazy smirk, fingers trailing idly over the instructor's bare chest. "Mmm, you can go now, darling."

He blinked awake, groggy but catching up quickly. "I—"

Manon's lips curled with mischief. "Shhh. You were divine, truly. But this is girl talk."

His mouth opened, perhaps to protest, but then he seemed to think better of it. He exhaled sharply, gathering his clothes from the floor, giving me one last lingering glance before mumbling something about another client and stumbling toward the door.

Manon rolled onto her side, watching his retreating form with an indulgent smile. "I'm sure you do. Now go on, sweetheart."

The door clicked shut. Manon turned to me, eyes gleaming with curiosity. "Alright, spill. What did he say?"

But before I could answer, the familiar buzz of another phone interrupted us. Manon, moving on instinct, snatched her phone off the nightstand and glanced at the screen.

She blinked, then gasped. "Oh, fuck yes."

I raised a brow, momentarily forgetting my own thoughts. "Good news?"

Manon's lips stretched into a wicked grin as she read the message again. "Vogue. Louvre. Lingerie. Me."

I sat up. "Wait, what?"

She twirled the phone in her fingers, her excitement practically vibrating off her skin. "Imagine—La Joconde between my legs. I think that might actually send Maman into cardiac arrest. Should I request a pose that makes her smirk look even more knowing? Maybe a little tilt of the hips, a hand in my hair—pure Renaissance scandal. The *Louvre*, B. Me, wrapped in lace, draped across centuries of history. The outrage it will cause, the sheer audacity of it—delicious."

She was beaming, already lost in the delicious anarchy of it all. And I was happy for her, truly. But my phone was still in my hands. And his message was still on my screen.

I had read it.

I wanted to talk about it. But Manon was too caught up in her own thrill, and I couldn't blame her. I forced a smile, pushing my concerns down for now.

"That's... incredible, Manon. You're going to look insane in those shots."

She preened. "I know."

I exhaled, glancing down at my phone again. The words stared back at me, curling around my ribs like a slow, constricting coil.

Yes, I was excited he had messaged me. But his words sat uneasily in my chest. There was something in them—something deliberate, something that felt like a challenge. I needed to talk to Manon about it, to get her advice on how to respond.

My phone buzzed again. I glanced down.

You are not home.

I exhaled sharply. Twice in a row? A potential show of impatience on his part. That was new.

You are not home.

A chill crawled up my spine. "Okay, that's... unsettling."

Manon peered over my shoulder, then snorted. "Again? Does he think if he says it enough times, you'll materialize before him? Maybe he's waiting for you in your apartment, lying in wait like some dark prince of dominance."

I exhaled, staring at the message. "I don't know if I should reply. Or go home. Or just... ignore it."

Manon stretched like a lazy cat, then smirked. "Ignoring him is an option, sure. Not the fun option, but an option."

I shot her a look. "What's the fun option?"

She grinned. "Showing up at home in something sheer and sinful, making him wait to see if you answer the door. Maybe you text him from inside, tell him you're busy soaking in a bath, dripping wet, and he should try harder next time."

I huffed, shaking my head. "You have a one-track mind."

"I do," she admitted shamelessly. "But let's not pretend you're not intrigued by this game he's playing. It's all very... Dorian, isn't it? Mysterious. Intense. Enough control to make you wonder what happens if you push back."

I pursed my lips. "Maybe. Or maybe he doesn't understand how texting works. Why not say what he wants instead of this whole paper note, messenger routine?"

Manon gave me a look. "B. If you think this man has ever 'said what he wants' instead of making people want to give it to him, you haven't been paying attention."

Before I could argue, my phone rang again. My stomach tightened. I didn't even have to check the screen—I already knew.

"Beatrix, there's someone here to see you," the doorman informed me.

Manon let out a low whistle. "And there it is. Another message in a crisp little envelope, hand-delivered like some royal decree. Seriously, B, do you think he owns a phone? Or is this his version of sexting?"

I wasn't listening. My pulse had already picked up, heat blooming low in my belly at the thought of another message waiting for me.

"Or maybe you're hot for the messenger, not the sender."

I laughed, shaking my head. "I need to get home."

Manon smirked, stretching luxuriously. "Mmm. Rushing off already? You sure it's him you're eager to see, and not whoever he sent? Because, B, if you end up in bed with the messenger, at least have the decency to call me."

I crossed the threshold of my building, pulse drumming with the remnants of urgency. The lobby was hushed, heavy with the scent of polished marble and expensive cologne, a sanctuary of wealth and quiet indulgence. One of Dorian's now-familiar messengers stood waiting—poised, unreadable, the very embodiment of his control. A silver tray balanced elegantly in her hands, the soft glow of the overhead lights reflecting against its surface like liquid moonlight.

She extended it toward me, the single envelope resting atop the mirror-like sheen. Every movement she made was deliberate, measured, like the man who had sent her. My fingers brushed over the thick, embossed paper, the weight of it pressing into my palm like a promise—or perhaps a command. No words passed between us; they never did. Silence was part of the ritual, part of the game.

I slid my finger under the seal, a small gasp catching in my throat at the quiet tear of the envelope. A faint trace of Dorian's cologne clung to the paper—smoky, dark, and utterly intoxicating. It curled around my senses as I unfolded the note, a slow bloom of anticipation spreading through my veins.

8pm. Tonight.

Where? His place? Another restaurant? Some secret, undisclosed location, tailored precisely to keep me guessing? The uncertainty twisted through me, sharpening my anticipation.

My breath hitched. Short. Direct. Assured.

Like him.

Heat coiled low in my belly, delicious and maddening. The invitation—so stark, so absolute—made my body respond before my mind could even catch up. There was no pretense of persuasion, no flirtation. Only expectation. The way it stripped me of choice while unraveling my restraint sent a slow, shivering thrill through me.

A slow shudder traced down my spine. The audacity of it. The sheer dominance in such a simple directive. The quiet confidence of a man who knew I would come.

The messenger inclined her head, a silent acknowledgment, before turning and walking out through the lobby's grand entrance, vanishing into the city beyond. I exhaled, but it did nothing to slow the quickening of my pulse. My thighs pressed together of their own accord, warmth pooling between them, the throbbing ache an undeniable admission of how much I wanted this.

I dialed Manon. She picked up before the first ring had even finished.

"*Enfin!* Tell me everything."

I read the note aloud.

Silence. Then, a pause so long I thought the line had dropped.

"…That's it?" Manon finally said, incredulous. "'8pm. Tonight'? No location? No instructions? No 'wear something scandalous and don't be late, *mon ange*?'"

"Nope."

"Hmm." She made a contemplative noise. "I shouldn't be surprised. He's a man of few words. And yet, he somehow makes those few words feel like commands."

I exhaled. She wasn't wrong.

"So where do you think he's taking you?" she asked, the excitement creeping into her voice.

"His place?" I guessed.

"Ohhh, the palace in the sky." Manon sighed dramatically. "Perched above the city like some billionaire Bond villain's lair. You know he owns the entire goddamn building. Keeps it empty except for himself because he refuses to share his walls with the rabble."

"I do recall hearing something about that," I murmured. "Didn't it cause some scandal? People wanted him to sell the other units, turn it into something useful—"

"And instead, he got new politicians in place who found his ownership perfectly reasonable." Manon finished smoothly. "Ah, the wonders of capitalism."

I smirked, but the thought of being taken up to that penthouse—where no one else was, where he was king of his own empire, watching the city below him—sent an undeniable warmth between my legs.

"Or maybe it's his office," I suggested. "Maybe he wants to go over the contract."

Manon barked out a laugh.

"Dorian Wolker, summoning you to his office to review terms? Oh, darling, I think this is less about clauses and more about consummation."

I rolled my eyes, but before I could protest, she pressed on.

"Honestly, this has all the makings of a classic case of mergers and acquisitions."

"Oh god."

"Yes, yes, merger of bodies, acquisition of Beatrix—" she purred. "I imagine he's quite the ruthless negotiator."

Heat licked up my spine.

"Fine, maybe it's a club," I offered, desperate to shift the conversation.

Manon made a dismissive noise. "No. That's not his vibe."

"What do you mean?"

"Clubs are for men who need an audience to feel powerful. Dorian doesn't need an audience. He doesn't even need a room full of people. His presence alone shifts gravity. He doesn't perform dominance—he *is* dominance."

I exhaled.

"So if it's not his office, and not a club..." I hesitated.

"Then it's somewhere else," Manon said, voice dipping into something almost conspiratorial. "Somewhere no one else knows about. Somewhere that doesn't exist on any public record. A room built solely for his own personal... tastes."

A shiver danced across my skin.

"A secret dungeon?" I joked, though my voice came out a little weaker than I'd intended.

"Pfft. A dungeon is for amateurs." Manon sighed, as if exasperated by my lack of imagination. "Try a secret kingdom."

My breath caught in my throat.

"And no matter where he takes you," she added, her voice smug, "one thing is certain."

I exhaled. "What's that?"

"...you're about to find out what it means to be under his rule."

I scoffed, but I couldn't ignore the sharp pulse of arousal that shot through me.

"I can't come over so we have to do this on video."

I sighed. "Manon, I've dressed myself before."

"Yes, and that's why I'm here," she shot back smoothly. "Video. Now."

I rolled my eyes but switched to video, propping my phone on the dresser so she had a full view.

"Strip," she commanded, taking a slow sip of her wine.

"At least buy me dinner first."

She sighed dramatically. "B, I need to see what we're working with."

As soon as I pulled the zipper down, letting the dress slide to the floor, Manon gave a satisfied hum.

"Much better," she purred. Then her eyes narrowed. "But before we get to the fun part, you need to get good and clean. Inside and out."

I rolled my eyes. "Manon—"

"No arguments, B." Her tone was playful but firm. "You've had quite the last twenty-four hours, and if you're about to step into Dorian's world, you're going to want to be at your absolute best. Call me back when you're... refreshed."

She hung up before I could protest.

I sighed, tossing my phone onto the counter before stepping into the shower. Water cascaded down my body, easing the tension from my muscles, but there was another tension that refused to dissipate so easily.

Dorian.

The way he looked at me. The way he made me wait. The way he had commanded, controlled, and yet held back.

I pressed my fingers between my legs, expecting a quick cleanse, but the moment I brushed against myself, the heat surged. My breath hitched as my fingers moved with more purpose, teasing, stroking, circling the ache that had been simmering inside me since the moment I read his message.

I leaned against the shower wall, one hand bracing myself as the other worked in slow, deliberate movements. My mind filled with images—Dorian's hands gripping my waist, his mouth at my throat, his body pressed against mine.

The orgasm hit me fast, rolling through me like a wave crashing against the shore. My legs trembled, my moan swallowed by the rush of the water.

I exhaled, tension finally easing, a satisfied warmth spreading through my limbs.

A few minutes later, I stepped out of the shower, toweling off before calling Manon back.

The moment the video call connected, she smirked, tilting her head. "Well, somebody looks freshly fucked."

I rolled my eyes. "It was only a shower."

"Uh-huh. You're flushed, B. Positively glowing." Her grin widened. "What is this now? Two? Three in a row?"

I shook my head, laughing. "This is probably the most I've had in a long time."

"As it should be," she said approvingly. "Life is nothing without sex. And you, my dear, have clearly been starving."

I couldn't argue with that.

"Now," she continued, clapping her hands together. "Let's get you dressed for whatever debauchery awaits."

And with that, we turned to the closet.

Manon's eyes flickered over the screen as I turned the camera toward my open closet, her lips pursed in assessment.

"We need layers," she said decisively. "You still don't know where he's taking you, so you have to be prepared for anything. Penthouse, boardroom, dungeon—"

"Dungeon?"

She grinned. "You *did* say he's the most dominant man you've ever met, *non?*"

I huffed but didn't argue.

Manon tapped a finger against her lips. "We want elegance, sensuality… but something that can be stripped away, if necessary."

"That sounds like an elaborate way of saying I need to wear lingerie under my dress," I muttered.

"B…" Her voice took on that authoritative, Parisian lilt that always meant she was about to make a statement. "The *right* lingerie. The kind that makes you feel powerful. Like the world should drop to its knees before you."

"Are you dressing me for Dorian or for myself?"

She met my gaze through the screen, all teasing gone. "Always for yourself first."

My chest warmed. Manon and I had our fun, but beneath it all, there was always this—her unwavering belief in who I was, and who I could be.

I turned back to my closet, letting my fingers trail over the delicate fabrics. Silk, lace, leather, sheer mesh— all weapons in their own right.

"Something black," Manon said, reading my mind. "Nothing virginal. Nothing too expected. Make him ache for it."

I pulled out a black lace bodysuit with a plunging neckline, sheer in all the right places, structured enough to sculpt my figure.

Manon let out a low whistle. "That one. Perfect."

I smirked. "And over it?"

She scanned the options, then pointed. "That."

I followed her gaze and pulled out a dress that draped like liquid obsidian—high-slit, low-backed, hugging my curves like a second skin. Understated from a distance, devastating up close.

I slipped into the bodysuit, feeling the lace press against my freshly cleaned skin, then slid the dress over it, the cool fabric skimming my thighs.

Manon sighed dramatically. "You look like a woman who eats billionaires for breakfast."

I laughed. "I'm hoping to keep up with one for dinner."

She waggled her brows. "Dessert is where things get interesting, *non?*"

I rolled my eyes but couldn't fight the grin on my lips.

Manon's lips curled in amusement as I turned the camera back to her, fully dressed.

"Neck bare?" she mused, tilting her head.

I glanced at my reflection, fingers skimming my exposed collarbones. "I thought keeping it open was more... deliberate."

Manon smirked. "*Très* deliberate. Leaving space for him to collar you, *non?*"

I scoffed. "Not even close."

She grinned. "Mmm. We'll see."

I rolled my eyes but didn't argue.

"Now, perfume," she instructed.

I reached for my usual, dabbing it at my wrists, my throat, behind my ears.

"And," Manon drawled, her voice teasing, "a drop at the—"

"I know," I muttered, already tipping a touch along the edge of my—

"*Bon,*" she said, watching approvingly. "You're learning."

I shot her a look. "I've always known. You're insufferable."

She laughed. "And yet, you adore me."

I exhaled, picking up my clutch. "It's a curse."

Before she could reply, my phone buzzed.

I glanced down. A call from the doorman.

Manon's smirk widened. "And there he is."

I answered. "Yes?"

"Miss, your car is here."

Manon stretched luxuriously, grinning. "Go on, then. Off to your mysterious, hopefully scandalous rendezvous."

I stood, smoothing my dress. "You're ridiculous."

She winked. "And you, *ma belle,* are about to have an extremely interesting night."

I smirked, stepping toward the door. "Let's hope."

CHAPTER
Fifteen

CLAUSE & EFFECT

The Rolls-Royce slid through the city like a ghost, its engine a whisper beneath me. I pressed my fingertips lightly against the leather seats, grounding myself. I had asked the driver where we were going—no answer. She hadn't even glanced at me in the mirror.

I should have been irritated. Instead, the anticipation curled in my stomach like a cat stretching its spine.

Where was he taking me?

The city blurred past, but then the car dipped underground, rolling smoothly into the private basement of one of the tallest buildings in Manhattan. *His* building. The one he had stripped of tenants, turned into his personal fortress in the sky. A skyscraper meant to house hundreds, reduced to a single ruler.

The car stopped. A door opened.

A woman stood there, impeccable in a black suit, tailored to a sharp elegance. Not a speck of dust dared cling to her, not a strand of hair out of place.

"Miss," she said. Not my name. A placeholder. A sign that she did not assume familiarity.

I stepped out, my heels meeting polished concrete. She turned smoothly, leading me toward a private elevator, tucked away in a shadowed corner of the basement. It was discreet, invisible to the untrained eye. No signage, no obvious buttons.

She lifted her hand and pressed her palm against a smooth, black pad.

A beat. Then the elevator doors slid open, soundless.

I stepped inside.

Polished wood, gold accents, leather-wrapped railing. But no buttons. No floors to select.

The doors closed.

Nothing happened.

Or at least, it felt like nothing. No sensation of movement, no shifting of weight. Stillness.

Then—

The wooden walls silently retracted.

And there it was.

The city sprawled beneath me in an endless stretch of light, a sea of glittering constellations. The buildings below, once towering, now insignificant.

I gripped the railing, my breath slow, steady.

The elevator kept climbing, but I couldn't feel it. It was as if I were floating, being lifted, rather than moved.

Then—

The ascent ceased.

The doors slid open behind me.

A voice. Deep. Controlled. Amused.

"I accept the terms of your surrender."

I turned.

Dorian stood before me, exuding effortless control, dressed in the kind of understated luxury that only bespoke tailoring could achieve. A black, long-sleeved Henley, deceptively simple, yet crafted from the finest cashmere blend, molding to the chiseled planes of his chest and arms as if it had been designed with his body alone in mind. Sleeves pushed up precisely to reveal the strong, veined forearms beneath—an intentional display of power wrapped in nonchalance.

His dark trousers, custom-fitted to perfection, hung with an ease that belied their precision, each line sculpted to his lean, muscular frame. Even the belt—matte black leather, hand-stitched, with a buckle that bore no ostentatious logo but whispered money in the way true wealth always did—spoke to a man who commanded rather than demanded attention.

For a microsecond—so brief it might as well have been a trick of the light—my gaze dropped.

Lower.

Heat pressed between my thighs before I could even register the slip.

I caught myself instantly, reining in the moment as if I had never faltered. My eyes snapped back to his, my expression smooth, my breath steady.

But he had noticed.

A smirk, the barest flicker of amusement, ghosted across his lips. I saw that. I enjoyed that.

A subtle shift in his trousers caught my eye. A flicker of movement, a slow tightening that told me, unequivocally, that I was not the only one affected.

"Surrender? That's a bold assumption." My voice was smooth, teasing, but there had been no hesitation in it.

Dorian's lips quirked, acknowledging the game. "Only if I'm wrong."

I took my time crossing the space between us, my heels clicking softly against the floor, letting him watch me. I saw the way his body held tension beneath the effortless ease; the way his fingers flexed, the slight shift of his breath as his gaze dragged down my body for a second before locking back on my face.

"If you've accepted the contract, then you know how this works." I let my words linger, watching his expression. "I'm not for the taking unless I want to be."

"I wouldn't have it any other way."

I let my gaze drift past him, to the art lining the walls. *Le Violon d'Ingres* by Man Ray—one of my favorites. A woman's body turned into an instrument, a thing to be played. Picasso. Klimt. Modigliani. The room was filled with pieces that spoke of possession, sensuality, desire made tangible.

I traced my fingers along the back of a chair, taking my time.

"You do have a taste for rare and beautiful things, Dorian." I glanced at him, eyes amused. "But I'm not something you can collect."

His smirk deepened, controlled. "No?"

"No." I met his gaze head-on, playful but firm. "Unlike these, I don't belong in a glass case, or on display for admiration."

His eyes flickered with something unreadable, something intrigued.

I took a step closer, letting the heat between us rise, enough to test how well he was keeping his composure.

"The real question," I continued, voice low and smooth, "is how well you take care of the things you already own."

I watched him for a reaction, but he gave me nothing—that same steady, deliberate control.

Then he smiled, slow and knowing. "Why don't you find out?"

I laughed softly, brushing my fingers against the chair again before finally sitting.

"I think I'll need a drink first." I tilted my head, watching him. "Unless your idea of hospitality doesn't include that?"

Dorian's gaze traveled over me, slow and deliberate, as if taking inventory of every inch of my body. There was a flicker in his expression—something considering, something on the edge of command.

I could see it forming on his lips before he even spoke. He was about to choose for me.

"Whiskey. Neat." I cut in smoothly, not bothering to hide my amusement.

His smirk flickered, his desire to control me warring with his appreciation for the game I was playing.

A pause. Then, he relented, moving toward the bar with a quiet exhale through his nose.

Dorian poured himself a drink alongside mine, the amber liquid swirling in his glass as he watched me.

"This whiskey isn't available anywhere else," he said, leaning back enough to look effortlessly in control. "Distilled exclusively for me—small batch, aged longer than anything on the market. You won't find it in any bar or collection."

I lifted my glass, took a slow sip. The burn slid down my throat, but it wasn't the drink making my body feel overheated. It was him. The moment. The unbearable weight of anticipation pressing between my legs.

But he couldn't know that.

So I leaned back, feigning indifference, letting my fingers trail lazily around the rim of my glass. "So it's old and expensive. Like everything else in this place."

His smirk deepened, eyes flashing with something darker, sharper.

I knew what I was doing. Pretending to be unaffected, acting as though I wasn't seconds away from wanting to tear this ridiculous game apart and take him.

"Tell me, Dorian—does everything in your life have to be exclusive?" I asked, tilting my head as if I truly didn't care about the answer.

He brought his glass to his lips, swallowing whatever answer he truly wanted to give. Instead, he simply said, "I have a very discerning taste."

I exhaled through my nose, lifting my drink in a mock salute. "Of course you do."

I swirled the whiskey in my glass, watching the way the liquid clung to the sides before settling. I took a slow sip, savoring the heat as it slid down my throat. The anticipation between us crackled, thick and palpable, but I refused to be the first to break.

"You do have quite the view," I said at last, feigning nonchalance as I turned toward the wall of glass. The city stretched endlessly beyond us, glittering under the night sky.

Dorian's gaze didn't waver from me, his presence as potent as the whiskey on my tongue. "It's even better from the terrace upstairs," he said, voice smooth, effortlessly controlled.

I knew what this was. A test. An invitation laced with challenge. He wanted me to show my hand, to betray my interest by leaping at the offer.

But I wasn't going to make it easy for him.

I shifted my weight, the dress slipping higher along my thigh, allowing the fabric to caress my skin in a way I knew he was watching. Then I turned back to him, lifting my glass to my lips once more, drawing out the moment, knowing damn well that every small movement of mine was designed to tease.

"Oh?" I tilted my head, swirling the whiskey again. "And what makes the view up there so much better?"

His lips curled, eyes darkening. "Perspective."

The single word sent a pulse of heat through me. He was reining himself in. I could see it in the way his fingers tightened around his glass, the way his gaze flickered for a microsecond to my mouth before snapping back to my eyes.

"I don't know," I murmured, tapping my nail idly against the side of my glass. "This one's already spectacular. Hard to imagine it getting better."

"You'd be surprised."

His voice was lower now, smooth like velvet, the weight of it settling over me. I licked my lips, purposefully slow.

He was waiting.

I let the silence stretch between us, tension thick enough to strangle. Every moment felt coiled, wound so tightly it was nearly unbearable. If I so much as leaned an inch closer, if I brushed my fingers along his wrist, it would be over. He would have me against the glass in an instant, and I would let him.

But not yet.

I placed my glass down on the bar with careful precision, running a finger along the rim, letting the silence stretch, thick and charged. His eyes followed the movement, his grip tightening around his own glass. He was waiting for me to give in, to yield to the tension crackling between us.

I met his gaze, unwavering.

"Show me."

The flicker in his eyes was instant—hunger, restraint, the coil of control pulled unbearably tight. He took another sip of whiskey, slow, deliberate, masking the heat simmering beneath the surface.

Then, without a word, he set his glass down and turned toward the stairs. Every movement was measured, dominant, his presence filling the space between us like gravity itself.

He didn't look back.

The air between us thickened as I followed him up the stairs, the soft click of my heels against the marble amplifying the silence. He moved with purpose, his broad frame cutting through the dimly lit hallway, his bespoke shirt stretching across his back, outlining the sheer strength beneath the fabric. Every inch of him was power held in restraint.

And he knew I was watching.

I made sure he was watching too.

With every step, I let my hips sway, the slit of my dress parting to reveal the bare skin of my thigh. I could feel the heat of his awareness, the way his body registered my presence even when he didn't turn to look.

We reached the top.

He pushed open a set of heavy glass doors, and the city spilled out before me, endless and glittering beneath the night sky. The terrace stretched wide, lined with dark, minimalist furniture, designed for indulgence—long lounges, low tables, the promise of a hundred decadent possibilities.

But my gaze was drawn to the edge.

A single step and it was nothing but air, the city sprawling below like something meant to be conquered.

Dorian stood beside me, watching, his drink still in hand. "It has a way of making you feel invincible," he murmured, voice low, smooth, meant to pull me in.

I turned to him, arching a brow. "Is that how you like to feel?"

His lips quirked. "I don't need the view for that."

I laughed softly, taking a slow sip of my drink, letting the burn of whiskey heat my throat, my chest, my limbs. "Of course you don't."

His gaze dropped to my lips.

For a moment, neither of us moved.

The city roared beneath us, but up here, in this suspended world of glass and air, we were alone.

Waiting.

Daring.

Every inch of my skin was awake, aware of him, of the tension between us, of how easy it would be to close the space, to let go of the control I was so carefully maintaining.

Instead, I turned, walking toward the edge, resting my hands against the cool metal of the railing, looking out at the city as if he weren't standing right there, as if the heat pooling between my thighs wasn't getting more unbearable by the second.

I heard him step closer, the air between us thickening with tension, charged with an energy neither of us acknowledged outright, but both of us felt. His presence was like a low hum against my skin, a heat that didn't touch me but threatened to.

"The view from here is... breathtaking."

His voice was slow, deliberate, rich with something unspoken.

I smirked, keeping my eyes on the shimmering skyline, fingers curling around the railing. "Is it?"

"Stunning."

I shifted my weight, the curve of my hips sharper, the tight fabric of my dress hugging every inch of my ass, perfectly framed and out of reach.

A sharp inhale behind me. The subtle tension in the air, thickening.

I could practically hear the clench of his jaw, feel the restraint in the way he hadn't yet reached for me.

The power of denial was intoxicating.

"You do have an eye for fine things," I mused, voice light, teasing.

His response was measured, controlled, but there was no mistaking the heat beneath it. "Only the rarest."

A slow smirk curled my lips.

I ran a fingertip lazily along the rim of my glass, ice clinking softly, the sound slicing through the thick silence between us. I could feel his eyes on me, feel the way they lingered on the lines of my body, the way he was imagining what it would feel like to finally reach forward.

"Tell me, Dorian," I murmured, stretching the moment like silk over skin. "Do you always admire from a distance?"

There was a shift, subtle but unmistakable. His breath was steady, but his silence spoke volumes.

"Not when something is meant to be touched."

A delicious shiver rolled down my spine, but I controlled it, breathing through the slow thrum of anticipation curling low in my belly.

I let the silence stretch, let the weight of it settle between us.

"Show me the rest of the terrace."

A challenge.

A command.

A test.

His pause was brief, but I caught it—a second of hesitation before he stepped back, turned; before he accepted the game I was playing and began leading me further into the night.

He led me deeper into the terrace, past the last glimpses of glass and steel, into something entirely unexpected. Here, the city disappeared. Towering trees stretched skyward, their thick branches blocking out most of the world beyond, save for the full moon peering through the gaps. The air was different here—cooler, laced with the scent of greenery, damp earth, and night-blooming jasmine. A hidden oasis, carved out above the skyline, untouched by the chaos below.

The ground softened beneath my heels, no longer cold stone but something closer to grass, something carefully cultivated to make this place feel... separate. Removed. Private.

And suddenly, I was intensely aware of the fact that no one could see us. No windows. No distant figures on neighboring rooftops. No prying eyes.

The realization sent a slow wave of heat curling through my core.

Dorian moved ahead, his broad shoulders shifting beneath the soft fabric of his shirt, his posture precise, controlled. His slacks fit him in a way that was almost sinful, the cut sharp, the fabric molding to his form, emphasizing the flex of muscle as he walked.

I watched him, my breath deepening.

Imagined him pinning me against one of these trees, my dress bunched up around my waist, his hands gripping my thighs as he—

I exhaled sharply, trying to reel myself in, but it was too late. The thought was there, seared into my mind, impossible to ignore.

Dorian stopped.

My heels continued their slow rhythm against the ground, deliberate, measured. He felt them. Knew I was still behind him, following, watching.

And wanting.

He hadn't turned yet, but I saw the shift in his stance, the slight tightening of his shoulders, the way his fingers flexed before he slid them back into his pockets. He was holding himself back. Keeping himself in check.

But he wanted me.

Badly.

He wanted to pull me into the shadows, press me into the tree trunk, tilt my head back and claim my mouth, my body—

But he wouldn't.

Not yet.

Not until I gave myself to him.

The tension between us coiled tighter, electric, humming through the air like something alive.

I dragged my fingers over my collarbone, as if adjusting my necklace—though, of course, I wasn't wearing one. A subtle movement, enough to make his gaze flicker lower and remind him of what might be there for the taking.

"It's beautiful here," I murmured.

Dorian's gaze traveled over me, slow and deliberate, drinking me in like I was something he'd been waiting for. When his eyes met mine again, his voice was lower, rougher, the restraint making it even more dangerous.

"You're beautiful here."

The way he said it sent a slow ripple of heat through my core. He wasn't talking about the terrace. He wasn't talking about the city spread beneath us.

He was talking about me.

Here.

Under the moonlight.

In this hidden, untouchable place.

With him.

I could feel how badly he wanted me.

But he was waiting.

Still waiting.

The air between us was thick with the unspoken. A pull so strong I could feel it in every breath. Every heartbeat. Every aching inch of my body.

"Are you always this poetic, or is it the altitude?"

He huffed a quiet laugh.

"You tell me, Beatrix."

I laughed, low and amused. "You're beautiful here? That's corny, even for you."

Dorian smirked, unbothered. "Horny, you said?"

Heat rolled through me, pooling low in my stomach. I held his gaze, daring him to flinch. He didn't.

"So, to be clear, you've accepted all the terms of the contract?"

His expression didn't change, but something in his stance did. "Yes."

I let the word settle between us, a thinly veiled acknowledgment of what that meant. "And you remember that the terms include my prior consent on everything you want to do with me?"

His jaw tightened but his voice remained smooth. "That's understood. Even if it was your revision."

I tilted my head, assessing him, his arousal as evident as mine. His chest rose and fell in a measured rhythm, but I could see the way his muscles tensed beneath his bespoke shirt, the control it took for him not to reach for me.

I let my gaze roam, dragging it over him from head to toe. Taking my time. Drinking him in the way I knew he was drinking me in.

God, he looked good enough to devour.

I felt the wetness between my legs intensify.

I met his eyes again, my voice smooth, teasing, but laced with challenge.

I let my gaze drag over him once more, slow and deliberate, taking my time like I was savoring a meal before the first bite. His body was pure temptation—broad shoulders, sculpted chest, the taut lines of his abdomen disappearing into the perfection of those tailored trousers. And lower still...

Then I met his eyes, lips curving in a knowing smile.

"For all your talk of consent, you've yet to give me anything to say yes to."

The night air was crisp against my skin, and despite the heat pooling in my core, my nipples had hardened. His eyes flicked down, noticing.

He tilted his head, a smirk playing at his lips. "Shall we go back inside?" His voice was smooth, controlled, with darker undertones. "Do I have your consent for that?"

I let the question hang between us for a beat, teasing him with the illusion of hesitation before I nodded. "You do."

He didn't touch me, didn't guide me. He simply turned, expecting me to follow, and I did, watching the way his body moved with precision, strength. The anticipation between us was thick, heavy, but neither of us would break first.

I let my gaze linger on *Le Violon d'Ingres* and pivoted to face Dorian, letting my fingers trail lazily down my own side, mirroring the curves of the woman in the photo.

"You do have a thing for collecting rare pieces," I teased, stepping closer, my voice dropping into something silkier. "But tell me... how do you like to display them?"

I moved to the edge of the couch, perching on the armrest, legs crossed. "Like this?" I mused, tilting my head, eyes locked on him. "Elegant, refined, a hint of seduction?"

He said nothing, but I caught the way his fingers flexed, the way his jaw tensed.

I slid off the couch and walked over to the glass coffee table, pressing my palms to it, leaning forward enough that my dress rode up my thighs. "Or maybe something a little more daring?" I tossed a glance over my shoulder, catching his stare locked on the curve of my ass. "A piece meant to be admired from every angle?"

His breathing had changed, but I wasn't done yet.

I straightened and sauntered toward the wall, placing my hands flat against it, arching my spine. "Or perhaps something restrained?" I glanced back at him, biting my lip. "Arms above my head, waiting—obedient?"

I let my fingers trail down the buttons of his shirt, a teasing touch that never fully pressed in. "Or..." I murmured, turning my back to him.

As I stepped forward, my movements ever so fluid, the space between us became agonizing, an inch separating his face from the curve of my ass. I arched my back, letting the dress cling to me in all the right ways, my hands pressing against my thighs as if steadying myself.

"Maybe you prefer your art in motion."

I tilted my hips, brushing the edge of his breath, feeling it ghost over the heat pooling between my legs.

"Bent over," I whispered, parting my legs ever so, feeling the fabric tighten around my thighs. "Spread open... ready to be taken."

My own words sent a pulse through my thighs, as tension stretched between us, thick and undeniable.

As the words "ready to be taken" left my lips, I felt it.

His grip. Firm, unrelenting, claiming my hips as if they had always belonged to him.

Then, before I could process the next breath, his teeth sank into my panties. Not roughly, not carelessly—but with devastating precision. A slow, controlled tear of lace as he pulled, shredded, and ripped them away, the fabric dissolving under his mouth like it had never existed.

Fuck.

The move was effortless. Masterful. Feral.

I shuddered. The barest whisper of his breath against my exposed, dripping core sent a violent tremor through my body. I braced against the cold glass in front of me, breath shallow, legs weak.

And then—his tongue.

Hot. Wet. Deliberate.

The first flick made me gasp—sharp, needy, my hips jerking into his mouth. He had me locked in place, hands gripping my ass, spreading me further apart as his tongue delved deeper, deeper, stroking over me with slow, devastating precision.

"Oh—fuck—"

The words jumped out of me before he doubled down.

Licking. Teasing. Taking.

I whimpered, a broken sound as he sucked me into his mouth, his tongue circling, stroking, flicking—fucking me with nothing but his mouth.

I loved it.

Loved how thoroughly he had me.

Loved how he was devouring me like I was the only thing he had ever hungered for.

My knees almost gave out, my forehead pressing against the Man Ray in front of me, my body shaking under the relentless assault of his mouth. Every inch of me burned, my body throbbing, pulsing under his tongue, the heat too much, too good, too *perfect*.

He growled into me.

That dark, low vibration sent me spiraling.

I shattered.

My orgasm ripped through me, violent and uncontrollable, my hips jerking, body convulsing as I came hard against his mouth. His grip never loosened. He held me, kept me still, kept me his, lapping up every shudder, every pulse, every last drop of pleasure.

I had lost my sense of time and place when I finally sagged, breathless, shaking.

I turned my head, trying to focus through the haze.

Dorian.

His lips glistened with me.

His eyes? Dark. Amused. Triumphant.

He traced his tongue over his lips, unhurried and deliberate.

"You were saying?"

CHAPTER
Sixteen

CONTROLLED EXPOSURE

I stretched, my body humming with the ache of last night, the silk sheets cool against my bare skin. Dorian's scent lingered in the air—sex, control, quiet dominance. My muscles protested deliciously as I shifted, the soreness a reminder of how thoroughly he had wrecked me several times over.

The insistent buzz of my phone pulled me from the haze. Video call.

I groaned, blindly reaching for it. Manon. Of course.

I swiped to answer, my vision still blurry with sleep. The screen flickered to life, and there she was—smirking, radiant, and practically naked in a place that should not allow such things.

I blinked. "Hold on. Are you in lingerie? At the Louvre?"

Manon preened, adjusting the leather corset cinching her waist, the sheer stockings hooked to garters, the absurdly high heels that should have no place in a museum.

"*Mais oui.*" She tilted the camera, showing off the grandeur of the gallery behind her, its priceless artwork a silent audience to her scandal.

"Can you believe this? La Joconde is literally right there. And I am wearing next to nothing. Maman will die."

I laughed, delighted despite the sheer audacity of it. "You're a menace."

She smirked, then turned her phone, and there it was—the Mona Lisa.

A masterpiece. A legend. And yet, in this moment, reduced to nothing more than the background for Manon's latest rebellion.

Manon's voice purred through the speaker. "Tell me that smirk isn't approving."

I shook my head, grinning. "She looks like she's questioning your life choices."

Manon gasped, mock-affronted. "Oh, please. If she had the chance, she'd do the same."

Manon turned the camera back to herself, adjusting the delicate straps of her corset with a practiced flick of her fingers. "Enough about me and my historic levels of scandal. Let's talk about you. You're still there?"

I exhaled, sinking deeper into the absurdly luxurious pillows. "Yes."

Her eyes narrowed, cat-like. "And yet, I see no Dorian in sight."

I gestured vaguely to the space around me. "Nope. Just me. And…" My gaze drifted to the chair where a single set of bespoke clothes had been left, along with delicate, expensive lingerie in my exact size. And a perfectly arranged breakfast—fresh fruit, pastries, eggs prepared the way I liked, and a glass of something green and probably nutritious.

Manon perked up. "Custom?"

I nodded. "Bespoke, down to the last stitch. Silk, lace—the works."

She whistled. "A man who ruins your lingerie, replaces it, feeds you, and still manages to disappear before dawn? That's practically foreplay."

I smirked, eyeing the absurdly fine fabric draped over the chair. "He didn't dress me in them."

Manon raised a brow. "Did he undress you?"

I shot her a look. "What do you think?"

She grinned. "And how are last night's… remnants?"

I let out a soft laugh. "I assume shredded. I didn't have the time or energy to check."

Manon exhaled dramatically. "This is beautiful. The man wrecked you, then left you couture and nutrients to recover. Truly, you are living my dream."

I rolled my eyes, but I couldn't deny the effect it had on me. The unspoken power play. The control he exuded even when he wasn't physically present.

Manon took another glance around the opulent museum setting she was standing in, then focused back on me. "So, tell me everything. Spare no details."

I hesitated for a beat, stretching my limbs beneath the sheets, feeling the delicious ache radiating through my thighs, my ass—everywhere he had claimed me.

"Where do I even begin?"

Manon smirked, crossing her arms, fully prepared to dissect every detail. "Chronologically, *mon amour*. And with the dirtiest parts first. So where did you end up last night?"

Manon leaned into the screen, eyes glittering with mischief.

I took my time stretching, enjoying the way her impatience practically vibrated through the phone. "His place."

She blinked. "That's it? His place? B, I was expecting something far more scandalous. A clandestine club, a leather-clad dungeon, a secret chamber filled with sins."

I smirked. "You sound disappointed."

Manon sighed dramatically. "Well, it's a little predictable."

I toyed with a piece of fruit from my breakfast tray, running my fingers along the fork's prongs. "I wouldn't call last night predictable."

Her eyes narrowed. "Go on."

I took a slow bite, letting the anticipation simmer. "No inch of me was left unexplored."

"Beatrix."

I swallowed. "No. Hole. Left. Uneaten. Unfucked. That man has range."

Manon gasped, clutching her nonexistent pearls. "You bitch."

I grinned. "You did say it would be a waste if he didn't wreck me properly."

She flopped back in her chair, exhaling loudly. "And did he?"

I ran a hand through my hair, feeling the delicious ache that still lingered. "Thoroughly."

Manon groaned. "Oh, now I'm jealous."

I smirked. "Should've asked to join."

She sat back up, wagging a finger. "Don't tempt me."

I laughed, finally relaxing against the pillows. "Oh, Manon, he had a point to prove."

Her eyes gleamed. "Mmm. I do love a man with something to prove."

I exhaled, remembering the way his tongue had worshipped every inch of me, the way his hands had gripped me with absolute possession. "I woke up very, very, very satisfied."

Manon sighed, feigning exasperation. "B, you're lucky I'm in Paris, otherwise I'd demand a live reenactment."

I grinned. "That would require me to be able to walk properly."

She howled with laughter. "Oh, *mon dieu*, he really did a number on you."

I lifted my coffee cup in mock toast. "To thorough men."

Manon laughed, shaking her head. "To thorough men."

CHAPTER
Seventeen

HOUSE RULES

Weeks passed, as I settled into the routine of new love. And while I chatted with her daily on the phone, I was glad to finally get to see Manon face to face again.

She slid into the booth across from me, oversized sunglasses perched on her nose like a shield against the world. "I have returned. Try to contain your excitement."

I smirked over the rim of my tea. "You look... expensive. And possibly jet-lagged. Or hungover."

She waved a manicured hand. "Maman has practically disowned me—again. She actually launched a full-scale campaign to exile me from French high society."

I took a slow sip, savoring the herbal bitterness. "And yet, here you are. More famous than ever."

She sighed, tapping a perfectly polished nail against her espresso cup. "Turns out, the French love a scandal even more than their so-called traditions. I've been knighted in the court of public opinion. They can't get enough of me."

I raised a brow. "France's most prized export?"

She grinned wickedly. "Oh, darling. I *am* France now. They call me 'a new era's icon of seduction.' I'm basically Brigitte Bardot meets Marie Antoinette... if Marie Antoinette had done a lingerie campaign in the Louvre."

I laughed, shaking my head. "Maman must be thrilled."

Manon lifted her espresso in a mock toast. "If she hasn't started drinking before noon yet, I'd be shocked."

I let her bask in the glow of her own notoriety for a moment before she turned her gaze on me, assessing. "Where the fuck have you been?"

I set my cup down. "Busy."

Her eyes narrowed. "Busy drinking... what even is that?"

I exhaled. "A custom herbal blend. Anti-inflammatory. Great for digestion and circulation."

She gave me a slow blink. "Your tea has goals now?"

I rolled my eyes. "It was recommended by my dietician."

She leaned back dramatically. "Ah, yes. The dietician. The personal trainer. The chef. You do realize you sound more and more like him every day, right?"

I bristled. "I do not."

She smirked. "B, I've been back for a week. A *week*. And this is the first time you've managed to see me. That is not the B I know."

I sighed, shaking my head. "I'm still me, Manon. Just... maybe more disciplined."

She tilted her head, a flicker of something unreadable in her expression. "Disciplined. That's a new one."

I ignored the implication. "So, what's next for the world's most scandalous model?"

Manon brightened, her playful edge returning. "I'm in talks with a few more brands. One in particular is scandalous enough to make Maman lose the last of her hair. And I have a proposal for you, too."

"Should I be scared?"

She smirked. "Only if you still have any reservations about being the most talked-about woman in the world."

I exhaled, watching her over the rim of my tea. "Go on."

Manon leaned in, her voice dropping to something conspiratorial. "It's time for you to step out of the literary world and into something even bigger."

"I'm listening."

And for the first time in weeks, I wasn't thinking about Dorian.

Manon stirred her espresso with a slow, lazy motion, watching me over the rim of her cup. "B, it's time."

"For what?"

She leaned in, eyes glinting with amusement. "To spread those pages of yours onto the big screen."

I snorted. "You make it sound like an OnlyFans subscription."

She grinned. "Even better—cinematic orgasms, award-winning moans, art with the right amount of filth. The kind that leaves audiences questioning their morals... and their underwear choices."

I took a sip of my tea, eyeing her. "And you've got someone in mind, I assume?"

She stretched, feigning casualness. "Oh, a very talented, very well-equipped director. Insatiable appetite for storytelling... and other things."

"How well do you know him?"

She licked a bit of foam from her lip. "Biblically."

I groaned. "Manon."

She sighed dreamily. "He's French, B. It would've been rude not to."

I shook my head, laughing despite myself. "And he wants to meet me?"

She smirked. "The moment he put his hands on my copy."

I gave her a flat look. "Your book copy, I assume?"

She wiggled her brows. "Oh, honey, he's been all over it."

I pinched the bridge of my nose. "And what's in this for you?"

She leaned back with a slow smile. "Oh, you know me. Supporting my best friend in her meteoric rise... and possibly securing myself a scandalous little cameo."

I exhaled. "Of course."

She twirled a piece of hair around her finger. "You do need someone to make sure the costumes are authentic."

I smirked. "You mean ensuring the lingerie budget is generous?"

She winked. "Details, darling."

I sighed, setting my tea down. "Fine. Set up the meeting."

Manon clapped her hands together, victorious. "I love it when you listen to reason."

I pointed a finger at her. "I'm regretting this already."

She grinned. "Give it time. You'll be begging for a sequel."

Manon tapped a manicured finger against her wine glass, watching me with that knowing smirk of hers. "So, tell me, B... the Most Influential gala. Are we making it official?"

I rolled my eyes, sipping my tea. "If by 'official' you mean announcing that you and I are the true power couple, then yes, absolutely."

She huffed a laugh. "You know what I mean. You. Him. Red carpet. Photographers capturing the smoldering gazes, the subtle touches, the unspoken confirmation that you've been thoroughly and repeatedly ravished—"

I held up a hand. "I am not some trophy for him to parade around, Manon."

She raised a brow. "Please, B. You're no trophy. You're the entire prize package, including the victory parade and post-game celebrations."

I shook my head, fighting a smile. "Regardless, no. I'm not walking in on his arm like some conquest."

She tilted her head. "You are, however, walking in on those legs, and I hope to God you let me dress them appropriately."

I sighed. "That's... still under negotiation."

Her eyes gleamed. "Oh? Negotiation with whom?"

I exhaled, setting my cup down. "I might let Dorian have a say in what I wear that night."

Manon gasped, clutching her chest dramatically. "Beatrix! Compromise? Have the stars aligned? Is this what love does to a woman?"

I gave her a flat look. "It's a dress, Manon, not a declaration of ownership."

She shrugged. "Mmm. But clothing is power, and if he gets to dictate what's draped over that body, I have to wonder... what does he get to do when it's off?"

I smirked. "You really want the details, don't you?"

She waved a hand. "Not right now. I'll get them out of you when you're drunk and sentimental. Right now, I want to know how he's making his grand entrance."

I leaned back. "Oh, he won't be paying attention to me. He's got a new prize to show off."

Her brows lifted. "And what new scandalous toy has he bought this time?"

I sighed, setting down my tea. "Not a scandal. He's excited about that buzzy tech darling responsible for the microscopic nerve-repairing robots. The ones that got banned for being too effective at fixing athletes. Apparently, helping people walk again is fine, but helping them run a second faster? All pretty boring stuff, really."

I shook my head. "Except... I think part of the fun for him was outbidding my father."

Manon's lips parted, then she let out a delighted ooh. "Now *that's* sexy. Was he smug about it?"

I exhaled a laugh. "Oh, deliciously so."

She grinned. "And yet, I assume you rewarded him accordingly."

I gave her a knowing look. "Are we done analyzing my sex life?"

She tapped a manicured nail against her glass. "Never. But fine, we can pivot to my next scandal."

She leaned in, eyes gleaming. "*Châtelaine.*"

I blinked. "*Châtelaine?*"

She grinned. "My new lingerie brand. Chanel and Hermès are backing it, but I'll have majority control. No meddling, no mother hovering, women wearing what they should to feel in control and make men absolutely weak if they choose to reveal it."

I let out a low chuckle. "God, that name. 'Mistress of the castle'—historically powerful, respectable..."

Her smirk turned wicked. "And a keyholder, B."

My brows lifted, catching the double entendre. "You really named your brand after a dominatrix role."

She raised her glass. "Why yes. Yes, I did."

I exhaled a laugh. "You do realize the moment the name comes out, conservative France is going to set itself on fire."

She purred. "Mmm, delicious, isn't it? Can you imagine the outrage? Lingerie, luxury, power, and me at the center of it? Maman might actually pack her bags and flee to the countryside."

I grinned. "And yet, she won't be able to stop it."

Manon's eyes gleamed. "I'll be the most famous Frenchwoman in the world, and the wrong kind of famous, which will make it so much better."

I shook my head, sipping my tea. "You are truly, spectacularly evil."

She winked. "And you love me for it."

I sighed. "I really do."

Manon raised her cup with a wicked grin. "To ruining everything our mothers hold dear."

I laughed, tapping mine against hers. "To scandal and restraint, in the right measures."

She took a slow sip, eyes never leaving mine. "And to you, winning the Orpheus Prize."

I exhaled, leaning back. "That's the plan."

"So tell me, B, how does one seduce the world's most elite literary minds?"

"With words, of course. The right ones, in the right ears, at the right time."

She nodded approvingly. "Which means this gala is the perfect opportunity. You'll be standing in a room with the very people who can make that happen."

I swirled the coffee in my cup, already running through the plan in my head. "The Orpheus Prize isn't only about literary excellence—it's about cultural impact. My book is everywhere, but I need the right people to say it's defining something bigger than itself."

Manon rested her chin on her palm, studying me. "Which it is."

I met her gaze with a small smile. "I know. But I need *them* to say it."

She tapped her cup against the table, considering. "Then let's make sure they do."

I narrowed my eyes. "Manon—"

She held up a perfectly manicured hand. "Relax. I promised, didn't I? No unplanned chaos. Just... a little strategic disruption."

I huffed a laugh. "I don't even know what that means."

Manon swirled the last of her coffee in her cup, a wicked glint in her eyes. "Of course, you need to captivate the judges. But let's not forget the real challenge."

I glanced at her over my own cup. "Winning the Orpheus Prize?"

She smirked. "No, B. Making sure your boyfriend is as desperate for you as the rest of the room."

I nearly choked. "He's not my boyfriend."

She waved a dismissive hand. "Fine. Your incredibly wealthy, absurdly dominant, completely obsessed with you *not*-boyfriend."

I set my cup down, leveling her with a look. "Not obsessed."

She snorted. "B, he literally cleared out an entire restaurant to watch you squirm under his gaze. He spent billions outbidding maman for the thrill of the game. And I assume, based on your glowing complexion and overall satisfaction with life lately, that he's been doing unspeakably filthy things to you."

I felt heat rise to my cheeks, but refused to give her the satisfaction. "You assume a lot."

Manon grinned. "And I'm usually right."

I exhaled, shaking my head. "The Orpheus Prize is the focus, Manon. Not him."

She leaned in, eyes twinkling with mischief. "B, the best way to win is to command every eye in the room. Make them all want you—intellectually, artistically, carnally."

I rolled my eyes. "Yes, because literary awards are so dependent on sexual tension."

Manon shrugged. "You say that, but don't underestimate the power of a room captivated by everything about you. And don't pretend you don't want to keep him watching, wondering, wanting. Men like Dorian don't lose control. But for you? He might."

I tapped my fingers on the table, feigning contemplation before deadpanning, "Manon, he already has."

She burst out laughing, nearly spilling her coffee. "Oh, B, you're in so much deeper than you pretend."

I rolled my eyes. "If the goal is to make him lose control, I might be playing the game on boss level."

Manon grinned, eyes gleaming with mischief. "That's why the most delicious thing you can do is steal it in your own slow, teasing, merciless way."

I exhaled, shaking my head, but a smile played at my lips. "You're impossible."

She raised her cup. "I prefer inevitable."

I clinked mine against hers, a silent agreement. "Then let's make sure this night is one for the ages."

CHAPTER Eighteen

DOCTOR, DOCTOR

Dorian had summoned me to his office, a sprawling, glass-walled testament to power, where the skyline bowed at his feet. The space was quiet, almost clinical, save for the rhythmic tapping of expensive shoes against polished marble. We were not alone—our respective trainers and nutritionists stood before us, meticulously dissecting every aspect of diet, sleep, and health. It was thorough, exhaustive, but I could sense Dorian's patience thinning. He thrived in control, but the mundane details of maintenance were beneath him.

One by one, the professionals were dismissed, leaving the two of us.

Or so I thought.

The door opened, and a woman entered—a specialist, I presumed, though she carried herself with an air of dominance that made me immediately wary. She was sharply dressed in a black pencil skirt and crisp white blouse, glasses perched on the bridge of her nose. She surveyed Dorian with the detached efficiency of someone about to take inventory.

Without preamble, she turned to him. "Strip."

I watched Dorian's jaw tighten, but he complied. He peeled off his bespoke shirt, exposing the sculpted lines of his body. His trousers followed, leaving him bare under the bright overhead lights. My mouth dried as my gaze lingered over his form, my pulse quickening despite myself. I had seen him naked before, had felt his power consume me in ways I still craved, but this? This was different. This was submission. Not to me, but to the clinical expertise of a woman who regarded him as nothing more than a subject to be measured.

She worked efficiently, using a combination of laser devices and traditional tape to record every precise detail of his body. I knew this was part of something larger—custom tailoring, data for his team to maintain his peak physicality—but it didn't change the way the air in the room had thickened.

Then, she reached the flaccid flesh between his thighs.

Without hesitation, she retrieved an electronic sleeve, sliding it over him with practiced detachment.

Small clamps were affixed to his nipples, a tablet in her hands glowing with data.

Dorian didn't flinch, but I saw the change in his breathing, the slight parting of his lips. A few taps on her screen, and the device hummed to life.

His member responded instantly, thickening, lengthening. My thighs pressed together as I watched him harden, his body reacting to the stimulation he couldn't control. Arousal coiled low in my belly, an insistent pulse of heat spreading through me. He was always the one orchestrating pleasure, dictating every moment of surrender. Yet here he was, body betraying him under someone else's command.

Dorian exhaled, fully erect, the veins along his shaft pronounced. His body strained, his muscles tensed. Then, with another flick of her fingers against the tablet, he came.

It was controlled, his body shuddering but not breaking, a low, guttural sound caught in his throat. The release was swift, clinical, yet my own body burned in response. I clenched my hands in my lap, resisting the urge to touch myself, to ease the ache forming between my legs.

The specialist ignored him a glance as she observed the data. "Good," she murmured, tapping a note onto her tablet. "Last measurement."

She retrieved a slender probe, and for the first time, Dorian hesitated for a fraction of a second, but it was enough. She pushed the lubricated device inside him, and a soft whir filled the space between us.

Dorian's hands fisted at his sides. His throat bobbed with a hard swallow, and I saw it: the moment when control slipped entirely from his grasp. His hips twitched, his legs flexed. With a deep, broken groan, he came again.

I was soaked.

The image of him, utterly undone, sent molten heat cascading through my veins. My fingers itched to drag over my own skin, to chase the pleasure that watching him had ignited.

The woman finally looked up. "I have what I need."

Dorian, still catching his breath, lifted his gaze to me, and for the first time, I wondered if he could see the arousal in my eyes; if he knew how badly I wanted to climb onto his lap and grind myself against the evidence of his surrender.

Then, she turned to me.

"Your turn. Strip."

I hesitated, my breath catching. My eyes flicked to Dorian. He met my gaze, and for the first time that night, he wasn't in control.

He was asking.

Not with words, but with his eyes.

Do you consent?

A slow, knowing smile curled on my lips.

I reached for the buttons of my blouse, slipping each one open with deliberate slowness. The silk parted, revealing glimpses of the lingerie I'd chosen—something intricate, something meant only for me, a quiet rebellion under the professional armor I wore. Manon had taught me well: lingerie was about power. And in

Dorian's presence, power was a currency I had no intention of surrendering easily.

I slid the blouse from my shoulders, letting it fall neatly over the chair beside me. Then, with measured ease, I unfastened my trousers and stepped out of them, my heels clicking lightly against the marble floor as I straightened.

Dorian hadn't moved.

But I felt him.

His gaze traced over me, a dark flicker of amusement as his attention dragged lower—to the unmistakable dampness at the apex of my thighs.

Damn it.

Heat curled up my spine, a slow burn of humiliation and arousal as I fought the urge to press my legs together. The tailored lace of my lingerie, delicate and precise, only made it more obvious.

He smirked.

The bastard actually smirked.

The specialist, however, was already moving. Unaffected, unfazed. She reached into her case and produced a small, black box embossed with gold lettering. With an economy of movement, she flicked it open and extended it toward me.

"Clean yourself," she instructed coolly. "We need precise readings."

I hesitated, caught between the sterile nature of her command and the very unsterile throb between my legs.

Dorian looked on with intent, waiting.

I took the box, my fingers brushing over the embossed surface before I lifted one of the wipes from inside. The fabric was impossibly soft, infused with something subtle—luxurious, expensive, like the kind of thing you'd expect to find in the restroom of a six-star hotel, not used to wipe away the evidence of your arousal.

I pressed the cloth between my thighs, a slow, torturous drag over my skin.

Too soft. Too much.

I bit the inside of my cheek as another pulse of heat rolled through me.

Dorian didn't move, but the energy in the room changed.

He saw.

I knew he saw.

And still, the specialist remained utterly indifferent, tapping on her tablet as though we were discussing quarterly projections instead of preparing for what was coming next.

"The measurements we take today," she continued, without so much as a glance at me, "will not only be used for tailoring, but for the production of custom sexual instruments."

I did not have the time to process the mention of custom sexual instruments before the specialist was reaching into her case again.

She withdrew a sleek, silver device—small, handheld, its curved blades encased in an elegant, minimalist shell. It didn't look medical, nor did it look overtly sexual.

It looked... like a fan.

I frowned. What the hell?

She powered it on, a soft hum filling the space between us. "I can't take precise measurements on someone in your current state."

My current state.

A flush of heat climbed my neck, my fingers tightening where they rested against my sides.

"Your body temperature needs to stabilize," she continued, adjusting the settings. "Excessive heat alters the readings. This will correct that."

I shot Dorian a sharp look, as if to say, *Are you serious?*

He leaned against his desk, arms still crossed, watching. His expression was unreadable, but the glint in his eyes? That was something else entirely.

Amusement.

Satisfaction.

The bastard was enjoying this.

Before I could form a retort, the specialist stepped closer and angled the device toward me. A controlled stream of cool air swept over my skin, first along my arms, then my torso. The sensation wasn't shocking—more of a gradual, creeping chill, a contrast to the molten heat still simmering inside me.

But when she adjusted the angle lower, the cool air ghosting over my inner thighs, my body reacted.

A sharp inhale.

A shiver.

My nipples, already taut from exposure, stiffened further. My body, trained to respond to sensation, rebelled against the sudden shift. The contrast between heat and cold sent a confused rush of sensation through me; almost pleasurable, in a strange, twisted way.

I clenched my jaw.

"Is this really necessary?" I forced out, my voice too steady to betray how much this was affecting me.

The specialist ignored my protest. "Your blood flow needs to neutralize. Otherwise, the readings will be inaccurate."

I exhaled through my nose, forcing stillness. I wouldn't give her the satisfaction of squirming.

After what felt like an eternity—but was probably only a minute—the specialist powered the device off and inspected her tablet.

"Better," she murmured, making a few notes. Then, without missing a beat, "Now, we can begin."

I swallowed down a response.

Dorian pushed off the desk, finally moving, finally speaking, his voice a smooth, knowing drawl.

"Try not to get too worked up this time."

I shot him a withering glare, but the traitorous pulse between my legs was already betraying me.

With my body sufficiently cooled and my dignity destroyed, the specialist resumed her work.

She measured with precision, hands moving over my limbs, cataloging every inch of me with the detached efficiency of someone assessing a mannequin.

Her fingers skimmed my collarbones, mapped the contours of my waist, traced the length of my legs. Every angle, every proportion, every subtle shift in muscle and bone was recorded in her tablet without comment.

Then, she reached my breasts.

Her hands pressed in, testing their weight, assessing shape and density. She cupped, lifted, compressed from the sides, from below—measuring resistance, elasticity.

"Well, at least I won't need a mammogram this year."

The specialist didn't even blink. "Mammograms are still necessary for long-term breast health. Ensure you schedule one annually."

Dorian exhaled a quiet breath that might have been a laugh, but when I flicked my gaze to him, he looked as composed as ever.

Of course he was enjoying this.

The specialist moved lower, hands firm as they traced my hips, my thighs. Then, without hesitation, she squeezed my ass.

Not once.

Not gently.

She palmed the flesh, fingers pressing deep, assessing from multiple angles, applying pressure in different ways.

I clenched my teeth. "Should I be getting regular checkups there, too?"

Nothing. Not even a flicker of amusement from her.

She simply continued her work, utterly unbothered, while Dorian watched with the distinct air of a man who was storing every second of this in his mind for later use.

I exhaled, determined not to let either of them see how much my body still wanted.

And I had a feeling the next part was going to be even worse.

The specialist retrieved a set of small, silver clamps, attaching them to my nipples with precise, impersonal efficiency. A quiet hum emitted from them as they calibrated, measuring sensitivity, firmness, and responsiveness. The cool metal sent a jolt of sensation through me as I swallowed back a gasp.

Dorian was watching, his eyes betraying his hunger.

"Lie back," the specialist instructed.

I hesitated for only a breath before complying, reclining onto the padded surface, feeling the cool air skim my bare skin. My thighs parted as directed, my body still primed from everything that had come before.

She pulled out a device.

I blinked.

It was an exact replica of Dorian's pride.

The same proportions, the same ridges and veins, the same thick weight. Even the material mimicked the warmth of real skin.

I let out a slow, incredulous breath. "If you're going to put that between my legs, wouldn't it be more efficient to use the real thing?"

Dorian smiled.

The specialist remained unbothered.

She tapped something on her tablet.

The device moved.

Before I could brace, it thrust into me with a precision that sent shockwaves of pleasure rolling through my body.

I gasped, my back arching, fingers gripping the edge of the surface. The sensation was too real. Every movement, every shift, felt like him. Deep, controlled, relentless.

I had no control.

The moment my body hit its peak, clenching around the device, it stopped instantly.

Not a slow withdrawal. Not an easing down.

Off, like a switch had been flipped.

I was left panting, aching, needing.

The specialist observed the data scrolling across her tablet, expression unreadable.

"Hm."

That was all.

Not impressed. Not interested.

Meanwhile, Dorian sat perfectly still, his expression composed. But I felt the heat between us. The tension.

And I knew that if we had been alone, this would have ended very, very differently.

The cooling device whirred to life once more, its artificial chill sweeping over my overstimulated body. I shivered, my muscles tensing against the unnatural temperature shift. The specialist didn't acknowledge my reaction, her gaze fixed on the scrolling data on her tablet.

After a few silent minutes, she finally powered down the device. Without looking up, she removed the replica from me with the same efficiency she had applied to every part of the process.

"You need to take a cold shower," she stated simply, typing something into her tablet.

I hesitated.

Dorian's bathroom was an extension of his domain. It would be foolish to assume that stepping into it, naked and vulnerable, wasn't part of the psychological game being played.

Still, I stood and walked toward it, my legs unsteady.

Inside, the space was as I expected—dark marble, sleek fixtures, everything exuding wealth and control. The shower was oversized, enclosed in glass, the kind of place built for indulgence. But there would be no indulgence now.

I twisted the handle.

Ice-cold water slammed against my overheated skin. I sucked in a sharp breath, my body protesting the abrupt shift from burning arousal to forced restraint. The sensation shocked me back into control, suppressing the raw need still coiled inside me.

This wasn't over.

Once I was sufficiently chilled—inside and out—I stepped out, drying off quickly, my mind already bracing for what came next.

When I returned, the specialist had cleaned and prepped everything, the Dorian replica resting back in her hands like a precision instrument.

"We'll continue where we left off."

I swallowed.

No preamble, no acknowledgment of what had transpired. Simply clinical progression.

She reattached the nipple clamps, the bite of them sharper against my cooled skin. This time, she added a third—clipping it much lower.

I exhaled through my nose.

Dorian remained still, watching.

Then the process resumed.

She pushed me through a sequence of measured stimulations, each building in intensity, meticulously tracking my responses. My body, primed and trained to react to his presence, didn't stand a chance.

A clitoral climax.

A breast climax.

An ass climax.

Each calculated, controlled, cut off the moment the data was gathered.

By the time she finally stepped back, my limbs felt boneless, my body spent. Sweat slicked my skin despite the earlier cold, my breath uneven. The only sound in the room was my own heavy exhale.

Dorian's arousal was palpable, a barely leashed force behind his composed expression. He hadn't moved, hadn't spoken—but I felt him.

Still, he remained controlled.

The specialist made a final note, then turned to me with one last instruction.

"I need one last set of measurements."

She lifted the replica of Dorian's member, wrapping her fingers around the shaft.

"Open your mouth."

CHAPTER
Nineteen

A BETTER OFFER

The evening had arrived.

Weeks of preparation, of whispered speculations and rising anticipation, had led to this.

The Influence Awards.

Dorian had dictated every detail: what lingerie would be against my skin, what dress would skim my curves, which heels would lengthen my legs enough to be commanding; The perfume—an exclusive blend he had commissioned, something deep and sensual, designed to linger long after I'd left the room. Even the shade of my lipstick, the precision of my eyeliner, the way my hair cascaded in controlled waves—each element had been curated with the same ruthless efficiency he applied to everything else in his life.

Not as submission, not as surrender. But as strategy.

Tonight was about making them feel me. The judges of the Orpheus Prize, the literary world's elite, the gatekeepers of legacy—they had to see me not only as a writer, but as inevitable.

I stood before the mirror, the final product of his machinations, and I felt it.

Power.

Sex.

Not overt, not crass. Enough to unsettle, to make them wonder if they were admiring me or being seduced by something they couldn't quite place.

Dorian sat across the room, legs spread in effortless command, watching. Assessing.

He hadn't spoken since the final touch of gloss had been pressed onto my lips. He was simply looking.

Waiting.

The final touches were complete.

The hairdressers and makeup artists, each one hand-selected by Dorian, stepped back, their work immaculate. No strand out of place, no detail overlooked. I was perfection—crafted, polished, refined down to the last gleam of gloss on my lips.

They murmured their goodbyes, gathering their kits and disappearing through the door. The moment it shut, a shift settled over the room.

Silence.

And Dorian.

He sat back in his chair, legs spread, one hand idly resting on the armrest, the other tracing the rim of a whiskey glass. His gaze moved over me with slow, measured intent, absorbing every inch, every decision he had dictated.

The gown—a statement of power without screaming for attention. The heels, high enough to alter my stance, to shift the way my hips swayed when I moved. The perfume—designed to linger, a ghost of scent that would haunt the air I left behind.

For long moments, he said nothing.

Then, finally—

"Come here."

I moved toward him, unhurried, letting him watch the way the silk clung to me, the way the slit revealed a tantalizing trace of my thigh with each step. When I reached him, he didn't touch me. He simply sat there, looking up at me, his expression unreadable.

"Turn around."

I did, my back to him now, my reflection captured in the mirror across the room.

His fingers found my waist first, a light press through the fabric. Then lower, along my hip. A slow, assessing touch that wasn't overtly sexual—but sent heat coursing through me anyway.

His fingers skimmed the zipper of the gown, lingering there.

"I want to make a few adjustments."

His voice was calm, deliberate. His hand disappeared into his pocket, and when it emerged, my stomach clenched.

There, dangling between his fingers, was the Luxuria Collar.

The blood-red Burmese Mogok Ruby caught the light, its fire flashing against the platinum and black-gilded gold. The diamonds glimmered like stars against shadow. The collar exuded power, opulence—ownership.

I went still.

"You should wear this," he said, his tone deceptively smooth.

"Should I?"

"It suits you."

"No."

His eyes darkened, but he didn't move. "No?"

"No," I repeated. "I am not something to be collared and paraded around like a prize you won."

Dorian tilted his head. "That's not what this is."

"Isn't it?" I folded my arms, gaze locked onto his. "You spent a billion dollars on that collar, and now you want me to wear it in front of the entire world. If you expect me to kneel next, you're going to be quite disappointed."

The tension in the air thickened.

"You're making this into something it's not," he said, voice steady but firm. "It's a piece of jewelry. A statement. You'll be the most powerful woman in the room tonight."

"I already am the most powerful woman in the room."

His jaw flexed.

"I accepted your terms," he said. "But power isn't always about refusal, Beatrix. It's about knowing when to take something, when to wield it."

"And you think this"—I gestured at the collar in his hand—"is something I should take?"

"Yes."

"No."

His eyes narrowed, the slightest flicker of something dangerous crossing his face. "Why?"

"Because I don't belong to you."

He took a step closer. "For one night, would it be so terrible?"

"Yes."

His patience thinned visibly. "Beatrix—"

"No."

The word lashed between us like a whip.

His fingers curled around the collar, knuckles whitening.

A long silence stretched.

Then, softer, quieter, he asked, "Why does it bother you so much?"

I stared at him, my heart hammering. "Because I don't trust what it means to you."

Something flickered in his expression.

Then, carefully, deliberately, he set The Luxuria Collar on the table beside him.

His surrender was subtle but absolute.

He exhaled through his nose. "Fine."

I was still rigid, still coiled tight from the confrontation.

He studied me. "If not this, then something else."

"Like what?"

"A concession," he said. "Something no one else will see. Something I will know is there."

I hesitated.

He had backed down. He had let go.

But not completely.

I considered him for a long moment. The silence between us was still thick with unspoken challenge.

Then I exhaled. "Fine."

The tension in the air didn't dissipate.

Instead, it shifted.

Dorian reached into another drawer, retrieving something larger. A velvet box.

Dorian's fingers traced the edge of the velvet box before he lifted it, revealing the contents inside.

A set of gleaming diamond-tipped nipple clamps, a set of weighted Ben Wa balls, and a slim, jeweled butt plug.

All exquisitely crafted and customized for me.

"These," he said smoothly, "were built to your precise specifications."

Every clamp, every weight, every inch—custom-made for your body."

A slow heat curled in my belly.

Dorian reached down, selecting one of the nipple clamps. He turned it between his fingers, the polished metal gleaming under the soft light. "The tension," he murmured, "was calibrated to the exact sensitivity of your nipples. Precisely calibrated to hold you at the edge."

He let the weight of the Ben Wa balls shift in his palm, the faintest clink of metal filling the space between us. "These are designed to rest perfectly inside you," he continued. "Not too heavy, not too light. A whisper of sensation with every step."

Then, finally, he lifted the butt plug. "And this—" His eyes met mine. "Made to fit you like a glove. The weight, the pressure, the way it sits when you move—all engineered for you."

"And you expect me to wear all of them?"

His lips curved.

"I expect you to do whatever you want to do," he said. "You made that clear earlier."

A test of power neither of us was willing to fail.

I held his gaze, the air between us thick with something heady, something dangerous.

Then, with unhurried grace, I stepped closer, sat, parted my thighs, and placed the tip of one heel, then the other, on his chest before piercing him with my gaze.

"What are you waiting for?"

His jaw tightened. With deliberate precision, he obeyed.

Part 3

REVISIONS

CHAPTER
Twenty

(D)EVOLUTION

Manon spotted me the moment I stepped onto the red carpet, her gaze locking onto me through the flashing lights and throng of reporters like a wolf spotting prey. She made a beeline for me, moving with her signature feline grace, wrapped Chanel, poured onto her like liquid silk.

"Chanel *and* Hermès? Should I be worried?"

She twirled, letting fabric catch the light. "Shocking, isn't it? I figured if I really wanted to terrify maman, I'd show her I can look the part of the dignified French icon she always wanted me to be." She leaned in, her voice dropping into a sultry whisper. "Of course, that's only the outside."

I smirked. "And what's underneath?"

She shot me a knowing look. "Oh, B, you know better than anyone—it's always what's underneath that's the most scandalous."

Her gaze raked over me, taking in every detail— the effortless sensuality in the way I carried myself.

"Well," she purred, "whoever put this masterpiece together has impeccable taste."

I gave her a teasing, unreadable smile. "That he does."

Manon's grin widened. "And tell me, *mon amour*, will you be taking home all the literary prizes this year, or only the ones that matter?"

I gave a dramatic sigh. "Oh, I suppose I could leave one for someone else... I could be generous."

She snorted. "Please. You're sweeping. The Orpheus Prize is a done deal, and every other one is waiting to engrave your name on their trophies. I can already hear the judges pretending like there was ever a choice."

I laughed, nudging her with my shoulder. "You flatter me."

She looped her arm through mine as we moved down the carpet, a few cameras capturing the moment—the two most dangerous women in the room, reunited.

"Only when it's warranted," she quipped, her voice turning more wicked. "Now tell me... what scandalous little number are you wearing underneath all this?"

I tilted my head, a flicker of mischief in my gaze. "Oh, it's definitely bespoke."

"And scandalous?"

"Let's call it all encompassing and immersive."

"Immersive," she repeated, rolling the word on her tongue like a sip of aged wine. "That's a... delicious choice of vocabulary, B."

I hummed, letting her linger in curiosity. She'd drag the truth out of me sooner or later, but I wanted to make her work for it.

She leaned in, her breath warm against my cheek. "Come on," she murmured. "I know that look. You've done something—*felt* something. And considering how exquisitely composed you are right now... I'd say it's something that makes staying composed a challenge."

I smirked. "Self-discipline."

Her eyes glinted with intrigue. "Oh, this is good."

We strolled down the carpet, faces poised for the cameras, her fingers idly tracing my spine as she studied me. "Tell me, B. Is it lace? Satin? Something with a little... pressure?"

I let the pause stretch, watching the curiosity flicker in her gaze. Then, ever so softly, I said, "Something with a firm grip."

Manon's gaze flickered downward, thoughtful. "Oh, you are bad."

I let my lips curve. "Took you this long to figure that out?"

Her eyes narrowed, playfully suspicious. "And?"

I toyed with her, letting the pause stretch before murmuring, "Weighted."

She let out a soft, sinful laugh. "You did not."

I took another step, feeling it shift again, the deliberate tease of something that belonged only to me, nestled deep.

Manon's nails dug lightly into my arm. "B—" she started, but her voice faltered.

"Something wrong?"

She let out a breathless, delighted laugh, masking it as a perfectly timed smile for a passing photographer.

"*Merde*," she muttered, shaking her head. "That's… committed."

I lifted a brow. "Would you expect anything less?"

Her cheeks were flushed now, lips parting for a second before she caught herself. Then she gave me a slow, knowing grin.

"And here I thought I was the most wicked one in this friendship."

I chuckled. "You still can be."

Her eyes flickered with interest, but then she sighed, squeezing my arm. "He still wins, you know."

I lifted a brow. "How?"

Her lips curved. "Because he doesn't even have to be here, and he's still got his fingers all over you."

The sheer audacity of it hit us at the same time. We shared a look, both flushed, aroused, and far too entertained by our own indulgences.

Like the devilish duo we were, we burst into laughter, heads tipping together in conspiratorial glee, the kind only best friends—and former lovers—could ever truly share.

As we stepped into the grand lobby, the hum of conversation and the clinking of glasses surrounded us, a well-orchestrated symphony of wealth and power. Manon and I were still locked in our private amusement, wrapped in the warmth of whispered secrets, when we crossed paths with him.

Dorian Wolker.

His presence was as controlled as ever—sharp suit, sharper gaze—but his expression was composed, formal. Distant.

For a moment, my body betrayed me, the carefully hidden sensations under my gown tightening, pulsing, heating in response to the sight of him. But I forced my posture into something equally composed, equally distant.

Manon, ever the performer, was the first to greet him.

"Mademoiselle de Rochemaure," Dorian said smoothly, offering the smallest inclination of his head.

Manon returned the nod with effortless grace. "Monsieur Wolker."

"Please, call me Dorian."

"Dorian, then."

He didn't extend the same courtesy to me.

His gaze flicked over, steady. "Miss Winslow-Hale."

I tilted my head, matching his cool detachment. "Mister Wolker."

The omission was deliberate. Calculated.

Manon, ever attuned to undercurrents, caught it immediately. Her eyes danced with mischief, but she said nothing—yet.

"I believe congratulations are in order for the both of you," Dorian said smoothly. "Your names seem to be shaping the cultural landscape as we know it."

Manon smiled graciously. "We do our best."

Dorian's gaze was unreadable. "Your upcoming venture is particularly intriguing."

Manon's smile didn't waver, but I felt the slight shift in her posture. The lingerie line wasn't public knowledge yet.

"Oh?" she said, feigning pleasant surprise. "And what have you heard?"

"Only that it promises to be... transformative."

I could practically feel the gears in Manon's mind turning, calculating where and how he could have learned about her plans.

She laughed lightly. "I do aim to make an impression."

Dorian inclined his head, his gaze cutting briefly back to me. "And Miss Winslow-Hale—your work continues to dominate literary discourse. The Orpheus Prize committee must be watching closely."

I held his gaze, keeping my voice poised. "One would hope."

Manon, always one to stir the pot, gave an easy laugh. "She does have a way with words."

Dorian exhaled softly. "Among other things."

It was so slight, so measured, that no one else might have caught the double meaning laced beneath the words. But I did.

The gentle yet insistent stretch of the plug conspired against me, a cruel orchestration of hidden indulgence.

I forced my breath steady.

Manon, oblivious to my struggle, tilted her head. "And congratulations to you as well, Dorian. Your latest acquisition was quite the spectacle."

Dorian took a measured sip of his drink. "It was an inevitability."

"Not much for competition, then?"

"Only when necessary." His lips barely quirked. "Though I hear I should extend my gratitude to your father."

My father had wanted that robotics company; had pursued it aggressively. And lost.

Dorian wanted me to acknowledge it.

"I'm sure he'll be glad to know he played a role in your success."

Dorian's gaze lingered, and for a fraction of a second, the space between us crackled—an unspoken battle of control, of restraint, of knowing.

Manon, ever the master of redirecting a conversation, took a sip of her champagne. "Well, it seems we're all having quite the year."

Dorian inclined his head. "It would seem so."

Then, with the same calculated ease, he added, "You should both pay close attention tonight. I have a little surprise in store—an unexpected demonstration of the company's technology."

I didn't react.

Manon, however, arched a playful brow. "Oh? Should we be excited?"

Dorian tilted his glass toward her. "You'll find out soon enough."

There was a pause, a breath of silence long enough for the weight of the encounter to settle.

Then Manon smiled, the perfect picture of effortless charm. "Shall we?"

I nodded, my voice smooth. "We shall."

And with that, we stepped away, leaving Dorian by himself—and me, still aching from the unseen touch he had left behind.

I was still recovering from the heat of Manon's teasing when I turned—and collided into a firm, familiar body.

A cool hand caught my arm, firm, steady.

Lucian.

The impact sent a shock through me, with a deep, undeniable shift inside me.

Everything inside me shifted, sharp enough to steal my breath.

My breath hitched, my thighs clenched, and I had to fight every instinct not to react, not to let it show, not to—

"Beatrix."

His voice was smooth, effortless—unaware he had wrecked me.

I forced an easy smile, masking the wreckage inside me. "Lucian. I figured we'd run into each other eventually."

"I suppose we were bound to collide at some point."

Manon slipped in beside me with her signature smirk. "You've been awfully quiet, Lucian. No new exhibits?"

Lucian exhaled the ghost of a laugh. "Busy with private commissions. More intimate settings. Things to be worn in the body."

Manon lifted a brow, her lips parting before curling into something wicked. "Now, that's intriguing."

Lucian's gaze flickered, barely perceptible. "Custom work only."

Manon hummed under her breath, tilting her head. "I imagine a perfect fit is crucial."

Lucian's mouth curved at the edge. "Essential."

Manon smirked, tapping a manicured nail against her stemware. "And you? Are you a patient man, Lucian?"

"When the subject is worth it."

"Perhaps I should schedule a session."

"Perhaps you should."

Manon let the words settle, then gave a slow, deliberate once-over of his frame. "Well, Lucian, from what I can see... you've already done some very fine sculpting of your own."

Lucian's smirk deepened, but he said nothing. He tipped his glass in a silent toast before slipping into the crowd, vanishing like a shadow.

Manon let out a slow, decadent sigh, her gaze shamelessly fixed on the taut curve of Lucian's ass as he walked away, his perfectly tailored trousers doing nothing to hide the strength of his thighs. "*Merde*, B. If he's the one who made what you're wearing, I don't know whether to be scandalized or impressed."

CHAPTER
Twenty-One

THE MISSING PIECE

The stage lights flared, illuminating the MC as he took his place at the podium, his presence carrying the perfect blend of charm and self-deprecation.

"Tonight is about more than influence," he began, letting the anticipation settle. "It's about power. The kind that shifts industries, redefines art, reshapes culture, and—based on some of the people in this room— possibly rewires human desire."

A ripple of laughter swept through the audience. Manon shifted beside me, crossing her legs leisurely, fingers idly adjusting the silk of her Hermès scarf.

"Let's start with innovation," the MC continued. "Dorian Wolker—because why buy the future when you can make it yourself?" He smirked toward Dorian's section of the room. "The man has taken tiny nerve-repairing robots and turned them into a billion-dollar industry. It probably won't be in sports, but I, for one, will be first in line to buy one if it can calm my nerves after a night like this."

The audience chuckled. I could almost feel Dorian's non-reaction from across the room.

"Politics." The MC turned toward Senator Ramona Guerra-Reina. "The woman who's been shaking up Washington so hard, I think even the statues are starting to sweat. No one's quite sure if she's a reformist or a troublemaker, but I'm sure after another six months, someone in Congress will have an answer."

Polite applause, a few knowing murmurs from the political class.

"Art." He gestured toward Lucian Moreau. "The man who doesn't only create pieces—you feel them. And in some cases, from what I've heard, wear them. On your body. Or, you know... in it."

A wave of laughter, some cheers from the crowd. Lucian merely inclined his head, an enigmatic smirk playing on his lips.

"And of course, literature." The MC turned toward me. "Beatrix Winslow-Hale. A woman whose words don't merely stir the soul—they light it on fire. She's got half the world reevaluating their literary tastes, and the other half questioning whether they've been doing sex all wrong."

The applause was loud. Manon nudged me, whispering, "Accurate."

I fought a smirk.

"And, of course, fashion and celebrity." His gaze landed on Manon. "Mademoiselle de Rochemaure, who has somehow managed to scandalize an entire country with nothing but a few pieces of lace, a museum, and the audacity of a woman who doesn't seem to have ever encountered a taboo she didn't want to break."

The room erupted. The French press had been in a full meltdown for weeks, and judging by Manon's pleased expression, she was soaking in every second of it.

"Between a certain now-infamous Louvre photoshoot and a few high-profile family disagreements," he continued, "she's proven that being French is more than an identity—it's an art form. And a headline-generating one, at that."

Laughter and applause filled the room. Manon tilted her head, basking in it.

Then, the MC placed a hand on his chest, feigning genuine concern. "I'll be honest, looking at this guest list, I'm unclear as to whether I am"—he exhaled dramatically—"wildly overdressed. And possibly... underperforming in multiple areas."

A roar of laughter.

"I mean, Lucian is sculpting bodies, Beatrix is writing things that make people reconsider their lives, and Manon—well, she's out here redefining what fabric is even for." He smirked. "If anyone's handing out influence tonight, please, for the sake of my self-esteem, throw some my way."

Manon laughed, eyes sparkling.

"But," the MC straightened, "if there's one thing we know about nights like this, it's that they come with surprises. Announcements. Power moves."

The energy shifted.

"So, my friends, enjoy your drinks, enjoy the company, and try not to drool... *too* much. Because I have a feeling by the time we leave here tonight, we'll all be talking about more than just influence."

Applause erupted. I glanced at Manon, who was practically glowing.

The night had followed its expected rhythm. Senator Guerra-Reina had spoken about people over billionaires, earning polite applause from the billionaires in the room. Lucian had spoken about art and sex, his voice rich with sensuality as he described creativity as an extension of desire. Dorian had, unsurprisingly, dominated the room with his announcement—his microscopic robots promising the potential to solve paralysis, to give sensation where none existed. He had even smirked as he added, "Until the technology is on the market, I'd recommend a stiff drink for your nerves." A tease at the MC's joke, but I had caught the way his eyes had flicked toward me, watching my reaction.

And now, the moment everyone would remember—Manon's entrance.

I stood with her in the dressing area, adjusting the final touches on her outfit. She had already left gasps in her wake, those catching glimpses of her in passing looking as though they had seen a goddess descend. But no one had yet seen the full effect.

"How do I look?"

I stepped back, arms crossed, pretending to scrutinize her like an art critic. In truth, there was nothing to critique. Manon was a vision of dominance and decadence, wrapped in a second skin of black leather. The corset dress sculpted her waist with merciless precision, zippers gleaming like whispers of temptation. Her boots stretched high over her thighs, making her legs look even longer, even more lethal.

"Like an expensive sin," I murmured, tilting my head.

She preened, giving a slow spin so the dress caught the light. "Leather by Hermès, little black dress by Chanel." Then she gestured to the men kneeling at her feet—harnessed, collared, waiting. Their collars each had a lock at the throat, a quiet symbol of ownership.

She smirked. "And, of course, my loyal subjects. Because what's a Châtelaine without some slaves?"

I exhaled, shaking my head. "You are going to make a scene."

"That is the point, darling," she purred, eyes glinting with wicked delight.

Then, suddenly, she paused, with a contemplative gleam in her eye.

I knew that look. That look meant trouble.

"What?" I asked, already wary.

Manon exhaled dramatically. "Something's missing."

I glanced at her outfit, the men, the grand absurdity of it all. "Missing? Manon, you have four men literally waiting to carry you inside."

Her lips curled as she turned to face me fully, her voice dipping into something dangerously smooth. "Something... internal."

It took me half a second too long to register what she meant.

My spine straightened. "No."

She tilted her head, gaze flicking downward, then back up, smug and knowing. "Yes."

I narrowed my eyes. "Absolutely not."

She sighed, as if I was the unreasonable one. "B, think about it. That ballroom, those cameras, the breathless anticipation." She leaned in, voice honeyed with mischief. "Me, standing in front of all of them... with your little secret inside me."

My body still hummed from wearing them. The heat, the unbearable pressure, the way they moved with every step.

I swallowed. "You want to make this even more scandalous."

"I *need* to make this even more scandalous."

I pinched the bridge of my nose. "You are impossible."

She grinned, nudging me playfully. "And yet, you love me."

I exhaled, already regretting this. "That is literally the only reason I'm even considering this."

Her eyes sparkled with victory.

With a resigned sigh, I slid my hands under my dress, pressing my lips together as I withdrew the warm, slick spheres. The sudden rush of cool air made me shiver. Manon watched, utterly captivated.

I held them up between us. "Last chance to back out."

"Do I look like someone who backs out?"

"You look like someone who has no idea what she's asking for."

She smirked. "I think I'll manage."

I let the pause stretch, watching her, making her wait for it. Then, finally, I took my time cleaning the spheres with a silk cloth, deliberately slow, deliberately torturous.

Manon was practically vibrating.

Then, kneeling before her, I looked up. "Spread."

She sat, then slowly put one leg on my left shoulder, and the other on my right. "Do me, B."

I pressed the first ball in, my fingers slipping effortlessly into the heat of her body. She let out a slow, decadent sigh, her gloved hands gripping my shoulders.

"Oh, B, they're deliciously warm."

Another, deeper. Her breath hitched, her thighs trembling.

"Still think this was a good idea?" I teased, fingers ghosting over her entrance.

Her grin was practically feral. "Oh, darling, this is the best idea I've had all year."

The last sphere nestled into place, and I lingered, feeling her body react to them. I rose to my feet, meeting her gaze.

"You're going to be a menace tonight."

She licked her lips. "That's the plan."

From the side of the stage, I watched.

Manon stood at the center of the room, draped in dominance, basking in the spell she had cast. The energy was pulsating, a living, breathing thing, held taut between the hundreds of bodies transfixed on her. The flashing lights of cameras; the slow, deliberate movements of the videographers capturing every exquisite detail of her entrance; her posture, the way the light skimmed across the leather of her corset dress; the dark gleam of her boots, the men beneath her, harnessed and collared.

Every single man and woman in that room wanted her. They might not admit it aloud, might not even fully understand it yet, but it was there, humming beneath the surface of their controlled exteriors. Arousal. Submission. Fascination.

It was impossible not to feel it. The ache in my nipples tightened under the clamps, sending sharp, hot shivers straight to my core. The plug in my ass pressed deeper, almost as if it had begun to pulse in time with the beat of the room's unspoken hunger.

Manon had them utterly enthralled.

The audience rose in an immediate ovation the second she uttered the name: *Châtelaine.*

The night was far from over. The audience merged into a singular gasp.

A collective, unrestrained sound of disbelief as she revealed her partners: Chanel and Hermès.

The crown jewels of French fashion, now under her command.

I watched as she stood there, taking it in, absorbing the weight of her own success. But I knew where her mind had gone. It wasn't to the applause, or the flashes of press cameras capturing her moment of triumph. It was to Paris. To her mother.

The vengeance in it all, the complete and utter dominance over a world that had tried to dismiss her as a scandal rather than a force—it was intoxicating. I could see it in her eyes. The power coursing through her, making her throb around the spheres I had pressed into her only minutes ago.

She found me in the shadows offstage, her lips curling as she gave me a slow, knowing wink.

She felt it, too.

This. *This* was the moment. Every headline tomorrow would belong to her.

I swallowed against the bitter edge of worry. Would there be room left for me? For my speech? For my chance to capture the judges and pull the Orpheus Prize into my hands?

But before doubt could settle in, Manon was turning toward the audience again, her voice as smooth and controlled as silk-wrapped steel.

"And now, my dear friends, I have the great pleasure of introducing someone who has redefined the written word. A woman whose voice commands as much attention as the body you see before you. My closest friend, my partner in crime, and the writer who has every critic, every scholar, and—if we're being honest—every one of *you* in this room begging to read her next sentence..."

She turned her head toward me, eyes glinting, as she stretched out her arm toward the wings of the stage.

"The incomparable Beatrix Winslow-Hale."

The room erupted again, the attention shifting, the energy cresting as Manon stepped down from the podium, her dominion momentarily passed to me.

She approached, the confident click of her heels lost beneath the applause. She was right in front of me, wrapping me in her arms, pressing a kiss to my cheek before murmuring, "I've hooked them, B. Now all you have to do... is reel them in."

I smirked, squeezing her ass—then giving it a swift, teasing slap. "Consider it done."

She sighed dramatically. "Mmm. You always did know how to send a girl off with a thrill."

The room was still humming with the aftershocks of Manon's spectacle, the air thick with the scent of leather, desire, and something close to submission. She had the entire world at her feet, and she knew it.

And now, all that attention—the raw hunger, the intrigue, the lingering arousal of the audience—had pivoted toward me.

I took a breath, feeling the bite of the clamps still teasing my nipples beneath the silk of my dress. A sharp ache. A reminder. The plug inside me sat heavy, deliberate, pressing into me with each slow step I took toward the podium. Dorian had ensured I wouldn't forget whose hands had been on me before I walked onto this stage.

Manon remained at the edge of the stage, arms folded, watching, waiting. She wasn't leaving. Of course, she wasn't leaving.

She had dominated the room, leaving it on its knees. Now, she was here to witness me do the same, in my own way.

"Well," I said, my voice like silk over steel, "that's quite the act to follow."

Laughter rippled through the audience, a slight release of tension, but not too much. I didn't want them relaxed. I wanted them hooked.

Manon smirked, tilting her head, her silent challenge unmistakable. *Your turn, B.*

I let my gaze drift across the crowd, catching the eyes that mattered—the judges, the literary elite, the journalists desperate for the next headline.

They were watching, waiting to see if I could command a room the way I commanded words.

I felt the deep, persistent throb of my body's awareness. The press of the plug inside me. The tight pull at my nipples. The edge of desire that had been simmering all night.

They thought I was here to speak about literature. I was here to give them something to remember.

The words poured from my lips, measured, deliberate, crafted to ensnare. It was the speech—one that would cement my name in literary history. A speech that would be dissected, quoted, whispered about in corridors of power, in smoky bars where writers and artists drank to excess.

And I had them.

Every single one of them.

The audience breathed with me, hung on every syllable. I was shaping the room, pulling them into my world, threading intellect and desire into something dangerous.

Dorian, seated front and center, was poised like a predator at rest. His face unreadable. No smirk, no arrogance. Watching. Drinking me in.

Owning me.

A shiver ran through me, and suddenly—

The clamps on my nipples tightened.

No.

Not tightened. *Activated*.

A flicker of pleasure licked through my chest, radiating outward, twisting low in my belly.

I swallowed, pushing forward, forcing my voice to stay even.

The butt plug pulsed.

Deep.

The pleasure shot through me like an electric current.

My knees weakened.

I gripped the plexiglass podium, fingers pressing into the smooth, cool surface.

This wasn't random.

This was him.

I darted a glance at Dorian.

His head tilted.

A command.

I forced my voice to remain steady, even as my body burned under his control.

The plug throbbed.

The clamps twisted.

A fresh pulse of liquid heat rushed between my legs.

My thighs clenched, desperate to suppress the ache.

I fought it, fought *him*.

But I knew he was winning.

The slickness between my thighs was undeniable, pooling, aching to be filled.

And he knew it.

He was watching me unravel, watching my breath hitch, my hips shift, my fingers grip the podium tighter—waiting for me to break.

Then, the plug vibrated.

A sharp, merciless pulse.

My hips twitched.

My breath hitched for a second.

And he saw.

Dorian's lips curled at the edges, subtle, predatory.

He was fucking me in front of a thousand people, and they had no idea.

My vision blurred at the edges.

My words faltered.

I tried to push forward, to reclaim control, but then—

I saw her.

Manon.

At the edge of the stage, chest heaving, lips parted, fingers digging into the curtain.

She was writhing, pupils blown wide, legs pressing together.

Her body arched. Her knees buckled.

Her mouth fell open in a silent scream.

And I knew.

The Ben Wa balls.

She was coming.

I felt her climax—her unraveling, her helpless surrender—and I couldn't stop myself.

My thighs quivered.

The plug pulsed deeper.

The clamps twisted harder.

A sound—raw, broken—escaped me.

I moaned.

Loud.

Shattering.

My legs gave out.

The heat between my thighs spilled over, arousal gushing down my legs, a violent, public orgasm, an undeniable surrender.

I crashed into the plexiglass podium, sending it clattering to the floor, the clear material reflecting the stage lights as it toppled.

The room gasped.

The audience froze.

The slickness pooled beneath me, my body wrecked with pleasure.

The last thing I saw before my vision blurred, before my body collapsed—

Dorian, smiling.

CHAPTER
Twenty-Two

CANCELLATION

The news cycle was relentless. Days had passed, but the firestorm refused to die. Everywhere I turned—television, radio, social media—my name was a scandal, a punchline, a warning.

I sat curled up on the velvet couch in my apartment, the dim glow of the city filtering through the floor-to-ceiling windows. Manon was sprawled across the other end, her Hermès scarf carelessly draped over the armrest, a glass of red wine in her hand.

She, of course, was thriving.

As for me, I was being erased.

Banned. Pulled from shelves. Disinvited.

They had reduced me to nothing more than a fallen woman, a deviant masquerading as an artist, an example to be burned.

Manon sighed dramatically, swirling her wine. "If they're going to crucify you, they could at least use a better headline. 'Smut Peddler?' Mon dieu, the lack of originality is offensive."

I exhaled, stretching my legs out. The ache between my thighs had finally started to fade, though my body still remembered. "You're not the one being erased."

Her dark eyes flicked to me. "No, *ma chérie*, but you and I both know that's temporary." She tilted her head. "They think they can erase you. But they can't."

I let out a humorless laugh, gesturing toward my phone, which had been buzzing non-stop with notifications I refused to check. "Tell that to my publishers. To every bookstore suddenly pretending I don't exist."

Manon made a dismissive noise. "American puritans have the memory of a goldfish. Give it a few weeks."

I picked up my wine glass, rolling the stem between my fingers. "It's not only the outrage. It's him."

He had done this.

He had pushed, pressed, invaded my body with his technology—in front of the world. And now, while I was drowning in the aftermath, he was silent.

My jaw clenched. "He hasn't contacted me."

Manon's expression darkened. "And what would you say to him if he did?"

I set my glass down a little too hard. "I don't know."

It was a lie.

I wanted to scream at him. I wanted to demand why he had done this, why he had taken my trust and used it against me in the most intimate, the most public way possible.

I wanted to drag my nails down his back and sink my teeth into his skin, punishing him for the humiliation — and for testing my control.

Manon stretched, taking another slow sip of wine. "You know, all of this"—she gestured vaguely—"proves how much power you have. They don't come for the weak. They burn witches because they fear them."

I let my head fall back against the couch, staring at the ceiling. "So, what do I do?"

A slow, wicked smile spread across Manon's lips. "You rise from the ashes."

Manon exhaled sharply, setting down her glass. The usual mischief in her eyes was gone, replaced with something dark. Something cold.

She swallowed. "I felt it too, B."

A shiver ran down my spine.

The ben wa balls.

She had been on the sidelines when it happened. And yet—she had felt it, too.

I sat up, gripping the edge of the couch. "Manon…"

She let out a breath, forcing a wry, humorless smile. "It wasn't as… dramatic for me. But I felt the same shift. The same…" Her fingers flexed against her knee. "Control. The moment it started…"

The wine in my stomach turned to lead.

"He did this to both of us," I murmured.

She nodded.

For a long moment, neither of us spoke. The only sound was the distant hum of the city, the muted voices of the world still discussing my downfall.

Then, Manon's expression shifted, sharpening with something dangerous.

"You do realize that might have saved you from something worse."

I frowned. "What?"

She turned fully toward me now, her body tense, her usual elegance traded for something harder. "You collapsed before he could take it further. The ben wa balls—they disrupted something. Maybe even short-circuited whatever else he had planned."

My fingers dug into the upholstery. "Are you saying—"

She met my gaze head-on. "He was planning worse, B."

I sucked in a breath.

Humiliation hadn't been the goal.

It had been the beginning.

Manon leaned in, lowering her voice. "I know you're still processing it. But we both know what happened." A pause. "And we both know what it was."

I felt sick.

The word hung between us, unspoken but heavy.

Rape.

Not with hands, not with force—but with power, with technology, with something so insidious that no one else even saw it for what it was.

Only us.

Only the ones who felt it inside us.

My throat was tight. "I should have seen it coming."

Manon scoffed. "You think I did?" She leaned back, shaking her head. "You trusted him. And why wouldn't you? He made you believe you had control." Her lips curled. "That's the real trick, isn't it?"

I exhaled shakily.

Manon crossed her legs, swirling the wine in her glass as she studied me like I was a puzzle with pieces missing.

"Let's go back," she said. "How the hell did you end up wearing all of that?"

I exhaled, pressing my fingers against my temples.

"I asked him to put them on me," I admitted.

Manon blinked. Then she let out a sharp laugh. Not amused—furious.

"You asked him?" she repeated, voice dripping with disbelief.

I swallowed. "I thought I was in charge."

Manon set her glass down, leaning forward, her movements slow and deliberate.

"Walk me through it," she said. "From the beginning."

I knew what she was really asking. Where did he start setting the trap?

I ran a hand through my hair. "It started with the measurements."

I rubbed my temples, knowing that once I said it out loud, I couldn't take it back.

"The ones they took on me. Weeks ago. In Dorian's office."

Her expression shifted instantly—suspicion deepening into something sharper. "Who's 'they'?"

I hesitated. "A specialist. A woman."

Manon went completely still.

I sighed, trying to find the words. "She was clinical. Professional. Nothing sexual about it. She had laser devices, electronic measuring tools, clamps—"

"Clamps," Manon repeated flatly.

"She measured everything," I continued. "Dorian, too. Every inch of our bodies. Our responses. Our tolerances."

Manon's jaw clenched. "And you didn't think that was the slightest bit fucking alarming?"

I swallowed. "I thought it was for sizing..."

Manon gave me a look so sharp it could have skinned me alive.

I exhaled. "I assumed it was to figure out the weight of custom-made toys. Nothing more."

Manon let out a bitter laugh. "You assumed."

I winced. "I—"

"You assumed Dorian Wolker wanted to make sure they fit well? Like a nice, tailored dress?"

I ran a hand through my hair. "I didn't think—"

"No. You didn't," she snapped. Then she pinched the bridge of her nose, inhaling deeply before exhaling slow, controlled.

I watched her reset herself, shoving fury down beneath the surface. But it was still there, vibrating, like a live wire beneath her skin.

Her voice was softer when she spoke again, but deadly calm. "So you thought he was making sure they weren't too heavy. Too loose. Too tight."

I nodded.

"And you didn't wonder why he wanted custom measurements of your nipples, your ass, your pussy—"

I flinched. "I do now."

Manon stared at me.

Then she got up and began pacing. "That bastard."

I didn't argue.

"He played the long game," she muttered, almost to herself. "This wasn't a last-minute decision. This wasn't some heat of the moment revenge stunt."

She stopped pacing, turning back to me.

"He built this." Her voice was cold. "He planned every part of this, B. He knew how it would end before you even put them on."

I clenched my jaw.

She tilted her head. "And you asked him to put them on you."

I shut my eyes. "Yes."

Manon exhaled through her nose, a slow, measured breath. Then she cursed viciously in French.

She crouched in front of me, grabbing my hands.

"We're going to fix this," she said. "But first, you need to understand—this wasn't your mistake."

I opened my mouth.

Manon squeezed hard. "No. Listen to me. He groomed you for this. Weeks of priming. A fucking medical-grade specialist. Precision-made sex toys. A collar as a distraction so he could offer you something that felt like a compromise."

I felt sick.

"He built the fall before you even climbed up the stage."

I inhaled, shaky. "I let him."

"No," Manon said fiercely. "He made you think you were in control. That's the cruelest part."

I nodded again, swallowing against the bile in my throat.

Manon's grip tightened.

"So now, B..." Her eyes burned. "Let's talk about how we burn him down."

CHAPTER Twenty-Three

OUT RIGHTS

I sat across from mother, the midday sun gleaming off the crisp white tablecloth, reflecting too brightly against the polished silverware. *Le Septième* was the kind of place where reputations were as meticulously maintained as the floral arrangements, where discretion was served alongside the *foie gras,* and scandal was only acknowledged in hushed, horrified whispers.

Jacques Marie Mage sunglasses shielded her expression, a silk blouse in the perfect shade of cream, her posture an unspoken condemnation of my entire existence. Her hair was unshaken. Her composure, unwavering. But I could feel the weight of her judgment from across the table.

She hadn't touched her food. Neither had I.

I sipped my coffee, though it did little to settle the tension between us.

"I suppose I should be grateful it wasn't worse," she said finally, stirring her espresso in slow, surgical motions. "Though I struggle to imagine how it could have been."

I set my cup down. "That's a refreshing perspective."

She lifted her espresso to her lips with an air of absolute poise, taking a small sip before setting it down with practiced precision. "You should have known better, Beatrix."

"I appreciate the support."

"This is support," she replied, as if she genuinely believed it.

I huffed a quiet laugh. "No. This is damage control."

She barely reacted, but I saw it anyway—the flicker of irritation, the faintest tightening of her lips.

"This family has worked for generations to maintain its standing," she continued, setting her spoon down perfectly aligned with the saucer. "And in one night, you turned it into the subject of late-night monologues and tabloid headlines."

I leaned back in my chair, crossing my legs, keeping my voice steady. "If you wanted a discreet daughter, you shouldn't have sent me to boarding school with the world's most debauched aristocrats."

"Yes. I do believe that's where the trouble started."

And there it was.

Manon.

It always came back to Manon.

"I warned you she was dangerous."

I let out a soft laugh, shaking my head. "Manon wasn't the one who put a butt plug and nipple clamps on me."

The words landed like a gunshot in a cathedral.

I let the words hang in the air.

Butt plug. Nipple clamps.

The sound of them, spoken aloud in broad daylight, at an exclusive restaurant where discretion was practically printed on the menu, felt like a bomb dropped in high society.

It wasn't the event itself that disturbed her. Nor the scandal or humiliation.

No, what truly unsettled her was hearing the explicit reality of it spoken out loud.

Hearing her *daughter* say it.

She picked up her wine glass, taking a deliberate sip, but I could see it—the way she gripped the stem a bit too tight, the way her fingers were a touch of white at the knuckles.

For once, I had unsettled her.

"Who?"

I let her stew in it for a moment longer. Then, I met her gaze, steady, unwavering.

"Dorian."

She blinked. Once. A single, sharp reaction—not fear, but fury.

She set her glass down with precise control, aligning it perfectly against the table's edge, as if she needed something firm to grip to keep from breaking the stem between her fingers.

The air between us tightened, charged with something icy and electric.

Her jaw clenched. The delicate tension in her shoulders turned to steel.

Pure, simmering, and deadly cold anger.

"He bought that company to please you."

I watched the realization settle—not only that Dorian had outmaneuvered my father, but that he had done so because of *me*.

Because of his desire.

His want.

He had used her daughter to take more from the family.

From her.

Her lips pressed into a thin, unyielding line, her fingers tensing against the pristine white linen of the tablecloth.

It was unforgivable.

Not only Dorian beating them.

But that I had been the reason he had done it.

She inhaled, sharp and composed, as if forcing herself to suppress the sheer violence of her thoughts.

When she spoke again, her voice was lethal.

"Is that what you are now?"

Her gaze locked onto mine.

"A prize to be won?"

I parted my lips to reply—to fire back, to cut through her insinuation with something sharp and deliberate—but my phone buzzed violently against the tabletop, breaking the tension like a slap.

I glanced at the screen.

My agent.

Again.

The call before? Ignored. The one before that? Silenced.

This was the third time she had tried to reach me since I sat down.

I exhaled, annoyed, but I knew I had to answer.

"Excuse me," I said, already reaching for the phone.

Mother said nothing, watching me with the kind of stare that could peel paint off walls.

I exhaled sharply and answered the call, already bracing for my agent's inevitable attempt at soft comfort.

The Orpheus Prize shortlist had been released that morning, and I wasn't on it.

I had figured as much. Since the collapse, since the lurid headlines, no one wanted to hand the most prestigious literary award in the world to the woman who had orgasmed on a stage in front of the elite.

I had prepared myself for that. It wasn't a shock. It wasn't even a disappointment, not really.

"If this is about the shortlist," I said, barely giving her time to speak, "I already know."

There was a pause. A small, sharp inhale.

"Well, sure," she said, her voice tight. "There's that."

Something cold crawled up my spine.

"But that's not why I'm calling."

I shifted in my seat, a flicker of unease tightening my ribs. Across the table, mother lowered her glass of wine, sensing the shift.

"Beatrix," my agent continued, hesitating for half a breath. "Your publisher is dropping you."

I must have misheard.

My grip tightened around my phone. "What?"

"They're pulling all of your books from print."

The words barely registered. It didn't make sense. My books were bestsellers. They were still dominating the charts. Even now, despite everything.

I swallowed, keeping my expression neutral. I would not react. Not here. Not in front of her.

I let out a small, disbelieving laugh. "Fine. I'll take them somewhere else."

Another silence. This one thicker.

I forced my hand to remain still around my cup. Forced my fingers not to curl.

"You... can't, Beatrix."

I blinked. "What do you mean, I *can't*?"

She sighed. I could hear it through the line, could feel her hesitating.

"Your contract," she said carefully. "It's not that simple."

My stomach lurched.

I didn't want to ask.

"What does that mean?" My voice was steady. I didn't know how.

"They own them."

My breath stopped.

Across the table, mother watched me, her face unreadable beneath her Jacques Marie Mage sunglasses.

"They own all of them, Bea."

I forced my fingers not to tremble. Brought my cup to my lips, even though I knew I wouldn't drink.

"They're keeping them."

The realization hit me like ice-cold water.

I had been cancelled.

No.

Erased.

I shifted, adjusting my posture, smoothing my blouse. I would not fall apart in front of her.

"Can I buy them back?" My voice came out too quiet.

Another sigh.

"They're not willing to sell them to you."

The ache in my chest spread.

Mother was still watching.

I lifted my chin.

Took a breath.

And pretended my entire world hadn't vanished.

I ended the call with a sharp tap of my finger. My phone felt heavy in my palm, like an anchor dragging me under.

I had no books. No publisher. No rights to my own words.

The weight of it settled into my bones, pressing against my ribs like a vice.

I forced a breath, placed my phone face down on the table, and lifted my eyes.

Mother was watching me with satisfaction.

She set down her wine glass with the kind of controlled elegance that had been drilled into me since childhood. When she finally spoke, her voice was smooth, polished, the edge of triumph barely concealed beneath a thin veneer of concern.

"Well," she said, taking in my expression. "Perhaps it's for the best."

I didn't react. Didn't flinch. Didn't let the rage clawing up my throat show.

Instead, I took a careful sip of my tea, letting the warmth coat my tongue, forcing myself to swallow the bitterness gathering there.

"For the best," I repeated flatly.

She nodded, the smallest tilt of her chin.

"I never liked those books of yours." A casual sip of wine. A flick of her wrist as she adjusted the sleeve of her blazer. "Smut, really."

I felt my pulse spike, but I willed my expression to remain impassive.

"They were my words!"

She sighed, shaking her head as if I were a child insisting that two plus two equaled five.

"Regardless," she continued, as though my defense meant nothing, "you've had your... rebellion." A pause. A deliberate choice of words. "It was entertaining, I suppose. And I *do* hope you got whatever it is you needed out of your system."

I exhaled through my nose, my nails pressing into my palm beneath the table.

Here it was. The moment she had been waiting for.

"You can't be serious," I murmured.

She smiled. A slow, knowing thing. "Oh, but I am."

I shook my head. "You think I'm going to walk away from everything I built?"

She tilted her head, her expression unreadable. "*You* built?"

Something sharp sliced through my chest.

"Yes," I said, voice firm. "I built this. I wrote those books. I found success on my own."

A small hum of amusement left her lips.

"Oxford," she mused. "Boarding school. Your travels. The tutors. The connections. Do you truly believe you've done this all on your own?"

I felt my teeth clench.

She continued, calm and relentless. "You have been groomed for success, Beatrix. That is what we do. We shape you. Prepare you." She gestured around us, as if to make a point. "You were never meant to waste it on... this."

I bristled. "This?"

She waved a hand dismissively. "Whatever it is you've been doing."

I leaned in, lowering my voice. "You mean writing."

Her lips curved, but there was no warmth in it.

"Porn."

I inhaled, reining in the sharp burst of anger threatening to unravel my composure.

"Literature," I corrected.

She tilted her head, considering me. "And what do you have to show for it now?"

My breath caught.

Silence stretched between us, heavy and suffocating.

She sat back in her chair, satisfied. "You're lucky, really. You have an opportunity now—come back to something real."

I shook my head, exhaling a sharp laugh. "You mean the family business."

She smiled, swirling the wine in her glass. "I mean respectability."

I stared at her.

She took a slow sip, savoring the taste before setting the glass down. "You've sullied our name enough. It's time to restore it."

I gripped the edge of the table, grounding myself.

"You actually think I would come back," I said, incredulous.

Her expression was unreadable, her tone mild. "I know you don't have a choice."

I laughed. Short. Sharp. A dagger of sound.

I pushed back from the table, the legs of my chair scraping against the stone terrace.

Mother didn't flinch.

I stood, adjusting my sunglasses, the weight of her gaze pressing against me even as I refused to meet it.

"You're wrong," I said, my voice sharp and unwavering. "I do have a choice."

She took a slow sip of her wine, her expression unreadable behind the tinted lenses of her Jacques Marie Mage sunglasses.

"And what choice is that, Beatrix?"

I leveled her with a look. "Not being you."

Her lips curved into something that might have been amusement—or victory.

I turned on my heel, walking away, my Celine heels clicking against the marble floor of the terrace. The midday sun burned hot on my skin, but it wasn't enough to chase the cold from my bones.

She thought she had won.

She always did.

I didn't rush. I didn't give her the satisfaction of a flustered exit. I walked with purpose, head high, through the secluded terrace, past the impeccably dressed diners who pretended not to have been listening. I could feel their gazes trailing after me, measuring, assessing. Judging.

Let them.

I reached the discreet archway leading to the restaurant's private exit, the city humming beyond it. I paused for half a breath, pressing my nails into my palm, grounding myself.

I would fix this. I would find a way back.

And I would do it without her.

CHAPTER
Twenty-Four

FAULT LINE

I barely registered the first knock.

Or the second.

It was distant, like a sound from another world—one I no longer belonged to.

I was too heavy, too slow. The room swayed when I tried to move. My stomach churned, warning me that I'd gone too far, but it was too late for warnings. I was past them.

Everything reeked—Macallan, absinthe, sweat, and something worse. The silk of my slip clung to my body, damp with liquor and sticky remnants of things I'd eaten without thinking. The couch was cold beneath my bare thighs, the air thick with stale indulgence.

Another knock.

Louder this time.

Then, a key in the lock. A pause. A breath. The door creaked open.

Footsteps. Hesitant. Measured.

A man's voice.

"...Miss Winslow-Hale?"

The doorman.

Even through the fog, I recognized him. A professional, polite man, the kind of staff hired to make the wealthy feel looked after without ever being truly seen.

He had seen too much now.

I heard his breath catch—smelled the sharp scent of his aftershave cut through the filth of the room. A shift of fabric, a step back.

Then, another voice.

Female. French.

"*Merde.*"

Manon.

The heels of her shoes clicked against the floor, faster than his steps, more deliberate.

A sharp inhale.

Then silence.

I felt her before I saw her—her presence, electric and commanding, even here.

Then hands. Warm. Steady.

"*Bébé*, talk to me."

Her fingers pressed against my shoulder, insistent.

I wanted to say something, but the words tangled in my throat, thick and useless.

Another shake.

"You need to get up."

The nausea swelled.

I groaned—barely more than a breath—and let my head loll to the side.

Manon cursed under her breath, something sharp in her tone, but she didn't pull away.

Instead, she turned to the doorman.

"Leave."

A pause.

Then a quick step backward, the door clicking shut behind him.

We were alone.

I squeezed my eyes shut, bracing for what came next.

Manon's grip tightened on my shoulder, steady, grounding. But the second she tried to lift me, my stomach lurched.

There was no warning.

A violent wave of vomit tore through me, spewing forward, hitting Manon square in the chest. Hot, thick, reeking. The force of it splattered down her legs, soaking into the plush carpet, seeping into the folds of her coat—Hermès, probably.

Manon yelped, recoiling.

"Oh, *merde!*"

Her gag was instant, visceral. She staggered back, arms lifted as if to ward off any further assault, but it was too late.

I slumped forward, too drained to care, my breath coming in uneven, ragged gasps. My limbs were leaden, my body a wreck of exhaustion, alcohol, and excess. A thin strand of bile clung to my bottom lip. I wiped it away, sluggish and unfocused, smearing it across my wrist.

Silence.

Then a sharp, measured inhale.

Manon stared at me, stunned. But beneath the disgust, beneath the sharp edges of anger and shock, was something worse.

Fear.

She crouched back down, slower this time, shaking her head.

"No. No, no, no. This?" Her voice wavered, but her fingers were sure as they brushed damp hair from my forehead. "This is not happening."

I blinked, barely processing the warmth of her hand against my cheek.

She exhaled, her breath tight. "Okay…"

Her hands slid under my arms, steady but unrelenting.

"You need a shower," she muttered, voice sharp with determination. Then, as if correcting herself, "A cold one."

I groaned, barely able to summon the energy to resist, my limbs sluggish and uncooperative. The idea of moving—of standing—felt impossible, but Manon wasn't giving me a choice.

"Up," she ordered, her grip tightening. "*Now*, Beatrix."

My body protested as she half-dragged, half-lifted me, my legs trembling beneath me. The world tilted violently, and I might have collapsed again if not for her strength.

The room blurred as we stumbled toward the bathroom, my stomach rolling, my skin fevered and clammy. I barely registered the opulence of the marble floors or the mirrored walls—details that had once mattered, now meaningless in the wreckage I had become.

Manon reached past me, twisting the shower handle. A blast of freezing water erupted from the rainfall showerhead, misting into the air like a warning.

I recoiled. "Too cold."

"That's the point," she shot back, shoving me toward it. "You need to wake the fuck up."

I barely had time to brace before she stripped me of my ruined lingerie, pushing me under the punishing cascade.

The moment the freezing water hit me, my body lurched violently in protest. A fresh wave of nausea surged up, faster than I could control.

I gagged, chest convulsing, and before I could turn away, vomit spilled from my lips, splattering against the pristine marble floor of the shower. It was mostly liquid—absinthe, whiskey, bile—burning its way up my throat before mixing with the rushing water, swirling down the drain in sickly green and gold ribbons.

Manon swore under her breath but didn't flinch. She reached for my hair, pulling it back with one hand while the other braced my shoulder, keeping me steady as I heaved again, dry this time, my stomach twisting painfully.

"Fuck, B," she murmured, softer now, rubbing slow circles into my back. "Get it all out."

I slumped forward, forehead pressing against the cold tiles, my entire body trembling. The water pounded down, relentless, washing away the filth but doing nothing for the ache settling deep in my bones.

Manon sighed, shaking her head. "You're a fucking mess, you know that?"

I blinked up at her, my vision still swimming, then let my gaze drop to the mess I'd made—her designer blouse clinging to her skin, streaked with vomit, the reek of absinthe and bile mixing with her expensive perfume.

A slow smirk tugged at my lips. My voice came out hoarse, barely above a whisper. "No. You're a fucking mess."

For a beat, she stared at me. To my utter disbelief, she burst out laughing. A real, full-bodied laugh, head tilted back, shoulders shaking.

"*Mon dieu*, you absolute disaster." She wiped at her ruined blouse, still chuckling. "You better be worth this."

Manon peeled off her ruined blouse with a grimace, tossing it onto the bathroom floor like it had personally offended her. She was still laughing, shaking her head as she kicked off her heels and wiggled out of her skirt, now speckled with the evidence of my spectacular collapse.

"*Mon dieu, bébé*, if you wanted me naked, there were better ways to go about it." She smirked, stepping out of her lace underwear and tossing them aside. "Honestly, anger sex would've been much more productive. Less bodily fluids. Well, different bodily fluids."

A groggy laugh pushed past my lips, weak but real. "You do have a point."

Manon flicked more water at me, rolling her eyes. "We're both covered in your bodily disaster, *bébé*. You think I'm scrubbing you down while marinating in this?" She gestured at the mess streaked across her chest, then dramatically down her legs. "Not a fucking chance. Scoot."

I groaned but obeyed, shifting as much as my weak limbs allowed. She stepped under the spray, sighing as the water hit her skin.

"You know, some women beg to be on their knees in front of me," she mused, running her hands through her hair, washing out the filth. "You? You projectile vomit on my tits."

A breathless laugh escaped me. "Well. I am unique."

"That, you are," she muttered, grabbing the soap and getting to work.

After, I sat on the only clean patch of couch left in the entire apartment, my head pounding so viciously it felt like my skull had been swapped for a bass drum. The towel wrapped around me felt too heavy, too scratchy, but at least I wasn't shivering anymore. I'd taken aspirin, but it hadn't kicked in yet, and judging by the state of the room around me, neither had my ability to process the absolute wreckage of my life.

The place smelled like stale alcohol, sweat, and regret. Takeout containers were stacked in some unholy monument to my self-destruction, an empty absinthe bottle teetering precariously on the coffee table like it was about to deliver the final insult and smash onto the floor. A half-eaten croissant had fused with the carpet near my feet. I didn't even remember ordering croissants.

Manon padded back into the room, also wrapped in a towel, her long legs bare and pink from scrubbing off my vomit. She took one look at the disaster zone that used to be my apartment and let out a low whistle.

"*Bébé*, we are not staying here. Not unless you want to die of airborne shame." She stepped over a pizza box that had calcified into a new life form and moved to the window, cracking it open. The sharp bite of winter air rushed in, slicing through the lingering filth. I sucked in a breath, letting the cold shock my system.

Manon turned back, giving me a once-over. "Stay put before you fall over again. I'm getting us clothes. No way I'm staying in a towel or borrowing anything that smells like *that*." She waved a hand toward the destruction before disappearing into my closet, muttering something about how she better find clean underwear in there.

I stayed where I was, letting the cold air scrape against my skin, trying to clear the fog in my brain. Manon was right—we couldn't stay here. The place was unsalvageable, at least until someone in a hazmat suit came in and set fire to half of it. I needed to be out, somewhere that didn't smell like last night's mistakes, somewhere that didn't feel like failure pressing down on me from all sides.

From the closet, I heard Manon rifling through my clothes, her sharp assessments floating back to me.

"*Non, trop mou*. This is not the day for soft." More hangers rattling. "Ugh, this needs to be burned. *Pourquoi*, do you even own this?"

I sighed, leaning my head back against the couch, waiting for the inevitable.

A moment later, Manon emerged, arms full of carefully curated selections. She was no longer only picking clothes—she was crafting an armor set. She tossed a black lace bra and matching thong onto the couch beside me, followed by sheer thigh-high stockings.

"Put those on first," she ordered.

I raised a brow at her. "We're leaving the apartment, not seducing a billionaire in his private jet."

Manon smirked, hands on her hips. "If we were seducing a billionaire, I'd be the one picking the jet. Second, this isn't about anyone else." She nudged the lingerie closer to me with her foot. "This is about *you*. You've been walking around like a ghost. That ends now. You know what I always say."

I exhaled. "Lingerie isn't for them, it's for us."

"*Exactement*." Manon's smile softened. "Get dressed, *bébé*. You need to remember who the fuck you are."

I rolled my eyes but grabbed the lingerie anyway. It was something to focus on, something tactile and grounding. As I slipped into the lace, feeling the delicate fabric stretch over my skin, I did feel a little more like myself. Like the version of me that existed before all of this—the woman who could own a room with a glance, who had people hanging off her every word, who was not some cautionary tabloid tale.

Manon stepped back out of my closet fully dressed, radiating effortless Parisian rebellion even in something as simple as a black cashmere sweater and perfectly tailored trousers. She had paired it with one of my structured blazers—probably stolen from an old designer collection I hadn't even remembered owning—draped over her shoulders like she owned every room she entered. The look was deceptively understated, but I knew better. Everything Manon wore was a weapon.

She flicked her hair over one shoulder and took in my half-dressed state with an impatient sigh. *"Bébé, tu traînes."*

"I'm moving, I'm moving," I grumbled, slipping into the silk blouse she'd chosen for me. It was loose enough to skim over my curves but cut to still suggest them. The trousers hugged my hips in a way that made me feel put together again; like I wasn't the disaster I had been an hour ago.

Manon smirked, watching me fasten the last button. *"Parfait.* Now put on your shoes so we can get out of this crime scene."

I exhaled sharply, rubbing my temples as I reached for a pair of boots. "Where are we even going?"

Manon reached for her bag and slung it over her shoulder, then leveled me with a look that was half-mocking, half-genuine care. "Somewhere that reminds you that you are Beatrix fucking Winslow-Hale. And not some sad little recluse who let one very public orgasm ruin her entire empire."

I shot her a glare, but the corner of my mouth twitched. She was trying to snap me back to reality in the only way she knew how—by dragging me out of my own self-destruction and forcing me to face the world on my own terms.

I grabbed my coat and shrugged it on, the leather heavy against my shoulders. "Fine. Let's go."

Manon grinned. "That's my girl."

And with that, we stepped over the wreckage of my apartment and out the door, leaving the disaster behind—at least for now.

NOX was one of those places that didn't exist, but commanded. Nestled behind an unmarked door in the depths of Tribeca, it was an exclusive, low-lit sanctuary where the elite nursed their vices in the most refined way possible. The walls were dark, the booths deep, the service impeccable. The scent of truffle oil and aged whiskey lingered in the air, mingling with the low hum of conversation. Even at this hour, the place was buzzing with the kind of people who didn't concern themselves with mundane things like morning or night. Here, time existed only in relation to pleasure.

The *maître d'* greeted Manon like royalty, and thus, by extension, me. We were whisked past tables of familiar faces pretending not to watch us, guided to a private corner booth that offered both seclusion and a trace of visibility for everyone to know we were there.

Manon slid into the booth with the effortless grace of someone who had been born to command attention, tossing her bag onto the seat beside her. I collapsed into my side like a woman barely held together by caffeine, alcohol, and whatever little will I had left.

Before I could even look at a menu, Manon snatched it away with a smirk. "*Non*. I'm ordering for you."

Manon scanned the menu with the focus of a woman preparing for battle. I barely had the energy to sit upright, let alone pretend to have an opinion on what I should be eating.

She signaled to the waiter—a devastatingly handsome man with cheekbones sharp enough to cut glass, his smirk betraying that he was well-acquainted with serving the very rich and very hungover.

"She'll have the avocado toast with chili flakes," Manon declared, eyes flicking to me with amusement. "Circulation. You need to be alive again, *ma chérie*."

The waiter nodded, jotting it down as she continued.

"And a classic omelet—soft, nothing too aggressive. But add caviar. She needs the nutrients. And she should always eat like a queen, even if she smells like a distillery."

I groaned, pressing my forehead against the cool table. Manon ignored me.

"The hash browns. Carbs will save her. And fruit—something hydrating. Berries, melon. No citrus, *pas aujourd'hui*."

The waiter hummed, his smirk widening. "And to drink?"

"Coconut water."

I made a noise of protest.

Manon shot me a look. "You need electrolytes."

"Fine," I grumbled.

She handed him the menu with a satisfied nod. "And the dark chocolate mousse to finish. Magnesium. Good for stress. Good for circulation. And..." she paused, eyes glinting, "good for keeping things... active."

The waiter's smirk turned positively sinful.

I threw my napkin at Manon. She dodged it effortlessly.

I leaned back, letting the warm atmosphere of NOX settle around me. For the first time in days, something in me felt a little looser. A little more human.

I glanced around the dimly lit space, taking in the lingering stares. A few men at the bar, a group of women whispering behind their cocktails. My scandal had only heightened my appeal in certain circles, it seemed.

Manon followed my gaze, then smirked. "See? You're still the most desirable woman in the room."

"You think?"

She sipped her water, eyes twinkling. "*Bébé*, some people dream of fucking a scandal."

Despite myself, I laughed. For the first time in days, I felt lighter.

I barely paused to breathe between bites, devouring the food like I'd crawled out of the desert. Every bite was salvation, every carb, every scrap of fat a desperate attempt to restore myself. My body ached for it, the need clawing at me like I could physically refill the emptiness of the last few days.

Across from me, Manon was the picture of effortless indulgence, dipping a strawberry into her champagne before sliding it between her lips, her eyes flicking lazily over the room as if she had all the time in the world.

"*Bébé*, slow down." She smirked, plucking a dark chocolate truffle between two fingers and letting it linger against her lips before taking a bite. "You look like you've been lost in the wild for a decade."

I waved her off, shoving another forkful of omelet into my mouth. "I have been. You saw my apartment. My diet over the last 24 hours has been absinthe and despair."

She sighed dramatically, licking a speck of sea salt from her fingertip. "Yes, well, let's not repeat that."

I took a deep breath, bracing myself for the words I hadn't yet spoken aloud.

I took another bite, feeling the weight of what I was about to say settle deep in my gut. "They're gone, Manon."

She tilted her head, watching me closely. "What do you mean, gone?"

"My books. Pulled from shelves, erased from their catalog. They're pretending I don't exist."

Manon stilled, her fingers hovering over her champagne flute. "*Putain.*"

I laughed, but there was no humor in it. "Oh, it gets better. They're not only refusing to publish me. They're making sure no one else ever can."

Her brows furrowed. "What are you talking about?"

"They own the rights, Manon." I set my fork down, suddenly no longer hungry. "It's in my contract. I can't take them anywhere else. I can't self-publish them. I can't even get them back."

Manon's fingers twitched around her glass. "That's insane."

I sighed. "It's standard."

Her expression darkened. "So what, they're locking them up forever?"

"Unless they change their minds." I let out a bitter laugh. "Which they won't."

She stared at me, lips pursed, tapping a manicured nail against the rim of her glass. "You should sue."

I scoffed, shaking my head. "It would take years. Even if I won, by the time I got my books back, my name would be buried. No publisher would touch me."

Manon exhaled sharply, sitting back in her chair, arms crossed. "This is because of him."

I swallowed, fingers tightening around my fork. "I know."

Manon swirled the champagne in her glass, watching me over the rim. She hadn't touched her truffles in a while, which meant she was thinking. Hard.

I knew that look.

"Say it," I muttered, stabbing at my plate, appetite fading.

She sighed, setting the glass down with a delicate clink. "I have an idea."

I exhaled sharply. "Of course you do."

She smirked, a dangerously calculating look filling her eyes. "I don't think you're going to like it."

I remained quiet.

Manon studied me for a long moment before leaning in, dropping her voice. "But it will get your books back."

I stared at her, my heartbeat suddenly loud in my ears.

"And," she added, trailing a finger through the condensation on her glass, "it will hurt him in the process."

I swallowed, pulse flickering between intrigue and apprehension.

"What are we talking about here, Manon?"

Her smirk widened.

"We're talking about making sure you don't fight this man, B." She plucked another strawberry from the plate, twirling it between her fingers.

"We're talking about making sure you own him."

Part 4

PLAN B

CHAPTER
Twenty-Five

ASHES

The scent of vanilla and bergamot candles mingled with the lingering aroma of espresso and dark liquor, creating an air of indulgence in my apartment. I lounged in my oversized armchair, feet tucked under me, wrapped in the soft comfort of a cashmere throw. On the outside, I was the picture of relaxed casual—silk lounge pants and an off-the-shoulder sweater—but beneath, lace and satin traced over my skin, a quiet reminder that I was still me. Still a woman who knew her own power.

Manon sat across from me, impossibly elegant in an outfit that effortlessly blended Chanel and Hermès chic—a cream-colored silk blouse, sheer enough to tease, paired with tailored high-waisted trousers and a thin leather belt that cinched her waist. Her gold jewelry caught the light as she lifted her glass, filled with an aged Armagnac she had selected from my collection without asking, as if she owned the place.

Of course, in some ways, she did.

She tilted her sunglasses down the bridge of her nose—the oversized, custom-built pair she had designed in collaboration with a Silicon Valley visual tech firm. A statement piece, bold and authoritative. One hundred percent Manon.

"Monsieur Wolker is obsessed."

Her voice carried that mix of amusement and something sharper—satisfaction. I let the words settle between us, watching the way her lips curled against the rim of her glass as she took a slow sip.

I exhaled through my nose, shaking my head. "Good."

Manon crossed her legs, the smooth leather of her Hermès slingback heels making a soft sound against the hardwood floor. "He's getting desperate. He wants to see me tonight."

I smirked, swirling the remnants of my own drink. "And?"

"I told him I'd think about it." She stretched her arms above her head, the silk of her blouse shifting against her skin, revealing the faintest sliver of her stomach. "Make him suffer a little."

I let out a low chuckle. "You're enjoying this."

Manon arched a perfectly sculpted brow, setting her glass down with a deliberate clink. "*Bébé*, don't pretend you're not."

I watched her for a long moment, then let my head fall back against the chair, exhaling. My voice was sharp, laced with anger and irony. "That poor man."

"That poor man?" She laughed, throwing her head back. "Please. He's spent his entire life bending people to his will. He's finally learning what it's like to be bent." She traced an invisible crack in the air with her finger. "And I do mean that literally."

I laughed, but it was a sharp, bitter sound. "*Mon dieu*, Manon."

She winked. "Don't '*mon dieu*' me. You're the one who gave me the go-ahead."

I sobered, the humor dissolving into something darker. "And you put your body on the line for it." My voice was measured, but the fury beneath it was unmistakable. "I don't take that lightly."

Manon stilled for a fraction of a second, then leaned forward, her gaze locking onto mine. "He violated both of us, B." Her voice was smooth, but there was something dangerous underneath. "But what he did to you? That was beyond."

I swallowed, my jaw tightening. Heat rose in my throat—not shame, not regret, but fire.

"He used me," I murmured. "Humiliated me. Raped me. Broke me in front of the world. Turned me into a spectacle, then discarded me like a broken toy when he had no more use for me." My fingers tightened around my glass. "Everything I built, everything I created—he destroyed it like I was nothing."

Manon's voice was steel. She leaned in, her voice softer, but no less sharp. "B, it's important he keeps believing you're broken. The moment he thinks otherwise, he'll try to regain control. We can't let that happen."

"Let him keep thinking that. Let him believe he won."

I exhaled through my nose, my grip relaxing, a slow, simmering rage settling in my chest. "He was wrong."

Manon broke the tension first, grinning as she tapped her perfectly manicured nails against the rim of her glass. "B, this is honestly the most fun I've had in ages. Between you being completely annihilated by that bastard and me achieving yet another stratospheric career high, things were getting dangerously lopsided. We needed some balance. Anyway, he's getting paranoid. France is not being kind to his businesses right now. He thinks my mother is behind it."

I smirked. "Perfect."

"He thinks it's retaliation for his having a relationship with me," she added, rolling her eyes. "As if my mother gives a damn about my love life. No, no, darling—he made the grave mistake of outbidding her for the Luxuria Collar, and now she's rearranging his entire world economy as payback. Honestly, it's poetic. It's the kind of exquisite, cutthroat maneuvering she built her reputation on. Honestly, if she weren't my mother, I'd be taking notes."

I exhaled, shaking my head. "He has no idea you're playing him."

"Of course not. He thinks he's taming me." She let out a delicate snort. "The audacity." She set her sunglasses down beside her, fingers trailing over the frame like an afterthought, her expression sharp with amusement. "He actually thinks he's winning. It's adorable, really."

I sipped my drink, watching her over the rim. "And what happens when he *does* find out?"

She shrugged one shoulder, utterly unbothered. "Then I fuck him over in a more spectacular fashion. And I'll be wearing something fabulous while doing it. Preferably in a shade that makes my eyes pop—because, darling, aesthetics matter."

Her smirk darkened, her fingers running idly over the rim of her glass. "But it's not only revenge. It's control. He thought he could make us submit, humiliate us, treat us like we were nothing. He made me kneel when he activated those Ben Wa balls—when I had no idea they were wired. Sure, he didn't know I had them in. But what he did to you, what he planned? That was deliberate, calculated. And unacceptable."

Her jaw tensed, a flicker of something raw flashing in her gaze before she steadied. "Now, he'll be the one to break. I'll tie him up, peg him, and I won't stop until he begs. Until he truly knows what it's like to have his body used as a tool for someone else's pleasure, with no escape."

She fidgeted with the sunglasses, the custom-built pair, her eyes gleaming. "And I'll have every second of it recorded. He won't see me, won't know who's behind it—only that he's helpless, that it's being documented. And when the moment is right, it'll go public. The whole world will see Dorian Wolker submit."

I laughed, shaking my head. "Remind me never to cross you."

"Oh, B, you never could." She raised her glass in a silent toast, and I clinked mine against it, the sound ringing between us like a promise.

I let my head rest against the back of the chair, finally allowing myself to exhale. It had been months since the gala, since my collapse—since Dorian tried to break me.

And for a while, he had.

But I was still here. Still writing. Still fighting. The scandal was beginning to slip from the headlines, replaced with newer, shinier controversies: Senator Guerra-Reinas investigating Dorian's financial dealings, the director Manon introduced me to sweeping awards across Europe.

And, of course, the anticipation around *Châtelaine*'s first runway show under the Eiffel Tower.

I glanced at Manon, curiosity piqued. "How's the show coming together?"

She smirked, swirling her drink. "Oh, you know. Chaos, couture, and a mild threat of international incident. The way I like it. But it's huge, B. The first big show for Châtelaine, and with Chanel and Hermès in the mix, it has to be flawless. The pressure is absurd, but also, have you ever seen me buckle?"

I snorted. "So, it's the biggest moment of your career, and you're handling it with a smirk and a perfectly tailored shrug?"

She grinned. "Obviously. But seriously, the logistics are insane. The Eiffel Tower as a backdrop? Iconic. But it means every detail has to be perfect—lighting, security, the guest list. Vogue wants an exclusive, the French press is circling, and Hermès insists on some absurd, ceremonial unveiling.

"And now, my mother is leading a campaign against it, rallying the old guard about the 'sanctity' of Parisian landmarks. It's all very noble, of course, except we both know she's still furious about the Louvre. The public is scandalized, which means they'll show up in droves. It's madness."

I laughed under my breath. "Poetic."

"Isn't it? On the bright side of life, you're no longer the controversy of the moment."

For the first time in a long time, I felt like I was stepping back into my own skin. Writing again, plotting over drinks with Manon—it was like waking up after a long sleep, stretching into something powerful and undeniable.

Starting over wasn't a setback; it was a chance to redefine myself on my own terms. I wasn't merely reclaiming my voice—I was sharpening it into a weapon. This next book wouldn't be good. It would be undeniable.

It would win the Orpheus Prize, and the world would remember just how good I was.

Manon watched me, a knowing smile on her lips. "You look better."

I rolled my eyes. "I feel better."

She studied me over her glass. "You're still dressing like a recluse."

I snorted. "I *like* dressing like a recluse."

She pointed at me, voice playful. "You need a new look. A comeback look."

I raised a brow. "You mean *your* kind of comeback look."

"Obviously." She tapped her sunglasses. "Something to say, 'fuck you' to the world."

"I don't need a look, Manon. I need a publisher."

She tilted her head, gaze glinting. "You have one, remember?"

I narrowed my eyes. "Manon."

She grinned, feline and dangerous. "It's time for us to move to plan B!"

CHAPTER
Twenty-Six

SMOKE SIGNALS

Manon's flight to Paris was only hours away, but she refused to leave without ensuring I was properly armed.

I assumed it would be simple—pulling a few favorites from my closet, let Manon choose something elegant.

I was wrong.

She arrived with boxes.

I leaned against the doorframe, arms crossed. "So my wardrobe is unacceptable?"

Manon swept past me, setting the boxes down with a flourish. "B, you're about to face Dorian for the first time since he humiliated you in public and attempted to annihilate you. You don't dress for that like you're going to brunch."

I eyed the topmost box. "I was thinking something clean, precise. A look that says, 'I'm thriving, I barely remember your name.'"

She snorted. "You don't need to convince him. You need to make sure he never recovers."

With a flick of her wrist, she untied the ribbon, lifting the lid to reveal jet-black leather—corseted, structured, unapologetic.

I blinked. "Subtle."

Manon's grin was wicked. "As a sledgehammer."

I ran a finger along the material. "Seems a little... aggressive."

She tilted her head. "You don't want him wondering if you're fine. You want him regretting that he ever thought you weren't."

I exhaled, shaking my head. "You really don't trust me to dress myself?"

Manon rolled her eyes. "B, dressing is one thing. But lingerie? That's the foundation. It does things to you. Straightens your spine, lifts your chin. And this"—she gestured at the corset—"isn't for him. It's for you. He'll think he's looking at a woman still in pieces. You? You'll know better."

"I trust you to be brilliant. But why be brilliant when you could be devastating?"

I smirked. "Devastating sounds exhausting."

Her lips parted, eyes glinting. "Please. You love exhausting when it means leaving a mark."

I huffed. "You're enjoying this too much."

"*Bébé*, I feed off this." She shoved another box into my hands. "And I didn't only bring the suit. I have something else for you."

I narrowed my eyes. "Should I be scared?"

She tapped the lid. "Excited."

I lifted the lid and let out a low whistle. It was the most exquisite lingerie I'd ever seen: supple black leather, embroidered with a gleam that caught the light like molten silver. The boning was sculpted, cinching, lifting, commanding.

I dragged a finger over the corset's edge. "So, you're saying I should stride in there like I own the place?"

Manon smirked. "No, B. You stride in there knowing you own the place, but making sure *you're* the only one aware of that. Let him think he's still in control until the moment he realizes he never had it."

I swallowed, the weight of the ensemble settling into my hands. This wasn't clothing. It was a declaration.

Manon crossed her arms, cocking a brow. "Now strip."

I snorted. "At least buy me dinner first."

She smirked, eyes glinting. "B, if I bought you dinner, you wouldn't make it to the meeting."

"I'd accuse you of having ulterior motives, but we both know you're shameless."

"Darling, if I had ulterior motives, you wouldn't be stripping alone. Now get moving." Her fingers drummed against her hip, watching as I slid my pants down my legs. "We have work to do."

I peeled off my bra, tossing it aside with a flourish. "You love bossing me around."

"Obviously." She held up the corset, black leather gleaming under the lights. "Arms up."

I obeyed, letting her fasten me in, feeling the firm grip of the boning cinch around my waist. It was tight, commanding— grounding. Manon's fingers skimmed over my back as she adjusted the laces. Firm pressure, unyielding. It forced me to straighten, shoulders back, chin lifted.

"You feel that?"

I swallowed, the warmth of her touch lingering. "Yeah."

"Good. Hold on to it." Her fingers trailed down my spine before she crouched, hands skimming my thighs as she slid the high-cut panties up my legs. The leather was cool, at first, but as it settled against my skin, molding to me, it warmed—like it belonged there. Like I belonged in it. The delicate chains brushed against my inner thighs, teasing, each shift sparking a new sensation.

I gasped.

Her voice was silk and sin. "Sensitive?"

"Shut up."

She chuckled, adjusting the garters. The stockings stretched over my legs, the leather smooth and supple, gripping me with perfect pressure. The sensation of being wrapped so tightly, encased in something built for power, sent heat curling low in my stomach. Every snap of a clasp, every slight tug, made something coil tighter inside me.

I felt taller, sharper, like every inch of my body had been carved back into something lethal.

It started as a flicker—small, almost unnoticeable. A low hum beneath my skin, a warmth that curled in the pit of my stomach. For months, there had been nothing. No spark, no heat, only numbness where something vibrant used to be. Desire had felt like a language I had forgotten, a rhythm I could no longer follow. But now—now it was returning, slow and insistent, like an ember reigniting after too long in the ashes.

The way the corset forced my breaths to deepen. The way the stockings held my thighs, a constant reminder of something gripping with the intoxicating promise of release. The way Manon's hands trailed over my skin, making sure I was perfect. It sent something heady through me, something I hadn't felt in too long.

It was arousal.

I clenched my thighs together instinctively, biting the inside of my cheek.

Manon stood back, her gaze raking over me like an artist surveying her work. "Look at you."

I turned to the mirror, half-expecting to see someone else. But the woman staring back at me was undeniably me. Except this me was regal, a dangerous body humming beneath the leather.

I exhaled sharply, heat pooling between my legs. My thighs pressed together of their own accord, my breath a little too shallow. I flicked my gaze toward the bathroom door, already calculating how quickly I could get there. "I need a minute."

Manon's smirk deepened. "A minute?" She stepped closer, her voice a purr. "B, do you need a toy, or will your fingers do the walking?"

Heat flared up my neck, but I didn't look away. "Go to hell."

She *tsk*ed, eyes dancing with amusement. "You need to get that under control, *ma chérie*. It would be a shame if you came in front of Dorian instead of making him suffer."

I spun on my heel and bolted for the bathroom, slamming the door behind me as her laughter followed.

Manon's knowing smirk was immediate. "Mmm. Sure. But make it quick. We still have to figure out how to cover this up."

The door barely clicked shut before my back hit it, my body already thrumming, burning, desperate. My breath came in short, ragged gasps, every inch of me alive, pulsing with need. My fingers were already sliding between my thighs, finding the slick heat that had been building with every brush of leather, every teasing clasp, every knowing touch of Manon's hands against my skin.

The moment I touched myself, the tension snapped. It was instant, electric—pleasure slamming into me so hard my knees nearly buckled. My head fell back against the door, my mouth parting, and I let it out. A long, wrecked moan, the kind that came from deep in the bones, the kind that released everything. The weight of months of doubt, of shame, of feeling like a ghost in my own skin—it all spilled out of me in waves of pleasure that didn't end, that kept cresting, kept shattering me in a never-ending loop.

The orgasm ripped through me like a firestorm, consuming everything weak, everything hesitant, leaving only raw, undeniable power in its wake. I wasn't simply reclaiming myself—I was devouring everything I'd lost and making it mine again. I was whole. No, more than whole. More than I had been before.

I exhaled sharply, my body still humming as I straightened, as I wiped the last remnants of hesitation from my skin. I adjusted the lingerie, let my hands skim over the leather, feeling the strength in every seam. My reflection stared back at me in the mirror, no longer questioning, no longer searching. The woman I had once been: powerful, confident, and in control.

I strode back into the room, chin high, every step electric. Manon, still lounging lazily against the bedframe, took one look at me, eyes widening before they gleamed with something like triumph. Her grin stretched slow and wicked as she let out a delighted, breathy laugh.

""There you are," she murmured, voice rich with something close to reverence. "The B I know. The B I love. Beatrixxx—the triple X threat."

Manon was already halfway into my closet by the time I caught up with her, tossing rejected options over her shoulder with ruthless efficiency. Silk blouses, tailored blazers, anything remotely structured—gone.

"I'm beginning to think you like making a mess," I said, watching as a perfectly good cashmere sweater hit the floor.

She *tsk*ed, unimpressed. "B, we have to sell the illusion. You can't walk in there looking like a woman who rediscovered her spine—and other parts of herself." She shot me a knowing smirk before yanking a sheer, over-sized knit from a hanger. "Ah, now this says devastation."

"That says 'forgot to do laundry.'"

"It's tragic. It's desperate. It's perfect." She held it up against me, assessing. "With the right styling, Dorian will take one look at you and think you're on the verge of collapse."

I sighed. "And that's a good thing?"

She tossed the sweater at me. "That's the whole point. You need him to believe he's throwing you a scrap, not walking into a trap. Now, put it on while I find something to make you look even sadder."

She turned back into my closet, letting out a low whistle. "I have to say, I'm impressed, B. The selection in here for making you look devastatingly undone is... extensive."

I crossed my arms. "They're comfortable."

Manon pulled out a slouchy, faded cardigan and raised a brow. "Comfortable doesn't have to mean 'I've given up on life.'"

"That is a perfectly good sweater."

She draped it over my shoulders dramatically. "If by 'good' you mean 'you look like you've been wearing it since your last emotional breakdown,' then yes, it's perfect."

I swatted at her. "I like that one! It's soft."

She held up a wrinkled linen dress, considering it. "Soft? B, we're not dressing for a spa day. We're dressing for a calculated demise."

I groaned. "I refuse to look like a complete disaster."

She turned, giving me a slow, amused smile. "Darling, you don't have to look like a disaster. You have to look like you *think* you are one."

I huffed, tugging the cardigan around me as she pulled out a pair of faded, stretched-out jeans. "Oh come on, these are too cozy."

"They scream 'my last shred of dignity left in a cab at dawn.'"

"You're impossible."

"And you're lucky to have me." She tossed the jeans at me. "Now, get dressed. We have a performance to stage."

I stood in front of the mirror, taking in Manon's handiwork. From the inside, I felt like the world was about to crumble at my feet, a storm ready to break loose at my command. Power hummed beneath my skin, a quiet, unrelenting force.

But the woman staring back at me?

She was wreckage.

The oversized knit draped over my frame like I had stopped caring, like I had thrown it on in a moment of cold indifference. The faded jeans sagged enough to look like I hadn't been eating; like I had given up on structure, on holding anything together. The cardigan slipped off one shoulder, exposing my collarbone in a way that wasn't elegant, but ghostly—like I didn't have the energy to fix it.

My hair, tousled, had the effect of restless nights and too many unslept hours. The slight smudge beneath my eyes hinted at a woman who had cried too many times to bother wiping away the evidence.

It was perfect.

Manon stepped forward, reaching into her bag and pulling out a pair of oversized sunglasses. "Put these on."

I raised a brow. "A final touch of mystery?"

She slid them onto my face herself. "I want him looking into your eyes and deciding they're puffy from crying. I want him to force you to take the glasses off and set them in front of him."

I looked... fragile. A woman past the brink of a nervous breakdown. Someone who might not make it through the week. Someone whose very existence teetered on the mercy of others.

Manon stood behind me, her gaze meeting mine in the mirror. For a moment, neither of us spoke. Then she exhaled, a slow, satisfied sound. "This is it."

I tilted my head, studying my reflection. "No way around it."

Her smirk was subtle, but I caught it in the glass. "None."

A quiet understanding passed between us. We had done what needed to be done.

I lifted my chin, letting the ghost of a smile play at my lips.

Manon's smirk widened and she tapped the side of my sunglasses. "Before we celebrate, there's something I want to show you. These aren't any sunglasses, B. They're part of the line I've been developing with the Silicon Valley team."

I turned to her, curious. "Oh? And what do they do?"

Her grin was positively feline. "Let me show you."

CHAPTER
Twenty-Seven

THE LONG BURN

The waiting area was designed to make me feel small.

Dark marble floors, sleek black furniture, high ceilings. A muted news broadcast scrolled overhead: Senator Guerra-Reyes' investigating Dorian's business dealings.

I twisted the hem of my sweater and kept my gaze down.

Behind the reception desk, a blonde sat poised in a tailored black suit and white blouse. She barely glanced up.

The soft click of heels against marble signaled another presence.

I flinched.

A second blonde approached—taller, bob razor-sharp, Louboutins striking the marble. Each step cut through the silence.

Her gaze landed on me, sweeping over my frame with slow, deliberate disdain. Her eyes lingered on my sunglasses, then moved on.

She had not wanted the meeting. Dorian had.

"Follow me."

I stood too quickly, tugging the sleeves over my knuckles. "Lovely office. New design?"

She didn't answer.

I swallowed.

She walked ahead, heels slicing the quiet. I followed. My steps sounded too loud.

I caught my reflection in a glass panel.

She checked with Dorian, then turned back to me, her stare lingering a beat too long. "Go in."

I hesitated.

The door clicked shut behind me.

Dorian stood with his back to me, phone pressed to his ear.

A pause. Then he turned.

His gaze landed on me, and for a fraction of a second, something flickered across his face—satisfaction.

Disgust.

His mouth tightened.

"Beatrix," he said, drawing out my name as if he were tasting it. "You look... different."

I let my shoulders droop, fingers gripping the hem of my sweater. "I—thank you for seeing me."

Hatred rose metallic in my throat. My hands trembled anyway.

"Take off your glasses."

I hesitated, then slid them off with unsteady fingers, blinking against the light.

His gaze locked onto mine, searching.

I didn't look away.

His lips twitched, satisfied. "Let's not waste time. Sit."

I placed the sunglasses on his desk, followed by my phone, screen facing up, and sat.

Dorian's eyes flicked to the phone, then to me. Without a word, he picked it up.

He reached into a drawer, pulled out a sleek, black pouch, and slid my phone inside. He pressed the seal shut with deliberate precision before setting it back on the desk beside my glasses.

"Just being careful," he said, his tone light. "Given everything happening in France. And, of course, the rumors about Senator Guerra-Reyes'... interest in my affairs."

He leaned back, fingers tapping against the desk. "I assume you understand."

I shifted in my seat.

"Of course," I murmured, voice small.

His smile sharpened. "Good. Now—"

The words ripped from my throat, sharp and violent, splitting the air between us.

"You raped me!"

CHAPTER Twenty-Eight

MOLTING

"You raped me!"

Dorian didn't flinch.

If anything, he seemed calmer.

He tilted his head, a smirk curling at the corner of his mouth.

"It was consensual."

My nails dug into my palms. "No, it wasn't."

"You ordered me to put the Ben Wa balls in. You told me where to put the plug. You lifted your chin when I clamped the nipple clamps on. You *wanted* it."

"I didn't know they had robots in them, Dorian! I didn't consent to that!"

"I'm not responsible for your lack of imagination."

"That's not how consent works. We had an agreement. I had the right to say no. You took that away from me."

"The whole point was to push you. To take you to the brink without letting you fall. You were supposed to control yourself."

I let out a bitter laugh, sharp and jagged. "Control myself? You made sure I had no control. You took away my agency."

"You say that like it wasn't the entire point."

"You planned this. The public humiliation, the exposure—you wanted to ruin me."

"You put yourself on display, Beatrix. I only gave the audience something worth watching."

"You're aroused by this. By what you did to me."

"You act surprised. You were meant to ride that line. You broke."

"If anything, you disappointed me."

I swallowed hard, my body vibrating with fury. He was enjoying this—the memory, my anger, the sheer power he still believed he held over me. His very being made me sick.

"No, Dorian." I forced my voice to steady, unyielding. "You broke me. But you made one mistake."

"And what's that?"

I leaned forward, letting the hatred burn through my voice, making sure he felt every inch of it. "You didn't realize I had Manon."

Something in his expression flickered—just for a second. Then he smiled, slow and dismissive. "That... is the only reason you're sitting here."

"Manon."

"Unlike you, she understands power."

"She put me back together. And now, you don't get to win."

Dorian leaned back in his chair, his smirk widening as he let his gaze drag over me in a way that made my skin crawl. Then, with a slow, deliberate motion, he palmed his crotch, rubbing himself through his trousers.

"You still have that effect on me, Beatrix."

I felt my stomach turn, but I forced myself to remain still. "You're disgusting."

His chuckle was low, indulgent. "Oh, don't be so dramatic. I'm feeling generous today."

"I don't need your generosity."

"Oh, but you do. You just don't like admitting it." He tapped the desk once.

"I bought your rights. Your entire catalog. I don't see them worth as much anymore, nor did your publisher."

"Why? "

"Because I could."

" Now I'm willing to be... gracious. So, I'm willing to give them back to you, under certain conditions. Consider it a parting gift."

"You think I'm supposed to be grateful?"

"I think you should recognize a lifeline when it's thrown at you. Who else would publish you now? Who else would dare invest in such... damaged goods?"

"If my work is going to be published, I want control over it. Full ownership."

"That's not how business works. Full ownership? Fantasy."

"It's not a fantasy. It's *my* work. My life. "

"Non-starter. I need to see a return."

"Fifty-one percent," I said immediately.

"Why would I agree to that?"

"Because I don't belong to you anymore."

"Done, under certain conditions."

I tensed. "What now?"

"Your next book... I'll guarantee it wins the Orpheus Prize."

I stared at him, stunned. I wasn't sure I'd heard him correctly.

"You think I want to win the Orpheus Prize because of you?"

Dorian simply watched me, a knowing smirk playing at his lips, his fingers tapping idly against the desk as if he had all the time in the world.

I shook my head, trying to quell the fury rising in my chest. "The only reason I didn't get it this year is *because* of you. And now you think I'd take it from your hands? You think I'd let you put your fingerprints on my success?" I let out a sharp, bitter laugh. "You're delusional."

He exhaled, slow and patient, as if I were a child refusing to understand a simple lesson. "Everything has a price, Beatrix. Even a prize. Even the ones people claim are given for 'merit.'"

I scoffed. "And you think you can just buy my career back for me? Buy my reputation?"

His smirk widened. "I don't think. I know."

A cold chill settled in my spine. "Then why didn't you do it when my life was spinning out of control?" I demanded. "If you had so much power, why let me crash?"

Dorian's eyes gleamed with something close to amusement. "Because you didn't ask."

I inhaled sharply. "You expected me to ask you for help? After what you did to me?"

He spread his hands, unbothered. "And yet, here you are." His smirk deepened.

I gritted my teeth. "This isn't an ask, Dorian. It's a negotiation."

"Oh, Beatrix," he sighed, tilting his head. "Everything in life is a negotiation. That's what you never quite grasped. The Orpheus Prize, your reputation, your career—they were never truly yours to begin with. They belong to the system, to the people who pull the strings. People like me."

I swallowed down the disgust rising in my throat. "You expect me to believe you can just decide who wins? That this whole thing is a farce?"

His smirk didn't waver. "You think judges are immune to influence? That they don't owe favors? That they don't have preferences?" He let out a low chuckle, almost pitying. "Beatrix, half of them are connected to me through business ventures, charitable foundations, even simple friendship. Do you really think anyone wins an award like that without someone ensuring the right doors open?"

His gaze flicked over me, slow and deliberate. "Just like how the right legs being open can do the same thing to the right doors."

I stiffened. "You're disgusting."

He grinned, full of mock innocence. "Am I? I thought we were being honest. Or do you think all these 'genius' minds win on talent alone? Talent is only as good as the people willing to endorse it." He leaned back, stretching lazily, watching my reaction. "Some are more willing than others."

I gripped the arms of my chair. "And you think that's supposed to make me want it more? If you have to hand it to me, it's meaningless."

He nodded as if he understood. "Which is why I'm offering to remove all obstacles in your path. You still write the book. It has to be... acceptable. But the right people will see it. They'll understand its 'importance.' And they'll vote accordingly."

"You think I would ever take it under those conditions? You think I'd let you taint it?"

His smirk widened. "Taint it? Oh, Beatrix. I will make it legendary."

I forced myself to hold his gaze, my stomach twisting. "And I'm sure there's a price for this... generous offer?"

Dorian leaned forward, his smirk sharpening. "Five conditions."

Conditions. There were always conditions.

"Five conditions," he repeated, as if tasting the number on his tongue. "That surprises you."

"Let's hear them."

CHAPTER
Twenty-Nine

TEMPERED

"We'll start with something simple," he said. "Your presence at Manon's show in Paris. At my side."

This wasn't about me. It was about Manon.

"You want me to be your date," I said flatly.

He chuckled. "Beatrix, don't be so crude. Think of it as a reintroduction. You've been in exile long enough."

"And why would I need you to do that?"

"Because I'm offering you a relaunch. Your books, under a new label, free from the baggage of your past."

"And this requires me standing next to you in Paris?"

"Visibility is everything, Beatrix. Your name will be back where it belongs."

"My name was fine where it was before you destroyed it."

"And now I'm offering to restore it. Under my terms, of course."

"And if I say no?"

"You'll have to claw your way back from obscurity," he said.

"But the industry doesn't wait for women past their prime. They want fresh talent. Easy to mold."

"Fine," I said finally. "I'll go."

"Good girl."

"You'll wear the plug, the Ben Wa balls, and the clamps again."

"No."

"You're reacting like I just asked you to walk on fire. This is about reclaiming control. "

"That's not closure. That's you playing another game."

" Maybe this time, you learn to resist."

I exhaled through my nose. "Resist?"

His smirk widened. "I can train you."

"You want me to let you train me to resist the same things you used to break me?"

"If you'd had better control, you would've enjoyed it more."

"That's your takeaway from what you did to me?"

"It's reality," he said smoothly. "You pride yourself on control. But you weren't untouchable, were you? You fell apart. And that's why you're here. Now prove it won't happen again."

"No."

"You're not even willing to try? To push past what happened?"

"I'm not putting all of them on again. That's not negotiation, that's humiliation."

His amusement didn't waver. "Then negotiate. One piece. You pick."

I swallowed, hating the game, hating the illusion of control.

"One," I said finally. "Only one."

Dorian leaned back, pleased. "Good girl. Now, which will it be?"

I hesitated, my mind racing. Dorian watched me, his gaze sharp, patient. He wasn't rushing me. No, he was savoring this, dragging it out because he knew this was where the real victory lay—not just in my choice, but in forcing me to deliberate my own humiliation as if it were a privilege.

The clamps were too visible.

The plug was impossible.

The Ben Wa Balls could be hidden.

Dorian's breathing had slowed, controlled, but his pupils were darker, his posture more at ease, his arousal simmering just beneath the surface.

"The Ben Wa balls."

"How fitting."

Dorian pressed a button on his desk. A soft mechanical whir filled the silence, and a hidden compartment slid open, revealing a case. A case I recognized immediately.

The Luxuria Collar.

He let the moment stretch, savoring it, his patience laced with amusement. He reached forward, opened the case, and turned it toward me. The collar gleamed under the lights, its intricate design a perfect balance of opulence and restraint.

"This is a necessary part of your rebirth."

"I'm not yours, Dorian."

"Aren't you? Until you agree to my terms, I still own the rights to everything you've ever written. In a way, you *are* mine. We're only negotiating the terms of your surrender."

"The last time we had a negotiation like this, you broke the terms. You raped me. You stripped me of choice. And now you want to sit there and talk about surrender?"

He leaned back in his chair. "The collar isn't a condition anymore, Beatrix. It's a gift. I'm *asking* you to wear it. Just me, *begging* you to put it on."

The collar sat between us, gleaming, waiting, its presence heavy with meaning.

The last time I had refused it, he took everything else.

I met his gaze, unwavering. "Fine, I'll wear it."

"The world may think I'm submitting to you," I continued, my voice like steel. "But you'll know the truth. I'm granting you this one."

Dorian let the silence settle between us, his satisfaction evident but restrained. He didn't gloat. "This next one," he said, "is about loyalty."

I knew what was coming before he said it, but the words still landed like a blow.

"You'll sever your friendship with Manon."

I said nothing.

"Well?" he said.

I kept my eyes on him.

He gestured toward the floor. "Come here."

"Kneel."

I moved. Pushing back my chair, rising to my feet.

I stepped around the desk. The heat between us grew heavier, suffocating. He didn't move, didn't shift, just watched, his focus entirely on me.

I lowered myself to my knees before him, my posture carefully neutral.

Without breaking eye contact, he reached for my phone on the desk. He turned it on, the screen glowing between his fingers, then extended it.

"Call her," he said, his voice smooth, measured. "Call Manon."

I didn't move.

He tilted his head, watching me, drinking in my hesitation like the finest wine. "Do it," he murmured, his voice dipping lower, richer with satisfaction. "I want to hear you say it. I want to see the look on your face when you tell her it's over."

His grip on control was razor-sharp now, his hunger barely restrained. This wasn't just about severing the tie. This was about witnessing the break, about savoring the moment. He wanted to hear the pain in my voice. He wanted to hear the shift in Manon's tone, the disbelief, the hurt. He wanted to watch me unravel and to know that he was the one pulling the thread.

I took the phone from his hand, careful, deliberate. It was warm from his touch. I stared at the screen, my reflection looking back at me, hollow, shattered—the powerless slave he wanted to see.

The number was right there, waiting. One press away.

I lifted my gaze to his, the phone heavy in my grip.

"Go on, Beatrix," he said softly. "Tell her goodbye."

The phone felt heavier in my grip than it should have. My thumb hovered over the screen for a fraction of a second before I pressed the call button, bringing it to my ear.

Manon picked up on the second ring.

"*Bébé*," she purred, her voice rich, indulgent, like she hadn't a care in the world.

Dorian's gaze flicked to me, sharp, assessing. He wanted to hear it unfold. He wanted to watch it happen in real-time.

I swallowed hard, my voice coming out restrained, as if I had been holding back tears. "Manon."

"What did he make you do, B?"

"A condition for getting my rights back... is that we cut ties."

Beside me, Dorian exhaled, satisfied.

"Oh, darling. That's what this is about? I should have known he'd try something so cliché."

"Manon, I'm serious."

"So am I. And I'm seriously unimpressed."

Dorian leaned back in his chair, watching me carefully, enjoying every flicker of hesitation, every beat of discomfort. His fingers drummed idly on the desk before sliding lower, disappearing from my view.

"This isn't up for debate," I continued, my voice stiff, brittle. "We're done."

Silence stretched between us.

Manon scoffed, sharp and indignant. "You're actually doing this. You're actually giving in to him."

I pressed my lips together, letting my breath stutter over the line, as though I were struggling to hold myself together. "I don't have a choice."

"You *always* have a choice, B." Her voice dropped, the first sign of hurt bleeding through. "Or maybe you just don't want to choose me."

"Manon, don't make this harder," I whispered.

"Harder?" A sharp, bitter laugh. "I didn't make this hard. You did, the second you decided to let him own you again."

I heard Dorian unzipping his pants.

"Say it," he murmured. "Tell her it's over."

I sucked in a sharp breath. "Manon, this is goodbye."

Manon let the silence stretch, the weight of it suffocating. Then, finally, she exhaled, sharp, incredulous.

"No. There has to be another way. You don't have to do this."

"There isn't another way," I said, voice low, tight. "Dorian already bought my rights from my former publisher. He owns me. It's done."

"He *owns* you? That's what you're saying? That's what you believe?"

"It's reality."

"No," she snapped, anger slicing through her voice now. "That's his reality, not yours. And you're just accepting it? After everything he did to you?"

"Manon," I whispered, my voice breaking just enough, "this is goodbye."

"No, Beatrix. I don't accept that." Her breath came hard, fast. "I don't accept that you would choose him over me. After what he did to you, after everything we—"

She cut herself off, the sound of something crashing in the background. Glass, maybe. A bottle.

Then, suddenly, silence. A violent exhale. And then, "Go to hell."

The line went dead.

"That," he murmured, his voice thick with pleasure, "was perfect."

I didn't answer.

"Now for the fifth condition."

His fingers slipped into my hair, caressing my scalp with a sickening gentleness. "Such a pretty pet," he murmured, his voice thick with satisfaction. His fingers pulling my hair, a possessive caress, a reminder that he considered me his.

"Be a good girl and show me how much you've truly surrendered."

The second the words left his mouth, I moved. My lips brushed against the tip of him, and that was all it took.

Dorian's entire body jerked. A deep, guttural groan tore from his throat as he lost himself completely. His grip in my hair tightened painfully, his hips stuttering forward, his breath ragged and uneven. He had been too pent up, too close for too long. The moment my mouth touched him, he exploded with a shuddering, broken gasp.

The tension left him in waves, his body convulsing, his fingers flexing in my hair, his chest heaving. His control—so meticulously maintained, so carefully guarded—was obliterated in an instant.

I stayed still, composed, letting him come undone, letting him drown in the mess of his own making, in the evidence of his own weakness.

His head tipped forward, his gaze hazy, lips parted as he struggled to steady himself.

Satisfaction warred with the remnants of his own ruin. His breathing was still ragged, but his smirk—slow, indulgent—began to return.

He thought he had won.

But he hadn't taken the one thing that mattered most.

My power.

CHAPTER
Thirty

FLIGHT PATTERN

The base of the Eiffel Tower had been transformed into spectacle, draped in luxury, humming with anticipation.

Towering fabric walls rose into the night, alive with project fashion films of French sensuality and craft.

Lace and silk whispered across screens, folding *Châtelaine*'s into the legacy of Hermès and Chanel.

The Champ de Mars had been reimagined into an open-air theater of extravagance, all champagne and speculation.

The Eiffel Tower loomed above, its iron lattice gleaming beneath the floodlights, as if Paris itself had bent to Manon's vision. The seating was a who's who of power—fashion titans, ministers, tech moguls, film stars, royals, and rock gods.

But outside the cordoned-off splendor, not everyone was celebrating.

The streets of Paris had been snarled for days, clogged with blacked-out SUVs ferrying the global elite from penthouses to the front-row. The air itself felt heavy, thick with the scent of exhaust and excess.

Environmental activists were out in force, furious at the private jets choking *Le Bourget* and the motorcades parading through the city.

Parisians, always eager to rebel against excess when it wasn't their own, had turned to the streets, waving banners condemning the suffocating indulgence, their chants swallowed by the sheer magnitude of the event.

Inside the spectacle, none of it mattered.

Presence was currency here. Missing it, exile.

The Eiffel Tower had seen a century's worth of grand affairs, but tonight, it belonged to Manon.

The car slid to a stop, and before the door even opened, flashbulbs were already firing. The moment I stepped out, I felt the energy shift, a ripple through the crowd.

The Luxuria Collar sat on my throat, its intricate gold filigree catching the Eiffel Tower's lights. It gleamed, a claim impossible to ignore.

For the first time since the auction, the collar had reappeared in public, and the realization moved quickly through the crowd, as Dorian was revealed as its mysterious owner.

The whispers started immediately, hushed voices threading through the crowd. My public collapse had been scandalous, but the collar was something else.

A different kind of scandal, not sex but ownership.

The Luxuria Collar, a relic of French aristocratic excess, had once graced the neck of Pauline La Soumise, King Louis XV's most devoted courtesan. It had always meant ultimate surrender made object.

And now, it was on *me*.

The outrage wasn't that it had resurfaced. It was its new ownership and gauche public display.

Dorian kept his hand at the small of my back, the weight of it meant to look like reassurance but feeling more like possession. He had checked before we left, smug in the knowledge I was wearing what he had chosen.

I smiled at him, soft, docile. Letting him believe it.

I hated him. Every second of this burned. I had perfected the art of pretending.

The gown Manon had selected for me was elegant, draped to hint at temptation without surrendering to it. A slit revealed the length of my leg as I walked; a shimmer of décolletage caught in the lights. The perfect balance—seductive yet sophisticated, a woman who belonged at the center of attention. My arm curled lightly around Dorian's, my lips tilted as if I were enjoying the moment.

He thought he had taken everything from me, but he would never take me. The silk on the outside belonged to his fantasy. Beneath it, I belonged only to myself.

The moment we stepped onto the carpet, the stares intensified. Some curious, some envious, some scandalized. Here I was, on the arm of the man who had made sure I disappeared.

Dorian held me close, his fingers pressing just enough to remind me of my place. He wasn't parading me. He was making a point.

Inside, the air was thick with anticipation and the hum of too many important conversations. Manon's show had already done its work; people were placing It in history before the first model stepped out. The projections on the fabric walls flickered with curated, decadent imagery: lace tracing over bare skin; flashes of Parisian architecture; a breath, a sigh, a glimpse of a hand sliding over silk. It was desire distilled into film, and everyone was watching.

Dorian guided me through the entrance with the effortless confidence of a man who believed he owned the room.

Eyes followed us as we moved through the crowd. My return had already set the press into a quiet frenzy, but the collar had elevated the moment to something more. The realization of what I was wearing had settled in now, shifting from gasps to analysis, from shock to meaning. The whispers were no longer about my sordid disgrace but about the statement wrapped around my throat. And, just as Dorian had intended, it wasn't me they looked at when they spoke of ownership.

It was *him*.

At his side, I was everything he wanted me to be. Poised, sensual, untouchable. I played my part so well I could almost believe it myself. The laughter, the demure glances, the effortless charm—I could feel the eyes on me, the assessments, the way people tried to determine whether I was truly lost to him. Whether I had become his.

Dorian's grip at my back tightened as we approached the central seating area. He leaned, his breath warm at my ear. "You're putting on quite a show," he murmured, smug.

I turned to him, my lashes lowering, lips parting in just the right way to suggest something indulgent. "Isn't that the point?"

He exhaled a quiet chuckle, his hand ghosting over my hip in approval, and then we stepped into the front row—where Manon was waiting.

She was exquisite, as always, her presence commanding without effort. A tailored cream jumpsuit, cinched at the waist with a delicate gold belt, high cheekbones accentuated by the softest touch of blush. Her hair was swept back, sleek, revealing the sharp cut of diamond earrings that caught the light with every slight tilt of her head.

But the moment her gaze landed on me, her expression hardened.

Her fingers curled around the stem of her champagne flute, but this time, it wasn't the only betrayal of emotion. Her lips, usually so poised, were pressed into a thin line, her stare colder than I had ever seen it.

Dorian felt it immediately. I knew because I felt his satisfaction in the way his grip on me flexed. He wanted this. Needed this. Proof that he had driven the wedge deep enough between us that even in public, Manon wouldn't mask her contempt.

For a moment, I let myself hesitate, my body going stiff beside him. It was for him, of course, for the performance, but it didn't make it any easier to see the coldness in Manon's eyes as she drank me in, as if I were nothing more than a disappointment standing in front of her.

Dorian, of course, saw none of the precision behind it. He was too pleased with himself. He gave Manon a slow, knowing smile, his voice rich with amusement. "Quite the spectacle you've put together, *ma chère*."

Manon tilted her head, her own smile lazy, indulgent—but not for me. She didn't even glance my way. "Spectacle? Dorian, you flatter me."

His fingers skimmed my wrist in what he probably thought was an absentminded gesture of possession. "It's not every day that a new empire is born," he said smoothly. "I had to see it for myself."

Manon's gaze flicked to the collar at my throat before returning to my face. Her nostrils flared, her lips parting, but she said nothing to me. Instead, she looked back at Dorian, eyes narrowing. "And of course," she said, voice light, "you couldn't resist bringing a relic of the old world to the new."

Dorian laughed. "You know me. I have a taste for history."

A slow sip of champagne, a perfectly arched brow. "Yes," Manon said, tone almost thoughtful. "But history is only useful when it isn't a cautionary tale."

Dorian's smirk tightened for the briefest of moments, just a flicker, before he recovered. But before he could respond, another presence joined our small circle.

Manon's mother.

Dorian and I were both caught off guard. I hadn't expected her to be here—Dorian clearly hadn't either—but then again, this was Chanel, this was Hermès, this was French respectability. Manon had done what her mother always demanded of her: she had aligned herself with tradition, with power. She had not only built an empire, she had built one that had the approval of the old guard. And with that, she had earned her mother's presence.

She moved with effortless grace, the kind of presence that silenced conversations without effort. Dressed in a sculpted black ensemble, understated yet undeniably powerful, she exuded the type of authority that required no adornment. Where Manon's coldness had been subtle, hers was absolute.

Her gaze barely flickered toward me before settling on Dorian, assessing him with the same sharp precision she had once reserved for the men who had tried to court her influence. A pause, the briefest beat, and then, "Dorian. What an... unexpected guest."

Dorian, to his credit, only seemed more amused, more entertained by the shift in the air. "*Madame,*" he greeted smoothly, inclining his head just enough to feign politeness, though there was an edge of satisfaction in his voice. "I wouldn't have missed it. Manon is making history tonight."

Manon's mother sipped her champagne, unhurried, unimpressed. Her gaze flicked toward the Luxuria Collar encircling my throat, lingering there before returning to Dorian.

"Legacy," she mused, letting the word settle before glancing at Manon. "It endures. Even when built in... unconventional ways."

Manon's expression didn't shift, but the tension in her jaw was subtle enough for those who knew her. "Unconventional doesn't mean unworthy."

Her mother's gaze flicked over the venue, the walls adorned with *Châtelaine*'s vision now fused with Chanel and Hermès, solidifying Manon's place in tradition. "Perhaps. The right alliances help."

Dorian, ever the spectator to power plays, smiled. "A name is only as strong as the empire behind it."

Manon's mother turned to him, assessing. "History is steeped in legacy," she said smoothly, her voice carrying the weight of centuries. "Manon's path has been... unusual. Distasteful, at times. But legacy is about endurance, not approval. And with Hermès and Chanel now entwined in it, she has made herself part of something lasting."

Dorian tilted his head, amused. "Even you can't deny the power of ownership."

The champagne flute in Manon's mother's hand barely moved as she spoke, her voice measured, her words deliberate. "Ownership is such a delicate thing," she mused, eyes flicking toward the Luxuria Collar resting against my throat. "It implies control, permanence, when in reality, it is nothing more than borrowed time. A momentary claim."

Dorian's smirk was steady, indulgent. "And yet," he said smoothly, "some claims last longer than others."

She ignored him, gaze settling on me instead. "It is distasteful, parading something like this. Do you even understand what you are wearing?" Her tone dripped with condescension. "This collar was never meant for display. It was not designed for the gaze of the common world. It was meant to be locked away, as its history should have been."

I swallowed, forcing my expression to remain neutral. She wasn't just disgusted by Dorian—she was disgusted by me.

"Crafted for private use, and now a public accessory. A *chienne*'s leash."

My stomach tightened, but I stayed perfectly still.

Dorian's smirk deepened. "Trophies are meant to be displayed."

Manon's mother turned her full attention to him, cold and unimpressed. "You vulgar American. You have no sense of history. You just think that displaying your plaything…"

Manon shifted beside her, fingers tightening around her champagne flute. "Maman—"

Dorian cut her off smoothly. "Let her finish. Unless, of course, you feel the need to protect my toys from your mother?"

I saw it. The flicker of anger, the briefest hesitation before she masked it. And Dorian saw it too.

I kept my gaze forward, pulse hammering. I felt like I was suffocating.

"Beatrix," my mother's voice cut through the tension, warm, composed, and utterly unbothered by the spectacle unfolding before her. My father was beside her, his presence steadier than I remembered, his gaze immediately shifting to Dorian with a cool detachment.

Manon's mother turned, her irritation ebbing as she assessed my mother. Something shifted in her expression—approval, perhaps, or at least the understanding that powerful families should remain aligned. "Claire," she said smoothly, inclining her head. "I was just discussing how certain things should never be paraded in public."

My mother smiled, sharp but polite. "And yet, here we all are."

The tension eased. There was a quiet camaraderie between them—one born of old money, of legacy, of the unspoken rule that those who belonged knew how to protect their own. And despite my mother's apparent warmth, I could feel the steel behind it.

My father turned to me, his expression softer than I expected. "You look well, Beatrix."

The words settled something deep inside me, though I dared not let it show. "It's good to see you both."

He nodded, then shifted his attention to Dorian. The warmth disappeared. "Mr. Wolker."

Dorian extended a hand, ever the performer, but my father merely glanced at it before reaching for a glass of champagne instead. There was no mistaking the coolness in his expression—resentment, carefully restrained. Dorian had stolen the robotics company out from under him, maneuvering in the shadows to claim something that had been meant to help future generations, not just one man's hunger for power.

"I hear you've been quite busy," he said mildly.

Dorian, to his credit, kept his smirk in place. "I try to keep things interesting."

"Interesting isn't always the same as meaningful," my father replied. "And certainly not the same as responsible."

Manon's mother took a slow sip of her champagne before adding, "*Noblesse oblige* is a difficult concept to grasp when one is still so focused on proving they belong."

My parents exchanged the smallest of smiles. They did not approve of my presence at Dorian's side, but they would not make a scene. Still, I could feel it in the way my mother's gaze lingered on the collar, in the way my father hesitated momentarily before he spoke. My name—*our* name—was not to be paraded in submission. They had tolerated my writing, even if they did not approve. But this? This was something else.

"Once you've achieved success, Mr. Wolker, you have a responsibility to more than just your acquisitions," my father continued. "You have a duty to society. Wealth is not just power. It is stewardship."

Dorian's jaw tightened, but he recovered quickly, his usual mask slipping back into place. "I suppose we all have different philosophies on what success means."

My mother hummed, glancing at me briefly before returning her gaze to Manon's mother. "Perhaps. But only one of them ever built something lasting."

The conversation shifted after that, but the weight of it lingered. Dorian had been put in his place, even if he wouldn't admit it. And for the first time since stepping onto that carpet, I felt something close to steady again.

The lights dimmed, the energy in the room shifting as the murmurs of conversation softened into expectant silence. The air was electric, every eye fixed on the towering projections that flickered to life on the massive fabric walls. Manon's vision, her empire, was about to take center stage.

At the front of the venue, President Laurent Moreau stepped forward, taking his place at the microphone. His presence alone was enough to solidify just how significant this night had become—not just for fashion, but for business, for culture, for legacy. He adjusted his cuffs, a practiced motion, before offering the crowd the kind of polished smile designed to put people at ease.

"Tonight," he began, his voice steady, warm, formal but not rigid, "we celebrate not just an extraordinary vision, but an extraordinary family. The name Rochemaure has long been synonymous with tradition, influence, and excellence. Manon de Rochemaure has taken that legacy and propelled it forward, forging an alliance between innovation and heritage, between modernity and tradition. Chanel, Hermès, and *Châtelaine*—a partnership of past, present, and future. A testament to what French craftsmanship has always stood for: excellence, beauty, and permanence."

He paused, letting the words settle, before adding, "And if she ever decides to run for office, well—then I will be very, very worried."

Laughter rippled through the audience, an easy, orchestrated charm offensive. Manon's mother inclined her head slightly, her approval clear. Moreau had tied Manon to her lineage, to her family's name, reinforcing its importance. It was just how she wanted the family to be seen—powerful, but anchored in legacy.

Then, Prime Minister Élodie Marchand stepped onto the stage. Her movements were deliberate, her presence sharpened to a blade. As she adjusted the lapel of her blazer, a hint of Châtelaine lace peeked through— intentional, unmistakable. A message to the crowd, to Manon. A reminder that she had her own alliances.

"Tonight is about more than legacy. It is about the future," Marchand said, her voice smoother, more intimate. "For too long, the world has dictated what women should wear, who they should be, and how they should be seen. What Manon has done is redefine that narrative—not by looking to the past, but by shaping a new way forward. Châtelaine is not just lingerie. It is a declaration. A reminder that femininity and strength are not contradictions, that seduction and power go hand in hand."

Applause rang out, louder this time, carrying a different energy. Moreau's speech had drawn admiration, a nod to heritage. Marchand's had ignited something else—momentum. She had tied Manon not to the past, but to progress, to disruption, to something undeniably modern.

Moreau's expression remained neutral, but there was a tightness at the edges of his smile. He had played his hand, but Marchand had played hers better. And Manon, without lifting a finger, had become the battlefield between them.

Manon's mother remained still, her earlier amusement shifting into quiet calculation. She did not agree with Marchand's framing—tradition was not something to be discarded in favor of a "new way forward." But she was pragmatic. If Marchand was to be the next President, the Rochemaure family would need to navigate that alliance carefully. Manon had not just reclaimed her place; she had positioned herself at the center of power. And that was something her mother could not ignore.

Music pulsed through the space, deep and commanding, the kind that thrummed through bone and demanded attention. The lights flared back to life, illuminating the vast runway stretching beneath the base of the Eiffel Tower. Manon's vision was no longer an idea—it was alive.

The Luxuria Collar was cool against my skin, a stark contrast to the warmth of the Châtelaine lingerie beneath my gown. It was armor and contradiction, power and restraint. No one here knew I was wearing it, except for Manon. But everyone could see the collar, the ever-present reminder of Dorian's control. The ben wa balls inside me shifted slightly as I crossed my legs, another silent reminder.

The first model emerged in a structured corset of molded leather and sheer silk, less seduction than command.

I had already seen the collection, but for the audience, this was a revelation. The murmurs grew, shifting from stunned curiosity to captivated admiration.

The collection walked a razor-thin line between heritage and revolution. There were nods to the past—Coco Chanel's radical independence, the structured rebellion of Jean-Paul Gaultier's tenure at Hermès—but they were remixed, reimagined. Traditional lace and satin of lingerie were slashed through with harness-like belts and tailored jackets. Silk garters were meant to be seen.

A model in a sheer bodysuit with a sharply structured bustier turned at the end of the runway, throwing a glance over her shoulder—not an invitation, but a dare.

From behind me, a voice murmured, "... *l'enfant terrible des de Rochemaure.*"

I smirked slightly, suppressing the urge to turn around. Manon would have found it amusing. Her mother, however, did not. I saw the flicker of annoyance cross her face before she smoothed it away, her posture impeccably straight. She had always wanted Manon to find her way back into the family's fold, but not like this. Not through irreverence.

The crowd has shifted from stunned to enthralled.

Beside me, Dorian exhaled sharply, his jaw tightening as he watched the runway. The murmur of approval from the audience, the way power shifted toward Manon with every step her models took, grated on him.

On stage, every step was a direct *fuck you* directed at Dorian.

Manon's mother gave a single, slow nod.

The final model walked, the music reaching its crescendo, the last look a masterpiece of silk and leather, structured and flowing all at once, feminine and forceful.

Then the lights around us went dark.

CHAPTER Thirty-One

FIREPROOF

The Eiffel Tower had gone dark. Gasps rippled through the crowd, a beat of silence stretching tight before a voice cut through it—smooth, assured, unmistakable.

Dorian.

"Noa Shalev doesn't stand a chance. She thinks LumeoTech is hers, but by the time she realizes what's happening, I'll have taken it from her hands. Women like her—like all of them—don't know how to hold onto power. They think they're players, but they never see the real game. And I? I take what I want."

The fabric at the base of the Eiffel Tower transformed into massive screens. High-resolution video flickered to life, revealing him—lounging, smirking, his arrogance on full display.

"The influencer awards? Please. They wouldn't even let me in, at first. Thought they could keep me out. But money talks, and now I make the decisions. I bought my way in, and once I was there, I made sure the right people won."

Beside me, Dorian stiffened. His fingers twitched. A flick of his tongue over his lips. Tiny cracks forming.

Another clip.

"Government scrutiny? It's a joke. I had the sports ban enacted just to drive the price into the ground. Now that I own it, I'll have it lifted. The right connections, the right payments, and suddenly, policy bends the way I want it to."

The murmurs in the audience sharpened into anger. I glanced at Dorian. His jaw clenched, his hand curled into a fist before he forced it open. Another video shift.

Dorian, massaging one of his custom-made dildos, dark amusement in his eyes. "Real women are disappointing. They think they're in control, but they're not. No one satisfies me unless they know they're mine. A slave to me. That's when they're at their best."

The disgust was visceral. Dorian adjusted his cuffs, trying to feign indifference, but his movements were too tight, too controlled. He was unraveling.

Then, the final clip.

"Your next book... I'll guarantee it wins the Orpheus Prize."

A beat of silence. Then, my own voice, steady and sharp. "You think I want to win the Orpheus Prize because of *you*?"

The weight of it landed like a blow. The crowd tensed, turning toward Dorian. Recognition dawning. Realization sinking in.

Then, a single spotlight snapped on, illuminating the center of the stage.

Manon and Noa Shalev stood there, microphones in hand, waiting.

The spotlight bathed Manon and Noa in a halo of light, their posture relaxed, their confidence unshaken. Sleek, stylish sunglasses graced their faces.

Dorian tensed beside me. He recognized the glasses. They were identical to the ones I had worn when I had come to him, supposedly broken, seeking his help to reclaim my rights.

I could almost hear the pieces snapping together in his mind.

Noa was the first to speak, her voice carrying effortlessly. "You didn't think you were the only one who liked to record things, did you?"

Manon smirked, adjusting her glasses with the same practiced ease she had when she'd removed mine in my apartment. "After all, people like to watch."

A perfectly timed double entendre. I had to bite back a smile.

The fabric walls at the base of the Eiffel Tower remained illuminated, but instead of Dorian's face, a new image appeared—a sleek technical rendering of IrisCoat, the revolutionary coating that turned any surface into a near-invisible optical recording device. Developed in secret by Noa and her team at LumeoTech, with manufacturing and refinement supported by Hermès and Manon's own Châtelaine brand, the glasses had recorded everything.

Every boast. Every manipulation. Every confession.

Dorian's chest rose and fell in rapid succession. He hadn't seen it coming. Not because it had been impossible to predict, but because he had been too confident in his own power to believe we could outmaneuver him.

Noa continued, her voice cool. "While you were busy assuming you were the smartest man in the room, I was receiving funding from Mr. Winslow-Hale."

Out of the corner of my eye, I saw my father smiling—calm, pleased, the expression of a man who had bested an opponent without breaking a sweat. This wasn't just about revenge. It was about power.

Manon's smirk widened as she addressed the crowd. "But this wasn't something I could do alone. A plan like this needed precision, patience... and the one person who has always been by my side. My oldest and dearest friend, Beatrix Winslow-Hale."

A new spotlight beamed onto me, illuminating both Dorian and me. The Luxuria Collar caught the light, its dark gleam a stark contrast to the furious, unreadable expression on his face.

Manon extended a hand toward me, an invitation. "Come on up, B."

Dorian's fingers curled into fists. His breathing had changed, no longer casual or even measured—it was clipped, strained. He could see where this was heading, the implications settling like a dead weight in his stomach.

The business world would devour him for this. He could talk his way out of scandal, out of accusations, but not out of his own words, broadcast to the most powerful people in the world.

His hand twitched toward his ring, pressing its stone down.

The response was instant: the ben wa balls inside me activated. I knew the sensation should have been overwhelming, but I felt almost nothing. I had trained for this, conditioned myself to resist. And, of course, the numbing cream didn't hurt.

Dorian expected to see me falter, expected my body to betray me. Instead, I sat still, my expression serene, meeting his gaze head-on.

His nostrils flared, a storm brewing in his eyes. This was slipping beyond his grasp, beyond any damage control he could manage.

For the first time in a long time, Dorian Wolker was powerless.

As the spotlight bathed me in its glow, I rose from my seat, a slow, deliberate smile spreading across my lips. Dorian's gaze burned into me, but I didn't acknowledge him. This moment wasn't his.

I was mine.

I stepped onto the stage, and the instant I reached Manon, she pulled me into a tight embrace. It wasn't just a hug between longtime friends. It was a victory, a silent declaration that we had won. The crowd roared, their energy electric, feeding into the triumph thrumming between us.

Manon pulled back first, her eyes bright with mischief as she reached into her pocket and pulled out a microphone. With a flourish, she handed it to me. "You might need this, B. Unless, of course, you'd rather let me do all the talking. Again."

I took it, shaking my head. "You wouldn't dare."

She grinned. "Oh, I would."

"Almost?"

She tilted her head, considering. "I could have been convinced you were miserable."

"Weeks of training." I gave a dramatic sigh. "You have no idea the restraint it took not to roll my eyes every time he opened his mouth."

Manon laughed, twirling her own microphone in her fingers before turning back to the audience. "But that's not all, *mes chéris*."

The massive screens flickered, and a new video played. Dorian's voice, smooth yet unmistakably desperate, filled the air.

"The collar isn't a condition anymore, Beatrix. It's a gift. A plea, if you will. I'm asking you to wear it. No obligations, no demands—just me, begging you to put it on."

Gasps rippled through the audience.

I lifted the microphone, exchanging a knowing glance with Manon. "You know, some gifts are just poisoned with an awful past."

Manon sighed theatrically. "It really is a terrible shame when men insist on giving bad presents."

"Right? And this one, especially—it belongs in a museum." I paused, smirking. "And since Manon still has to make amends for that little Louvre scandal—"

Manon clutched her chest dramatically. "Ugh, will I never be free from that?"

"No, and I enjoy reminding you of it."

Laughter rippled through the crowd.

I let the amusement settle before continuing. "Thanks to Manon, I recently had the chance to have a chat with Prime Minister Marchand. We talked about legacy, power, the weight of history. And we agreed that some things should not be owned—especially not by men who see them as tools for submission."

The audience murmured, anticipation thick in the air.

"Which is why I am gifting the Luxuria Collar to the Louvre, where it will be displayed behind glass—not as a toy for rich men to put women down."

Applause erupted, the reaction seismic. I turned to the front row.

" Élodie, would you do us the honor of helping with this transfer?"

The Prime Minister stood, a smile gracing her lips as she made her way onto the stage. Manon reached behind me, her fingers brushing my skin as she unclasped the collar. For the first time since Dorian had fastened it around my neck, I felt its weight lighten, its claim over me severed, and its curse over generations of women lifted.

As she held it up, the audience roared, the flash of cameras catching every angle. In the front row, Manon's mother and my parents clapped approvingly, pride evident in their expressions.

I turned to Dorian but his chair was empty. On the edge, a few paparazzi were shooting his disgrace as he scurried out.

EPILOGUE

AFTER CARE

A few months had passed since Paris.

Manon had remained in France, where success required witnesses and victory demanded repetition. *Châtelaine* had stopped being a daring new label and become something worse for its enemies: established. The French press had tried, at first, to decide whether it was fashion or provocation, heritage or insult, revolution or branding. In the end, it had become the only thing that mattered.

And I had come home, reclaiming my territory without having to rely on family.

The public room at NOX glittered around me in its usual language of low light, discretion, and appetite. Velvet banquettes curved through shadow. Crystal caught candlelight. Power sat at neighboring tables pretending not to stare. The club had always understood something most of the world did not: that the most dangerous people were rarely the loudest. They were the ones invited back.

I was halfway through a conversation with a woman whose expression suggested she had read every word I had ever published and underlined the ones that made her feel less alone.

"I mean it," she said, leaning closer, one hand wrapped around the stem of her martini. "Your last book changed the way I think about power. About intimacy. About not apologizing for wanting what I want." Her mouth tightened, just briefly. "And you should have won the Orpheus."

I smiled into my glass. "There's always another book."

Her gaze sharpened. "What he did to you. What they did after. It was disgusting."

"He belongs to my past now," I said.

Then I let the pause stretch just long enough to make her lean in before I added, "Fortunately for me, the past is excellent material."

That got the laugh I wanted.

"Then I'll be first in line for whatever comes next."

"You and half the city."

She smiled, pleased by that, but then something behind me caught her attention. Her expression changed—

not surprise, exactly. Recognition. Awe, sharpened by affection.

I did not need to turn around.

"I should let you two have this," she said, already rising.

I stood before I could think better of it.

The room had shifted. Not dramatically. NOX was too disciplined for that. But attention bent toward the entrance all the same, as if the air itself had made space.

Manon crossed the room like she had never left it.

Her heels marked the floor in a rhythm I knew as well as my own pulse. She was all cream and gold to-night, a study in French precision softened only by the wicked curve of her mouth. Success suited her the way sin did: as if it had been waiting for her all along.

Before she reached me, I was already smiling.

Before I could say her name, she was in my arms.

She held me tightly enough to make something deep in my chest unclench as her familiar scent folded around me. So did memory. Boarding school corridors. Laughter. Survival.

"*Mon dieu*, B," she murmured against my cheek. "I leave you alone for one season and suddenly America belongs to you."

"Please. New York only behaves for me because it knows you could arrive at any moment and make things worse."

Her smile widened. "That may be the sweetest thing you've ever said to me."

"Don't get sentimental. It's unbecoming."

"Too late. Paris has me glowing."

The old unease that had lived in me for months—the tautness, the private bracing, the expectation of impact—eased with embarrassing speed. That was the problem with loving someone who knew where every version of you was buried. You could spend months hardening yourself into something glittering and untouchable, and then she would sit down across from you and suddenly the room would feel breathable again.

"You missed me."

I lifted my glass. "Only in the way one misses oxygen."

She placed a hand over her heart. "*Bébé*. Say another thing like that and I'll start believing you have feelings."

"I do have feelings."

"For me?"

"Mostly irritation."

"Ah. Balance is restored."

We clinked glasses.

"Now. Tell me everything I missed, and make it entertaining."

"You mean besides my meteoric rise and your transformation into the patron saint of leather-clad national panic?"

She tilted her head. "I mean the important things."

I let my fingers run once around the rim of my glass. "The auction was a success. Every piece sold. Millions moved."

"And?"

"And the money landed exactly where it needed to."

That pleased her. I saw it in the way her mouth softened—not into sweetness, never that, but into something quieter and far more intimate.

Les Louves had always been like that. Dangerous not because they announced themselves, but because they did not need to. They moved through the world the way a blade moves through fabric: efficiently, leaving damage that was only noticed once everything started coming apart.

"Good."

I smiled. "Lucian was there."

That got her attention immediately. "And?"

"He looked exactly as he always does. As if carved by someone with exquisite taste and terrible restraint."

She sighed with feeling. "My favorite kind."

"He asked after you."

Manon's brow lifted. "Did he?"

"He was very composed about it."

"Which is always the sexiest way for a man to suffer."

I laughed. "Lucian doesn't suffer. He endures."

"Mm." She considered that. "That may be even better."

It was one of the things I liked most about Lucian, and one of the reasons he remained so dangerous in a world like ours: he had never wanted to own either of us. Not really. He looked at Manon like sunlight on a blade. He looked at me like I was something rare enough not to touch carelessly.

Men in my life were not usually generous with restraint.

"Did he seem happy?" she asked, and there it was—that tiny shift beneath the teasing, the place where her curiosity became sincerity.

"Yes," I said. "And still in love with impossible things."

She gave a soft, private smile and looked away, as if she had no business being moved by that. "Then he's in excellent company."

I let that sit between us for a beat.

"Élodie is settling in?"

"Settling?" she said. "No. She's stripping the old guard for parts."

I had read enough international coverage over the past months to know that Élodie Marchand had not entered office intending to be decorative. She was precise, unsentimental, and profoundly uninterested in being underestimated—a quality that made her instantly legible to both of us.

"And you?" I asked lightly. "Still keeping her well dressed and badly behaved?"

Manon's smile turned cryptic. "I am keeping France in excellent hands."

"That sounds suspiciously like seduction."

"That sounds suspiciously like strategy."

"With you there's rarely a difference."

She raised her glass toward me in acknowledgment of a fair point.

Manon tilted her head, studying me with that feline intensity that always meant she was about to pounce. "So, ma *chérie*, tell me how many women are currently in love with you."

"What a boring question."

"That many, then."

"Publishing is not a harem."

"Not with that attitude."

I tried not to laugh. Failed. "I run a press, Manon."

"You run a machine that takes women everyone else underestimates and turns them into forces." She leaned forward. "That's hotter."

There were worse ways to describe what I had built. After Paris, after the fallout, after discovering exactly how fragile institutions became when enough money and panic hit them at once, I had stopped waiting for permission from old ones. If they wanted to shut one door, I would buy the building across the street and open ten more.

The women on my list were smart, hungry, furious, messy, difficult, ambitious.

Perfect.

Manon knew that better than anyone.

"You love it," I said.

"Of course I love it. You're making publishing look predatory in the hottest possible way."

"That may be the nicest thing you've ever said to me."

"Please. I've said much nicer things to you. Usually naked. Sometimes even in bed."

I smiled into my drink.

Then, because I knew where this was headed and because she knew I knew, she asked, "So. Do I have to sleep with one of your editors to get on the list, or am I allowed to submit directly?"

"You would be an administrative nightmare."

"I would be your bestselling nightmare."

"That part, I believe."

She rested her chin lightly against her knuckles and gave me a look so soft it almost escaped notice. "You'd publish me."

"If the manuscript was any good."

"Cruel."

"Professional. Besides, I know you just want to be on my roster of powerful women to bed them."

She leaned in, voice dipping. "B, I was your *first* powerful woman."

She placed a hand over her chest, in mocked shock. "And the cruelty of rejection! After everything we've been through?"

I smirked, lifting my glass. "Welcome to publishing."

Manon leaned back, her smile all wicked amusement. "Speaking of cruelty, how are dear old mom and dad?"

I exhaled, swirling my drink. "Suspiciously... proud."

"*Monsieur and Madame* Winslow-Hale? Pleased?"

"Try not to faint."

"I'd hate to cause a scene."

"Mother has decided that surviving publicly is a kind of pedigree. She still disapproves of my books in theory, but in practice she enjoys being related to someone people quote at dinner."

Manon smirked. "As she should."

"And father..." I paused, because some pleasures deserved timing. "Father has been very busy."

"Oh, this sounds promising."

"He saw the opening when the investigations hit. Once the contracts around the robotics company started collapsing, Dorian had no room left to posture. He sold."

Her smile sharpened. "At a loss?"

"At a humiliating one."

"Delicious."

"He folded what was left into Noa's company."

That pleased her in a different way—less theatrical, more exact. "And?"

"And Noa now has control of the whole operation."

Manon exhaled slowly, savoring it. "There is nothing so erotic as watching a man lose something he assumed was his by birthright."

"In Dorian's case," I said, "by ego."

"Same difference."

She was right, of course. Men like Dorian had always confused temporary access with entitlement. The correction, when it came, was usually expensive.

"And father adores her," I added. "Which, coming from him, is practically a public works project."

Manon laughed. "He's right to. Noa's terrifying."

"Competent," I corrected.

"Terrifyingly competent."

There was a shift near the entrance, subtle but immediate. Not the hush that followed beauty. Not the bend in attention that came with glamour. This was different. Cleaner. The kind of recalibration that happened when someone entered a room carrying actual consequence.

Manon's smile widened. "Speaking of the devil."

Noa Shahar stood just inside the room, all clean lines and contained force, scanning the club with the expression of someone assessing an unfamiliar machine and deciding how many parts she'd need to replace to improve it. She wasn't uncomfortable exactly. She was simply not performing ease for anyone, which in a room like NOX amounted to a quiet act of domination.

When she spotted us, her posture altered by barely a degree.

I lifted a hand.

She crossed toward us without hurry.

"Took you long enough," Manon said as Noa reached the table. "I was beginning to think Silicon Valley had finally devoured you whole."

Noa slid into the seat beside me and gave her a dry look. "It tried. I improved the terms."

I laughed.

She looked good. Not in the decorative sense—though she was striking enough to turn heads she would never bother to count—but in the more meaningful one. Grounded. Sharper somehow. Like someone who had stopped wasting energy pretending other people's discomfort with her mattered.

"You belong here less than anyone I know," Manon continued conversationally, "and yet somehow you still make half the room look underdressed."

Noa accepted the compliment the way she did most things: without theatrics. "That's because half the room mistakes expensive for intelligent."

"See?" Manon said, glancing at me. "Terrifying."

Noa's mouth twitched.

There had been a time when the world insisted on translating women like Noa into something smaller before it would accept them. Cold instead of disciplined. difficult instead of exacting. lucky instead of brilliant. Silicon Valley was especially creative in the ways it tried to patronize women while profiting from their work. Noa had survived that culture long enough to stop needing its approval. What remained was cleaner, harder, more useful.

Which was exactly why Dorian had underestimated her.

"Congratulations," I said.

She turned to me. "For what?"

"For taking his toy apart and rebuilding it correctly."

A brief flash of humor crossed her face. "It was poorly engineered."

Manon closed her eyes in pleasure. "Oh, marry me."

"No."

"Cruel again. What is it with powerful women in my life denying me simple joys?"

I said, "Your definition of simple is criminally unserious."

"Thank you."

Noa looked between us, amusement flickering now. "I've missed this."

Noa was not warm for sport. She was precise, even in affection. Which meant when she offered something, it usually mattered.

"We've been busy," I said.

"So I noticed."

Her eyes held mine for just a beat longer, and beneath the room, beneath the laughter, beneath the very expensive alcohol and the cultivated appetite of NOX, another truth moved quietly into place:

we were no longer improvising survival.

We were building structure.

Manon, naturally, broke the silence before it became emotionally useful.

"You two have become suspiciously competent together."

"Jealous?" I asked.

"I don't get jealous."

Noa said, "That sounded unconvincing."

Manon placed a hand against her chest. "I am wounded by the lack of faith in my emotional maturity."

"Your emotional maturity," I said, "once was paraded at the end of a leash."

"And yet I couldn't be tamed."

Noa, to my delight, laughed.

The room shifted again.

This time the change was more pronounced. Conversations lowered. Attention didn't just bend; it organized.

Ramona Guerra-Reyes had arrived.

She moved through NOX with the brutal efficiency of someone who did not need introduction and had never confused charisma for authority. Politics had sharpened her, but it had not made her soft around the edges. If anything, it had clarified what kind of blade she was willing to be.

She spotted us immediately.

Manon watched her approach with the slow satisfaction of a woman who appreciated a well-assembled table.

"Well," she murmured, "now it's a party."

Ramona reached us and did not waste time on pleasantries.

"Ladies."

There was history in the single word. Pressure. Intelligence. The kind of caution earned the hard way. Ramona had known Dorian before all of us had. Before the scandal. Before the contracts and the collapse and the very public lesson in what happens when ambitious men mistake cruelty for inevitability.

She set one hand on the back of the empty chair and looked from me to Manon to Noa, measuring, confirming, deciding, and sat.

And just like that, something invisible locked into place.

Not quite a reunion. Nor indulgence, though there would always be some of that where Manon and I were concerned.

A table of women the world had tried, and failed, to contain.

Manon wordlessly lifted her glass.

I raised mine.

So did Noa.

Then Ramona.

Crystal met crystal in a soft, lethal little chorus.

And in that moment, I understood, with the kind of clarity that only arrives after you have already paid for it in blood and spectacle and humiliation, my redemption.

Not through revenge or reinvention, but thanks to the women who had stood beside me when it cost more than what they would get in return.

I thought of the first line I had ever truly lived.

Some people may drag you to hell.

I looked around the table.

But others you follow willingly, because you know they'll always be on your side.

— THE END —

ABOUT THE AUTHOR

Jean Thesquare is a New York based author.
AcClaim is their debut novel.
Everything else is a rumor.

More at https://www.sultryverse.com